PRAISE FOR
DEFINITELY, MAYBE

"FIVE STARS. Craig Oliver is amaz̲   ̲ ̲ s English mannerisms, to his simplistic views, ̲ ̲ ̲ ̲ his ability to bake with alcohol when his heart gets shattered is amazing. I really love this character."

—*Scattered Thoughts and Rogue Words*

"These guys ... are smoldering together."

—*Joyfully Jay Reviews*

PRAISE FOR
CERTAINLY, POSSIBLY, YOU

"I am totally having a moment with this series."

—Dahlia Adler, LGBTQ Reads

"I am loving the Sucre Coeur Series as a whole and the fact that we can continue to see characters from *Definitely, Maybe, Yours* not only woven into the narrative of book two, but also supportive and involved in helping Mari and Sarita stay together. I really can't wait to see what happens in the next book *Absolutely, Almost, Perfect.*"

—*G Jacks Writes Reviews*

ABSOLUTELY, *almost*, PERFECT

LISSA REED

interlude ✦ press. • new york

For Alana
With all the love and sparkles in the world...
This one is for you, Magic Girl.

Trouble is just like love, after all;
it comes in unannounced
and takes over
before you've had a chance to reconsider,
or even to think.

—Alice Hoffman

"**A**LEX," SAYS THE WARM, PATIENT VOICE OUTSIDE THE bathroom door. "You can't live in there forever."

Alex considers. Sure, he can live in here forever. It'll be a little cramped, and the fuzzy blue bathroom rug he's sitting on is in no way as comfortable as the double bed, and of course he'll need some help with food and all—but yes. Yes, he can manage. It will be fine.

On the other side of the locked door, Craig sighs. "Alex. We both knew this day was coming."

Cross-legged on the rug, Alex leans harder against the door, closes his eyes, and takes his fifth deep breath in as many minutes, inhaling through his nose and exhaling through his mouth, exactly as his therapist instructed. He's getting a little light-headed from all the calming breaths, but maybe Dr. Laborteau was onto something with her emphasis on breathing. Then again, maybe the half a Xanax he took at the start of this debacle wasn't hurting anything either.

There's a whine at the bathroom door, and, when Alex opens his eyes, a tiny pair of caramel-brownie-striped Yorkie paws reaches into the crack underneath, scrabbling on the white tile. Fitz whines again; the barest hint of his damp, black nose pokes between his paws.

"Fitz will miss you terribly if you take up residence in there, babe," Craig says, his voice a bit more distant and accompanied by the clatter of broken pottery being dumped from a dustpan into the trash bin. "Come out; come feed him his breakfast. He loves it when you feed him his breakfast."

They both know Fitz loves breakfast, period. Alex shakes his head. This emotional manipulation is beneath Craig's standards. He's usually *much* better at it.

Craig's next sigh is right by the door. "Alex."

"I'm fine in here." His voice is too high; there's a shake in it that no number of calming breaths will eradicate. Alex narrows his eyes and glares at the cause of this mess, which rests next to his right fist on the blue shag rug: a perfectly innocent ivory square, an envelope, neatly addressed to *Craig Oliver and Alexander Scheff* in a clear script. From the upper right corner of the envelope, Queen Elizabeth II's eternally youthful stamped profile gazes steadily into an unknown future.

The envelope is crumpled where his right hand clenched it at about the same time his left hand released his mug of tea. He remembers the shatter as the mug hit the floor and Craig's yell of shock, but it all gets blurry after that.

Inside the square little envelope is a square little card: *The families of Chloe Antonia Pennant and Duncan Joseph Oliver cordially invite you to witness the joining of two hearts in matrimony...* The date of the occasion is October twenty-second. That date burned itself into Alex's brain the moment he read it. Doomsday.

"You know, it's my brother," Craig says. "My *estranged* brother, whom I've not seen or even spoken to much for nearly half my life. By rights, I should be the one locked in the loo being upset. Although, in either case, I say again that we knew this was coming. We've known since May, Alex. It's now July."

That doesn't mean I have to like it. He had managed to put it out of his mind, helped at the time by several generous measures of top-shelf vodka provided by their friends whose baby shower came screeching to a halt when Craig's mother called with the news of the wedding. Alcohol, however, is not an option now. Not at six o'clock on a Wednesday morning. Besides, his Xanax bottle has a large label advising against it.

Alex squints one eye and continues to glare at the invitation. It's an irrational action, but he's doing it anyway. This is one hell of a way to start a day. They have plans: work, for both of them—Craig to Sucre Coeur, the bakery where he is half-owner, Alex and Fitz to the photography studio Alex owns with his best friend Connor; then together to a party thrown by their friends Devesh and Sunil to watch and celebrate the season finale of *Dance Nation* and see where in the top four their friend Maritza would place. Today was supposed to be a good day... but then, *this.*

"Alex. Please don't make me go downstairs to use Theodora's loo. We're out of coffee; I have nothing to offer her. At this hour of the morning, that's lethal." Craig's long brown fingers poke underneath the door, patting around in search of Alex's hand. "I support your need for isolation, you know that I do, but I'm too young to let my business partner strangle me to death for waking her before sunrise."

Alex lets Craig's hand find his, and their fingers just touch in the narrow space. Guilt swirls in his stomach. *Craig* comforting *him* is the wrong way around. Not for the first time, he wishes he could rummage inside his head, into the dark reaches where his anxiety crouches, and pluck it out, smother it to death.

Looking at the cracked white plastic light fixture over the mirror, Alex takes one more long, slow breath. The Xanax really is working. He's almost ready to face Craig.

Craig clears his throat. "If you don't want to go, you don't have to. Mum has made it perfectly plain that I'm not getting out of this one, but you're in the clear, Alex. I can tell them you're afraid to fly or something. They'd understand that; my Aunt Lorraine can't get near an airport without having a fit."

"I'm not having you tell your family I'm afraid to fucking fly. Jesus Christ!" The words burst out of Alex, and, without further thought, he spins around and yanks the bathroom door open. Craig's sitting cross-legged, leaning against the door frame with Fitz curled in his lap. His face is tired and concerned, which makes the guilty lump in Alex's stomach expand. "I'm sorry, Craig."

Craig sets Fitz aside, gets to his feet, and reaches down to offer Alex a hand up. "I know. Listen. Go make yourself another cup of tea; feed Fitz. I'll shower and shave, and then we'll sort it all out, all right?"

Alex doesn't have Craig's confidence in their ability to sort, but he follows his marching orders. Twenty minutes later, he's seated at their tiny, butcher-block kitchen table with fresh tea, hot buttered toast, and a soft-boiled egg for each of them; the wedding invitation sits next to his plate. Fitz, from his feeding station in the back corner of the kitchenette, is making obscene noises as he smacks and snorfs his way through his own breakfast. Everything is in order, calm and quiet but for the nagging worry at the back of Alex's brain. Well, that's been there as long as he can remember; there's nothing he can do about it.

"Breakfast, fantastic. Thanks, babe."

Smelling of soap, a blue bath towel slung around his hips, Craig drops a kiss on Alex's forehead before he takes his own seat. He slides the Ivory Square of Doom to his side of the table. "Right, we have to work this out."

"Do we?" Alex cuts a finger of toast and dips it into his egg. He concentrates on the simple task so he doesn't have to look Craig in the eye. "I mean, really. Neither of us actually wants to go. Why *can't* we just RSVP with a sad but firm *no* and send them the nicest thing on their registry?"

Silence stretches long enough that he does look up. Open-mouthed, Craig stares at him. A forgotten toast finger drips egg yolk onto the tabletop. "You..." Craig shakes his head and puts down the toast. "You spoke to my mother. Many times you faced this woman on Skype or Facetime and had actual conversations with her and you still somehow think that is a reasonable course of action." His eyebrows lift, and he lets out a low whistle. "You know, I've held your balls in my hand. Were they brass all this time, and I just missed it?"

"Oh, come on, Craig." Alex runs a hand through his hair. "Yes, I spoke to your mother. She's nowhere near as scary as mine."

"See, now, there's an excellent reason for both of us to go to this damn wedding, so I can show you in person exactly how wrong you are." Craig lifts his mug of tea and coughs out a laugh. "Your mother is frightening, I grant you: half my size and twice as intimidating as I can manage on my best day. In fact, our mothers would get on like houses afire, which should give you an idea as to why I, at least, cannot get out of going to this wedding." He takes a sip of tea, sets the mug aside, and reaches over the table to catch Alex's hand in both of his. "Alex, even apart from my mother's insistence... Chloe is one of my oldest friends. I have to do this for her. But I'd rather not do it without you. I know it won't be easy, but I need you there with me."

At the sight of their joined hands, a lump grows in Alex's throat to match the one in his stomach. "It's just... your family..."

Silence falls again, interrupted only by Fitz tap-tap-tapping across the checkerboard linoleum of the kitchen floor and whining to be picked up. Craig scoops him up and scratches Fitz's fuzzy little ears. "They won't bite, Alex. They're just..."

"Just people, just your family, I know." Alex's chest tightens. "Just your mother, your father, your sisters, your brother who you don't even like, and I guess there's an Aunt Lorraine now, and this Chloe chick and God knows who else gathering for the Wedding of the Century, where they'll get to meet Craig's neurotic train wreck of a boyfriend and judge us. They'll judge me for being an uptight, deadbeat American and you for *clearly* having some kind of episode, to decide that I was an appropriate choice for a boyfriend."

The lump in his throat swells and cuts him off.

Family.

Craig's family, to Alex, is the grainy laptop-camera picture of his small, pale, sharp, smart mother Moira seen in their twice-weekly calls. They catch an occasional glimpse of Craig's tall, lanky father Stephen with a pen tucked behind his ear and a stack of math exams in his hands as he ambles through and smiles at them. The siblings, well, none of them have showed up on any of the calls thus far, so Alex views them almost as mythological creatures or endangered animals.

They're not real people. They're... they're computer people. Computer people are far away and not alarming at all. Computer people can't judge.

Across the table, Craig holds the wedding invitation between his index fingers and uses his thumb to spin it in a lazy circle. "You're being too hard on yourself, as usual. They'll love you. They won't judge you, and, for the thousandth time, you're not a deadbeat."

"I'm not?" Alex can't help a snort. Sitting back, he crosses his arms over his chest. "I left a perfectly good advertising job to open a photography studio. I struggle to break even every month, let alone turn a profit. We live on beans and spaghetti and cereal because I'm bringing in half of what I used to make before we moved in together."

"That's your dad talking again, Alex. What you are is a former advertising professional, who is now making a name for himself in the Seattle photography scene. They don't write up deadbeats in *F-Stop Magazine*." Craig raises an eyebrow. "It's not about the money; it's about the art, remember? My mother can totally appreciate that." Moira Oliver, known professionally as bestselling author Moira Cunningham, has been writing since Craig and his older brother were babies. Has been writing as a career *because* of Craig and his brother as babies, Alex has heard her joke. Craig has a point. His mother has never known anything but self-employment.

Fine. Moira is unlikely to judge. Stephen, on the other hand, is a mathematics teacher at the secondary school Craig and his siblings attended. Despite his always affable, slightly absent appearance, Alex is certain that Stephen must have some reservations about his son dating a deadbeat artist. "Okay. Your dad?"

"Has a soft spot for snarky, creative types given that he married my *mother*," Craig points out with perfect, inescapable logic. "Also, he was very proud of me for becoming a partner in a successful bakery business while still managing a solid freelance writing career. He's fine."

Alex closes his eyes. "I hate it when you're logical."

"It happens to be my turn. You had yours last week when you talked me out of adopting another dog." Alex hears a sip and then a soft clink as Craig sets down his tea mug. "So. Did you want to move on to my siblings?"

"Can I stop you?" Alex asks, opening one eye and then narrowing it.

"I'm on a roll." Craig picks up his discarded toast finger, pops it into his mouth, and grimaces at the cold egg. "My sisters are teenagers. They judge everyone. Be nice, but honest, about Jasmine's art, and don't touch Jade's cello, and you'll be fine. Duncan…" He lifts a shoulder in a shrug, but the effort this casual gesture costs him is visible. "Duncan is going to be more concerned with me, or not concerned at all, and I don't know what's worse, or which I prefer."

Craig squirms. This uncertainty is an unfamiliar weight, and, for the first time in their relationship, Alex can see the teenager Craig must have been: confused, constantly at odds with an older brother he wanted desperately to get along with. Craig doesn't talk about Duncan much and never explained their estrangement to Alex. Alex never wanted to pry; it was something that hurt Craig, and the last thing he wanted to do was hurt Craig.

Alex does have some remaining concerns: How will they afford it; will they be able to take a week off work; can they bring Fitz? But this all fades in the face of wanting to support Craig in the way that Craig has always supported him. Craig was there for him while Alex wrestled his way through the dark aftermath of his relationship with his ex, Jeff. He was patient and loving through Alex's anxiety diagnosis. He stood by Alex when Alex and Connor decided to open their own photography studio.

Compared to all of that, what's one measly family wedding?

Alex kneels next to Craig and wraps his arms around his boyfriend, his partner, the love of his life. "Did they ask you to do the cake?"

Craig shifts in his chair, the burgundy faux-leather squeaking beneath him. "Yes. Chloe did, last week."

"Okay." He rests his head on Craig's arm. "I could do the photography; we could offer that as part of our gift."

Craig is still for a moment. Then he twists in Alex's embrace and sets Fitz down before he takes Alex's face in his hands. His kiss is long, soft and sweet, full of gratitude and relief. "Thank you," he whispers, touching his forehead to Alex's. "Thank you. I love you."

Later, Alex will reflect that it's odd, the first day of the rest of his life landing on a Wednesday. Nothing ever happens on Wednesdays. What are Wednesdays? Only the middle of the week, nothing special.

No wonder he never saw it coming, he'll think, though he'll also have to admit that spending a good chunk of it freaking out in the bathroom was a bit inauspicious.

Important days, he will decide, should always come with warnings.

 *Chapter One*

"'**G**O GET FITZ AND YOUR BAG,' HE SAYS. 'I'LL BE RIGHT out,' he says."

Wary glances from passersby alert Alex to the fact that he's not quite mumbling under his breath, but he doesn't care. He is tired. He is angry. He is—unless one counts Fitz, in his carrier slung across Alex's chest—alone in the swirling ocean of humanity that is Heathrow Terminal Five.

He is on his last ragged nerve and in desperate need of coffee and a shower.

Alex drags his suitcase to a halt and glares at the shop front sign just ahead: a sign that reads *WH Smith* and not a damn thing about coffee. His huff of contempt is explosive. "'There's a coffee shop right around the corner,' he says. And yet this is not a coffee shop, is it, Craig?" His laugh is only a little hysterical. "Oh, wait. You can't answer me. Because you're not *here*."

Alex shoves his suitcase against a wall next to what is emphatically not a coffee shop, lifts the strap of Fitz's carrier over his head, and sets it gently on the floor. Then he leans against the wall, closes his eyes, and takes many long, slow, deep breaths until the urge to strangle someone passes.

It takes a couple of minutes.

Trouble began the minute they stepped into the passport control area at Heathrow.

"Oh, no," Craig said, as he hitched the strap of his carry-on farther up on his shoulder. "Shit."

"What?" Alex glanced at the three lines of people Craig was studying with such despair.

"Ah, I..." Craig sighed. "I didn't realize there were so many British passengers on the flight."

"So?"

"So, as a non-UK, non-EU citizen, that's your line," Craig said as he pointed at the shortest of the three. "But I hold dual citizenship. I am still a subject of the dear old Queen and I'm using my British passport to enter the country. So this one is mine."

At this point, Craig indicated the longest line, a good three dozen people deep at least. That's when Alex's ears filled with the sound of a radio stuck between stations and his rationality flew right out the window.

"Go out—get your bag—Fitz." Craig's voice came in distant and vague, broken up by the radio noise in Alex's brain. "Coffee—corner—arrivals—get decaf—be there—babe?"

Alex registered every other word or so and a comforting kiss on the cheek as he was pushed off into his line. He went through the motions in a daze before being funneled out into Terminal Five and swept along to baggage claim.

And now he is here. Craigless. Coffeeless. Clueless.

England is not off to a good start.

"'Get decaf' had to be a joke," he mumbles as he pushes away from the wall to grab his suitcase and the pet carrier. "Fuck jet lag. I cannot face this family without caffeine."

"Oh, you have got to be Alex."

Alex freezes. Oh, no. No. No, no, no.

Unless Craig experienced an impossibly spontaneous and thorough gender switch in the last half hour, this is not the voice Alex wants to hear saying his name.

He's still hungover from the flight and the melatonin he took to sleep through most of it. His hair is a wreck; he caught a frightening glimpse of himself reflected in a glass partition on the moving walkway. His breath does not bear thinking about. And Craig is not here.

"Alex? It *is* you, right?"

He has no choice. Heart sinking the considerable distance into his shoes, Alex opens his eyes.

"Over here." A wave catches his attention, and Alex glances to his left. The sweet, clear voice belongs to a gorgeous woman with smooth, brown skin and a lovely, if hesitant, smile. "Hi?"

"Chloe," he wheezes, while darkness infringes on the outskirts of his vision. "You're Chloe Pennant. The bride."

He might be verging on a panic attack, but a zing of triumph goes through him. Alex has photos of everyone involved with this wedding circus; he studied a file he made of them, and his work is paying the fuck *off*. Craig thought he was taking things a bit far, but here it is, proof that Alex was entirely right. Somehow, he resists the urge to drop everything he's holding and pump his fist in glee.

"So formal. Call me Chloe, or just Cee is fine, too." Chloe's face brightens into a much larger and more certain smile, and Alex's sight begins to clear in its sunshine; the black edges melt away from his peripheral vision and resolve her into an actual person, clad in loose jeans and a black-and-red-striped rugby shirt she's practically swimming in. She's nearly as tall as he is, with big, sparkling brown eyes, lots of curly, dark hair piled atop her head, and if her smile is any indication, a personality that's just about its own separate entity. She hurls herself forward for a hug, which forces him to let go of his suitcase to catch her.

"This is fantastic! I'm so happy to finally meet you. We waited ages. Craig texted to say you were getting out first, alone, so we kept an eye out for you. Oh, this is Jasmine," she says and pulls back to point to a smaller, younger woman in jeans and an oversized, paint-spattered blue sweater. Her dark hair hangs in long twists around her surly, but pretty, face. "Craig's sister. Jazz, say hey."

Jasmine lifts an eyebrow and removes an earbud from her left ear. "Hi. I'm not into hugs."

"Works for me." Alex rubs a hand over his eyes and tries to stifle a yawn. As he focuses on Chloe, details from his file entry on her float to the surface. "Chloe. Right. You're the sheep-fister."

As soon as the words are out, Alex's face all but bursts into flames. *No!*

Chloe is, more accurately, a large-animal veterinarian. But the legend in the Oliver family annals is that her reintroduction to Duncan took place in a barn, with Chloe elbow-deep in a sheep that was enduring a difficult birth. It is one hell of a story.

If only it wasn't stuck quite so firmly in his subconscious. His regret is swift and instantaneous.

Jasmine cackles, and Chloe, raising a skeptical eyebrow, takes a step back from Alex. "You want to rephrase that?"

"I want to take it back." He groans into the palm of his hand and wishes he could melt into the linoleum. "I want to take it back and then I want you to kill me."

"I would, but I expect Craig would be unhappy with me, and anyway, I am fairly certain that I don't want to get married in a prison chapel." Chloe's laughter bubbles under the surface of her voice. "I will, however, let you make it up to me by buying me a coffee. There's a place just—"

"Around the corner, I know." He sighs and lifts his head. Chloe is biting her lip, clearly trying to hold in her laughter. Her eyes glitter, and Alex shakes his head. "Okay. Point the way. I am desperate."

"Yes, I can see that." Chloe loops one arm through his and uses the other to grab his suitcase. "I'll do you a favor and tell you now that Craig's father is waiting for us at the coffee place. Maybe don't say anything until you get some coffee into yourself?"

Behind them, Jasmine snickers. "Craig texted again. He says don't let Alex drink anything with caffeine."

"Craig is mean, and the situation is dire. I was just publicly accused of bestiality, so I get to make the call." Chloe winks. "But we'll compromise. How does half-caf sound?"

The knots in Alex's chest and stomach loosen, and he can't help but grin at his new friend. Maybe he will survive this week after all. "Craig was right. I do like you."

"Wholesale misinterpretation of my career aside, I might just like you, too." When she smiles, Chloe's nose crinkles at the bridge and lends her an elfin air. "And if you promise not to have me sectioned for untoward behavior with animals, I'll let you come to my parents' farm and feed some abandoned lambs with me sometime this week."

Alex mouth twitches. "That really shouldn't be as effective a bribe as it is."

"Nobody can resist baby sheep. Nobody." Chloe is obviously pleased with herself. "Deal?"

"Deal," he says, disengaging his arm so that he can offer her a handshake. She accepts with an impressive grip. Alex's eyes water.

"Boring," Jasmine sighs, with a tug at her earbuds.

Chloe's head whips around to glare over her shoulder. "Be nice."

"I am being nice." Jasmine steps up, grabs Fitz's carrier from Alex, and continues forward without breaking stride. "I could have just stolen the puppy and taken off."

Alex and Chloe are left staring in her wake. Chloe shakes her head. "If you could bottle teenage contempt, it would strip the rust off a shipwreck—none too gently, either." She loops her arm back through Alex's and sets off at a brisk pace. "She's a good kid. Just..."

"Sarcastic." With careful attention to whatever the hell he's saying, it's probably safe for him to talk. "It's fine. I've always been curious to know what I'd have been like as a teenage *girl*, and here we are."

"I heard that." Jasmine aims a scowl over her shoulder.

"I have no regrets," Alex shoots back. His reward is a dark glare through the thick twists of Jasmine's hair. His fingers itch for his camera, and he grins at her. Craig's sister is as terrifying as Alex expected, but in a fun way. And Chloe strikes the perfect balance between spunky and sweet. He's still nervous about meeting Craig's father, but the women have certainly managed to take the edge off Alex's anxiety.

Maybe Craig was right. Maybe this won't be too bad.

"You seem to have relaxed," Chloe comments as they meander through the terminal. "I'm glad. I asked to be part of the whole..." She pulls her hand free to make air quotes. "'Welcome Team' thing, you know."

"Yeah." His hands entirely free, Alex has no idea what to do with them. He runs one through his hair. It's already a disaster; how much worse could he make it? "So we could talk about wedding arrangements on the way to the house?"

Chloe blinks. "Hmm? Oh, no. Not really. I mean yes, but also no. That is, Craig mentioned that you were wound up about meeting us. The original plan was that *everyone* would be here."

An icy chill tickles Alex's spine at the very thought, displacing a prickle of irritation at the idea that he's been managed by Craig and his well-meaning concern. "Oh."

"So I made sure everyone else had something to do or somewhere else to be except for the three calmest of us." Chloe beams. "Jade arguably would have been a less sarcastic choice than Jasmine, but she's busy rehearsing the music for the wedding, and a little sarcasm never killed anyone."

Managed or not—there's that prickle again, with a touch of resentment and the distinct sensation of being patronized to keep it company—Alex has to admit he's grateful not to have to face the entire Oliver gang when he's fresh off the plane. With a little effort, he shrugs off his irritation. He is determined to be a pillar of strength for Craig this week. "I'm pretty sure your entire comedy industry is predicated on that notion," he says, allowing another grin to slip out, a grin that slips right back in when he spots the sign for Costa Coffee and anxiety makes his nerve endings dance a jig. "Oh, boy. Dad time."

Chloe's hand is warm on his arm. "He's really great. I promise." The reassuring touch disappears as Chloe throws her arm up in a wave. "Hey, Mr. O! I got him!"

A copy of *The Guardian* folds down, and Stephen Oliver's face looks up with the affable smile that Alex has seen so many times in a Skype window. It's Craig's smile, bright as anything and the warmest of welcomes. But Stephen's face is older; his skin is a bit darker than Craig's and lined here and there. His graying dark hair is cropped into close, tiny curls against his head, and his facial hair is shot through with silver.

Still, the resemblance is incredible. Alex's nerves settle as he takes in what Craig will almost certainly look like in twenty years, assuming that Craig will ever wear wool slacks and well-pressed, tucked-in button-downs. "Mr. Oliver."

Stephen stands and offers his hand. "Not you, too. It's Stephen, and I hope you'll call me that. Chloe here never does." Laugh lines crinkle the edges of Stephen's brown eyes, eyes that are so very like Craig's, and his handshake is firm. "Makes me feel like the neighborhood dotty old dad."

"You *are* the neighborhood dotty old dad, Mr. O." Chloe sweeps over to the table, where Jasmine is already tucked in a chair with her knees up, clunky boots planted on the seat, and Fitz's carrier on the table in front of her. Chloe parks Alex's suitcase nearby and flops down in the next chair. "I've been calling you Mr. O since I was in primary school. Marrying Duncan can't change old habits overnight."

Stephen retakes his own seat and indicates an empty one next to him for Alex. "You've been with my son for how long now, Chloe? Statistically speaking, I should think—"

"Dad, no, don't bring maths into this, *please*," Jasmine groans. "We're not at school; give it a rest."

"Jazz, maths doesn't—"

"Take a day off. We know, Dad." Surprising them all, Craig's greeting is a sleepy chuckle from behind them just before he drapes himself over Alex in a lazy, tired hug. "Hello. Am I ever glad that experience is over."

"Me too." Alex wants to collapse against his boyfriend in relief. No matter the mild patronizing or his slight irritation, no matter how funny and kind Chloe, Jasmine, and Stephen are, the most fundamental truth of his life is that Craig is home, Craig is refuge, Craig is a place for Alex to catch his breath, and he could really use a moment for that. But he's also okay with getting beaten to the punch by the others, who jump up and swarm Craig with smiles, hugs, and sheer joy and pull him into a swirl of chatter.

Chloe leans down and whispers, "Now's a good time to go grab *whatever coffee you want*." She winks at him and gives his hand a squeeze before she hugs Craig for a bone-cracking third time.

She has a point, but Alex stays seated with his eyes on the flurry of activity amongst the Olivers: three pairs of laughing brown eyes, animated hands, and identical brighten-the-world smiles. Chloe, of course, fits in smoothly with her bounce and shine, as if she's always been one of them, which, Alex supposes, she has been, really.

Next to them, Alex cannot help but notice that he himself is distinctly uptight. His own family isn't like this. His parents are practically a living parable of opposites attracting: his German-American father so reserved and calm next to his boisterous Russian mother. Dieter and Marina love Alex, but they never went in for hugs, and Marina only lets her laughter rip when she's with her brothers and sisters. Alex's memories are mostly of his father telling him how hard he needed to work, of his mother expecting him to toe the parental line without question, of both of them shuttling him to one carefully chosen extracurricular activity after another.

Maybe the coffee run was a good idea after all. Alex wanders over to the counter and orders coffee for the group, but keeps an eye on the Olivers and their happiness and exuberance. *What might it have been like to have a family like that?* He loves his parents and appreciates all that they provided for him: the education and the work ethic and the intellectual nurturing. His paternal grandparents' quiet delight in his interest in photography and their surreptitious encouragement under the nose of his father's disapproval, that was a good memory too. And of course, he had his cousin Samantha, as close as a sister from the time they were in diapers.

Alex's life has been a little rocky, and he's definitely made some tremendously stupid choices along the way, but he had every advantage and then some. That's something to be grateful for, and he is, most of the time.

It's just that... something like *this* might have been nice, too. Would it have made a difference in the choices he made and the attitudes he espoused? Would he have felt less guilty about dropping his advertising career? Would he have done better in school? Would he have been less of a little shit?

Maybe he would have been a little shit no matter what.

There's a comforting thought.

Alex gathers the five coffees and pushes his way back to the table, where everyone's sprawled over their chairs, chattering a hundred miles a minute, and so absorbed that Craig, leaning toward Chloe with his chin in his hand, hardly notices when Alex slips a cup into his other hand.

"So you're really doing this DIY?" Craig asks Chloe. "That's incredible. My friend Poppy is a wedding planner, and I know from watching her that it can't be easy. She's always having meltdowns over glitter and catering and where to seat people."

"But doing it ourselves means we can afford to take a proper honeymoon, not just rent a leaky tent on the Isle of Wight." Chloe mouths her thanks to Alex when he pushes a coffee over to her. "We're still just a pair of struggling veterinarians. We may be the best in the area, but we're still not exactly drowning in clients." She shrugs and smiles, completely at ease. "I'd much prefer to take all the annoyance and stress of the last several months and make it pay into a nice week on a beach in Spain, thank you. It's worth it. And really, it hasn't been so bad."

"Speak for yourself." Jasmine's dark eyes roll as she scowls. "If I have to untangle one more giant knot of fairy lights, I'm taking off for Manchester, and you're on your own."

Craig pats his sister's knee. "I'll give you a hand with that, Jazz."

"No, you'll be too busy baking cake and getting fitted for your kilt," Chloe, all impish grin and sparkling mischief, informs Craig. "Which I get to watch, by the way. Got to make sure everyone's looking good for the day."

That's a pleasant attention-grabbing distraction. Alex has been having some very nice dreams and daydreams of Craig in a kilt ever since he found out that was going to be the order of the day, and he would give a lot to tag along to Craig's fitting. "Can I—"

"I'll text you some photos if you help Jazz," Chloe stage-whispers with a wink and, *yes*. Yes, that is an acceptable compromise, because pictures are a permanent record and untangling strings of lights with Jasmine is likely to be a relatively quiet enterprise, and as much as he is enjoying the boisterous racket of this family, he is also sure he will need an occasional break from them, especially if *this* contingent is the calm one.

Yikes. Alex takes a gulp of coffee.

Chloe picks up her conversation with Craig, and her voice is a little too casual. "Did I tell you that David's doing the flowers?"

"David?" Craig asks, sharply enough to send alarm shooting up Alex's spine. "Not David Morgan?"

Chloe turns her coffee cup around in her hands, not taking her eyes from it. "The very one."

"But he lives in Leeds. He's a nurse, not a florist." Craig's sharp tone melts into bewilderment. "He can't do your flowers. Why isn't his dad doing your flowers?"

"His dad... Mr. M had to go into care, Craig." Biting her lip, she looks up at last. "You haven't heard?"

"No, I—oh." Light dawns in Craig's eyes. "The dementia, yeah?"

Stephen breaks in with a nod. "It kept getting worse, and Mrs. Morgan just couldn't keep up, you know? She only ever did the books, didn't know much about the flowers. And of course she's getting on, herself."

"Of course," Craig mutters, and Alex is definitely not going to start a fan club over the slightly goofy smile that's begun to grow on his boyfriend's face.

Oblivious to the tension that suddenly encircles the table—that clears up which side of the family Craig got that from—Stephen goes on. "So, the shop was closed for months until David could get free from the hospital and come home. They thought at first that he would care for his father, but it was more complicated than they expected, so... there you have it. James went into care, and David decided to reopen the shop so that his mother had something to do to fill her days." His smile makes no indication that he notices anything amiss. "It's nice that he did. No one liked having Morgan's closed; they've been there so long. And he's doing the wedding at cost." Stephen sips at his coffee. "Says hello, by the by."

Craig's smile is still half pleased, half confused. "He never wanted to run the shop; he liked nursing. I thought. I mean, it was all he talked about doing, ever."

Chloe takes Craig's hand. "Of course he likes nursing. But he wanted to take care of his parents and he always had a knack for the arrangements. You know that; you worked with him in the shop when we were kids." She smiles. "I don't think he minds. Truly."

But Craig still seems befuddled and even slightly unhappy, and Alex is more than a little uncomfortable with the visible sense of deep investment that Craig has in this nurse, this florist, this nice, parent-caring guy named David—whoever he is.

Alex's stomach churns the coffee as if it's trying to make butter. *Jealousy.* Christ, it's been so long since he experienced it, he didn't recognize it at first. And it is just as unlikable as Craig's interest in David. "So," he begins, struggling to maintain some semblance of casualness. "Who's David?"

Chloe's smile is bright, much too bright. "Oh, he ran around with us in school."

"More than that. He was my first boyfriend, Alex. You remember." Craig's interruption is gentle. "And a friend, yes, but we did date for a little while when we were younger." He casts a lopsided smile at Chloe. "We're not really in the business of keeping secrets, Cee. I know you meant well, but no need." Dismissing the topic, he picks up Alex's cup. "Is this decaf?"

"No. Back off." Alex tugs the coffee cup back and hopes that his scowl of annoyance over this David person is accepted as a mock scowl over the attempt to police his coffee. No one told him there would be an ex-boyfriend. And he remembers David now, or at least the passing mention of him very long ago: Craig's first kiss. Oh, he is liking this less by the second. "I needed at least some caffeine."

And to his relief, Chloe helps him with the ruse. "When we found him, he was half asleep and completely without a filter, Craig," Chloe chides. "I was not sending him in to meet the rest of the family in that state; he'd be totally unprepared. I am not heartless!"

Chloe is definitely his new best friend.

But she is not Craig's best friend, at least not at the moment. "But caffeine... we're never going to get to sleep at a decent hour now." Craig's smile droops, and he sets aside his own cup. "I was trying to fight the jet lag. Damn."

Jasmine raises an eyebrow, and a chuckle escapes. "What gave you the idea that you were going to get to sleep at a decent hour? You know we're going back to the house, and it's barely ten o'clock."

"But it's just Mum and everyone; they'll let us get off to bed—" Craig stops as everyone at the table avoids looking at them all at once, and Alex pushes his own coffee aside when anxiety makes his stomach heave. "Oh, no. You didn't."

That cannot be good. Just when Alex thought he might be out of the woods...

Pressing her fingertips together, Jasmine takes a deep interest in the ceiling of the coffee shop. "Jade and everyone. They're at the house practicing."

"That's Jade and her girlfriend Frankie; she plays the flute. And their piano player friend they both used to date, I forget his name but he's there," Chloe explains to her coffee. "Also, Duncan texted me to say he picked up David from the flower shop to come say hello to you in person."

"Tristan. The piano guy's name is Tristan," Jasmine volunteers to the napkin dispenser. "His parents are way into opera."

The tension is now so thick, even Stephen can't miss it. He is very intent, however, on assembling a tiny building out of stirring sticks and sugar packets. "Your mother had the idea that she'd get a few of the neighbors to come for dinner and stick around to welcome you home, Craig." He's the first one to slide a glance their way, and it's a split-second one. "Mrs.

Fitzgerald will probably bring those little chicken vol-au-vents that you always liked."

Craig closes his eyes, and the tiniest of groans emerges from his mouth. "You did."

Alex's stomach begins to meander slowly southward. "Is it... a party?"

And Craig can only nod. "So it would seem." His hand covers Alex's and squeezes. "Sorry, babe. I thought we'd have a chance for a more gradual introduction and an early night. Silly of me to think I'd get out of a welcome party. You up for it?"

Not really.

Alex's hand, under Craig's, squeezes into a fist, and he looks around the table at the four nervous Olivers and their soon-to-be new addition. He's flown all day and is mentally still about eight hours behind the rest of the group. His stomach is in knots, and now he's about to face all the rest of Craig's family, plus a saintly, flower-peddling ex-boyfriend, several more teenagers, and neighbors who were never on the agenda.

Craig swore everything was going to be fine. This is Alex's lesson to never again lose sight of the fact that the love of his life is a pie-eyed, boundless optimist with a Texas-sized capacity for underestimation.

For one wistful moment, Alex wishes for a bathroom with a sturdy lock, but for just the one moment.

He did, after all, promise to be the pillar of strength this week.

Alex sucks in a breath. *I made it this far. In for a penny...* "I need another coffee. A big one. Fully caffeinated. And a comb and some powerful breath mints. Anyone want to help me out, here?"

He's mostly joking, but, to his astonishment, his request galvanizes just about everyone into action, and, wow, doesn't he just wish he could have that superpower full-time. It would make his wedding photo shoots a hell of a lot easier.

"I'll get the coffee." Chloe bounces to her feet to make a beeline for the counter.

"Smith's has mints, I think." Stephen stands. "I'll go see what I can find. I told your mother I'd bring home the latest *Vogue* anyway, Craig."

Craig nods at his father and bumps Alex's shoulder with his own. "I have your comb in my carry-on. If you give me a minute, I can find it. You forgot it on the sink this morning." He manages to get in a hug and a kiss as he scrambles to his feet. "I'll go dig it out."

Alex can only stare after them. "Jesus. It's like watching an army jump into action."

"You're not wrong."

And he nearly jumps out of his skin. He forgot about Jasmine.

Alex expects her to laugh at his fright, but she's still curled up quietly in her chair with one hand picking at a splotch of what might be yellow paint on the cuff of her pale-blue sweater and the other holding her coffee cup balanced on her knee. Her dark eyes watch him with curiosity.

Finally, setting the cup aside, Jasmine unfolds one leg at a time, settles her booted feet on the floor, and tosses the long twists of her hair back to level a steady stare at him until he really begins to squirm. "You're freaking out." She picks up a stirring stick to chew on.

"Actually, I'm doing my level best not to." Alex dismantles Stephen's construction project very slowly, very carefully. "I'll be fine."

Her gaze doesn't waver, and he gets the distinct impression that he's not going to be able to bullshit Jasmine any more than he can her brother. Cool and amused, she tilts up her chin. "We won't kill you, you know."

Alex is not at all reassured, and, since she reminds him so strongly of himself as a teenager, he's fairly certain that this was her exact intent. He draws himself up, grasping for the old shell of cocky confidence that used to be his second skin. It doesn't fit quite as closely as it used to, but it's what he's got. "I did assume your family wasn't the murderous type, yes."

"We're not." Something that might be half a smile tilts her mouth, and her eyes twinkle. "But we'll probably make you wish you were dead."

So much for confidence.

 Chapter Two

WAS IT ALWAYS THIS SMALL?

It's his first glimpse of home in far too long, and all that comes to Craig's mind is, *Wasn't it bigger?*

He's gotten used to Seattle. He's accustomed to the urban sprawl punctuated by tall buildings and the Space Needle, to coffee shops on every corner and a Metro stop in each direction, to hustle and bustle, to a world so loud, the sound of it eventually became background noise.

Ingatestone, in contrast, is quiet and green and dark with dim and infrequent streetlights illuminating clutches of low little houses as they enter the village. *It's a horror-movie village,* comes the thought, and he only just manages to muffle his snort of laughter to his fist.

"Craig?" Stephen calls back over his shoulder.

"I'm fine, Dad. Sorry. Post-flight cough, you know how it is." Craig is very glad indeed that it's too dark for anyone to see his face. That would give up the game in an instant. "I'll be fine as soon as we're in the house and I can get something to drink."

And with any luck, dodge the throng of neighbors, family… my ex-boyfriend.

Ugh.

He's been dwelling on this since he heard about it. It's not that Craig isn't excited to see David. No. Wait. That's not true. He isn't really excited—quietly pleased, maybe, a little baffled at the idea of David giving up nursing to run his family's flower shop, but no, not excited. Craig glances across the van, where Alex broods, clutching tightly to Fitz's carrier while he gazes out the window. *How could I be excited about it?*

It was cute how Alex thought he hid his sudden fit of jealousy at the airport. Craig sighs as quietly as he can. There's not a whole lot he can do about the jealousy, though, as ever, he wishes he could fix it or go back in time to prevent it from bubbling up in the first place. Damn Duncan. There was no need to drag David to this party; it was sheer petty—

Oh, if Duncan hadn't done it, Mum would have called David and badgered him into it. David's family as much as Chloe is. Let's try to be at least a little *fair to Brother Loathsome.*

Duncan doesn't deserve that much, but Craig does have a vested interest in keeping the peace as much as possible this week. Plenty of people have vested interests, at that; Moira, for example, would be happy if her sons could get along for once, and Chloe would be happy if her wedding wasn't blighted by familial strife. Craig has no desire to stoop to Duncan's level in front of Alex. There's too much at stake.

Craig Oliver, resident peacekeeper and milquetoast, all in the name of family harmony. He rolls his eyes and tries to stifle a rising tide of resentment at the unfairness of it all. *Isn't it past time for Duncan to grow the hell up?*

Right. Because at the age of nearly thirty-four, Duncan is likely to do that now.

Jasmine leans over the back of the seat and startles Craig out of his increasingly sour thought spiral. "Hey." She folds her arms to make a pillow for her head and gazes at him. "What's up? Is it weird? Being home, I mean?"

He's grateful for the distraction. "A little," he says, and it's not a lie, at least. There is definitely weirdness afoot. But he casts that aside and forces a smile for his baby sister. "The last time I was here, you'd just got braces on your teeth. You and Jade didn't even come up to my shoulder."

He catches a glimpse of a bashful smile before Jasmine buries her face in her arms. "It's been that long?" she asks, somewhat muffled.

"So it would seem. I notice the braces are gone." Craig twists in his seat to poke at his sister until she lifts her head. "It's so strange that you're almost all grown up. I still remember helping Mum with changing your nappies."

"Less of that in front of the new guy." Jasmine socks him in the arm. She jerks her head to indicate Alex, who looks over with an uncertain smile. "I have a reputation to uphold."

It's nice to have siblings he does actually like. "Right. So you don't still have that enormous stuffed bunny I brought with me on my last trip, then."

Jasmine ducks her head with a giggly little snort. "I didn't say that," she mumbles, eyes a-twinkle. She shakes her hair back and props her chin in her hand. "I like him," she whispers, nudging Craig with her elbow. "Jade's going to die; he's so cute. It'll give Frankie fits all week."

"Poor Frankie," Craig chuckles. Maybe he can get Frankie and Alex to hang out this week and be jealous together. *Hmm. Probably, that's asking for trouble.*

"I think maybe I scared him a little back at the airport, though," Jasmine confesses. "Didn't mean to. The look on his face was priceless when I implied we were more into torture than killing, but I hope I didn't make shit weird."

"I'm sure he's fine, whatever you said," Craig says, not entirely sure that's true. Alex has hardly said a word to anyone but Chloe on the drive from the airport. "Tired and nervous, that's all he is. He knows what a joke is, Jazz, I swear he does. It..." Craig checks on Alex again. His boyfriend is stiff as a poker, very much the picture of someone who wouldn't mind terribly if he melted into the upholstery. "It just might take him a few hours to get the joke."

"Here we are!" Chloe turns in her seat, bouncing and clapping with unbridled glee as Stephen steers into the drive alongside the big white house. "Ahh, I'm so excited; wait till you see everything."

"Mum made us paint welcome banners." Jasmine sits up straight. "I got the rest of the art club to help out, so they're pretty great, if you ask me."

"And I'm sure Jade and Frankie and Tristan are still playing." Chloe opens her door, swings down to the ground, and tilts her head to listen. A smile spreads across her face. "It's my processional! They're practicing my processional! Come on, Alex!" She bounces over to yank Alex's door open and pulls him right out of the van. "You have to hear this. They're so good; you'll love it. Do you like Haydn? They're amazing..." Her voice fades as she leads Alex to the back of the van to gather luggage.

Craig pushes his own door open; only his sister's impatient pushing gets him out of the car faster than at a crawl. "I'll get your bags," she tells him, flinging an arm over his shoulder. "Go on in."

"Yeah?" He glances at her. "You sure?"

"Yeah, yeah, go on in, get the fuss over with." She grins widely. "Everyone's really excited, Craig. Even your old swim coach cracked a smile when Jade told him you were coming back."

"Old Man McInnerny? Smiling?" Craig manages to laugh at the mental image of his dour swim coach actually smiling. "Wonders will never cease. All right, I'm going."

Yeah. He is definitely a fan of having at least one sibling he likes.

But now it's time to face the music. Craig draws back his shoulders and hurries down the little pathway to the front door. The door—painted a glossy navy blue and mounted with a shiny brass knocker, just as it has been for as long as he can remember—is cracked open just a bit, enough to let the sweet strains of Jade's cello stream into the night. The mellow drone is cushioned by light piano and augmented by the silvery trills of an expertly played flute.

Craig slips through the door, presses himself into the shadows of the foyer, and peers through the doorway that leads into the front room to see if he can find the rest of his family before they find him.

Success.

He spots his mother first. Her shock of short, dark curls halos the youthful face that belies her fifty-two years; her blue eyes are bright as she watches Jade and her friends play. With a peaceful smile, she sways a little to the music.

Jade is easily spotted next, the cello of course being a dead giveaway. Head bent, she is intent on the music stand before her and looks for all the world like the utter antithesis of her twin. Her dark hair, woven into dozens of tiny braids, is drawn back into a large bun at the nape of her neck. Her jeans and pink sweater are free of the paint splotches that mar Jasmine's clothing; she wears a pair of pristine white sneakers as opposed to clunky boots. Her face is serene; the smooth, brown skin of her brow is untroubled as she draws her bow across her strings.

Next to Jade stands a small, round girl with a nimbus of blonde waves that glows in the low light of the lamps. A silver flute shines in her hands. She has to be Frankie, and the earnest, thin boy at the piano is obviously Tristan. They're playing brilliantly, as well as any classical musicians Craig's heard in Seattle, and he can't help but flush with pride. His own sister! He can't play an instrument to save his life, and here's his baby sister, a virtuoso.

Craig's lip curls as his eyes find Duncan standing just behind Moira. Duncan's face is expressionless despite the beautifully played music. No change there. Duncan never was able to appreciate most art forms. Craig allows his gaze to drift over some dozen or so neighbors he hasn't said boo to in years, and then there's David in the back corner with his dark hair tousled and his green eyes bright. Dark stubble lines his jaw and stands in stark contrast to his fair skin. Standing in front of a brightly painted *Welcome Home, Craig and Alex* banner, he's good-looking as ever and in a way that sets off butterflies in Craig's stomach. David is tall and broad-shouldered, and the way he looks in his leather jacket almost distracts from the way his eyes dart around the room.

God, he looks good. Wait. Where did that come from?

Right. Craig is so not ready to walk into that room.

A soft whine sounds around his ankles, and Craig crouches to find the family Welsh springer spaniel snuffling at his socks. "Newton!" he whispers, ruffling the spaniel's floppy ears. "How are you, boy? You remember me, yeah?"

His friendly pats are greeted with a sharp bark, and Newton bounces up to lick his face before barking again in obvious delight. "Newton, no, shh, shh, come on; they'll hear you."

The music cuts off with a screech, and Moira's voice rises above a sudden buzz of murmurs. "Hello? Is someone there?"

Damn it. Okay, then. Ready or not.

Brushing brown and white fur off the front of his sweater, Craig gets to his feet. "Um. Right. Hello. Sorry, Mum, it's just m—"

"Craig!" Jade's shriek fills the room, and he has about two seconds to register her joy before she's hurling her cello aside for Frankie to catch. She shoots to her feet and bolts across the family room in a blur, jumping at the last minute to wrap herself entirely around him and squeeze him tight. He's only just able to grab hold of her and keep the both of them from crashing to the floor. "Craigcraigcraigcraigcraig!"

"Hey there, Jade." Between his laughter and her stranglehold around his neck, it's hard to get the greeting out. "Jesus."

"Sorry." She releases him, climbs down, and hugs him around the ribs. "I'm just so happy to see you!"

"I'm happy to see you, too." He still can't quite breathe, and she's got him clamped in a vise, but it doesn't matter. He does try to pull back and get a good look at her, though. "God, and I thought Jazz looked all grown up. You're not allowed to become an adult, hear me? I was just feeding you mashed peas yesterday!"

"Oh, shut up." Jade lets go and backs up, bouncing on her toes. "You're here! I can't believe you're here finally. Why didn't you say anything when you came in the door? Where's everyone else?"

"Here." Stephen pushes through the door with Craig's carry-on in one hand and a suitcase in the other. Jasmine and Chloe behind him carry Alex's bags. "Get this stuff to... oh, let's say your mother's office, will you, girls?"

"On it." The twins disappear into the crowd of neighbors that's suddenly blocking the entry into the family room, and occasional squeals of pain mark their progress as Jasmine makes no effort to prevent a heavy case from rolling over some hapless neighbor's foot.

Moira's pushed her way to the front of the scrum and stands before Craig with a scowl of mock annoyance. "That's a fine greeting for your mother, isn't it? Sneaking in through the door like some kind of thief in the night and not a single hello for me, is that the way of it? And I was in labor with you for a full day, I'll have you know. Craig Andrew Oliver, is this how you're going to treat me?"

"God, I missed you, Mum." Craig grabs his mother, taking in the smell and feel and sound of her all at once for the first time in years. He grips her as tightly as Jade grabbed him and doesn't want to let go. He has to close his eyes to hold back the needle-sharp tears he refuses to shed in front of everyone else. "I'm so happy to see you; it's so good. Oh, Mum."

"Ah, darling boy. It's good to see you, too." All sarcasm is gone from Moira's voice. "It's always too long between visits, love. Let me have a look at you." She steps back and gives him a good once-over. "Tall, strong, and handsome like your brother. I did raise me a good pair of boys." Cocking her head, she surveys him. "Love clearly does you good. Now, where's this Alex of yours? I'm almost more excited to meet him than I was to see you!"

With a laugh, Craig takes a look around, only to frown in worry when Alex isn't anywhere in the room. "I don't... didn't he follow everyone in?"

"No." Behind Craig, the front door swings slowly open and, oh, there Alex is. He stands in the doorway taking deep breaths with his white-knuckled fists around the strap of Fitz's carrier. He'd combed his hair at the airport, but a certain fluffiness in the dark strands is clear evidence of nervous finger-ruffling.

"Sorry. I needed a minute." His smile is crooked and a little forced; he must be bristling with nerves and anxiety.

Slowly, Craig reaches out to take Alex's arm, but he's beaten to the punch by Moira, who isn't nearly as slow or careful. She has seized Alex in a hug and yanked him into the house before either Alex or Craig fully grasps what's happening. "Ooh, look at you. If circumstances were very different all around, I think you and I would be having a nice long talk in a cozy dark room, you lovely fellow, you." Her wink is salacious, and her giggle is bright. "You're even more good-looking in person. And so tall!"

Alex has time to cast one startled glance at Craig before Moira pulls him into the center of the crowd and starts introductions. "Everyone, this is Craig's partner Alex. Isn't he lovely? Let's give him a grand welcome! Oh, and you brought wee Fitz. Hello, little love; oh, let's have him out of the carrier..."

And that is the last Craig sees of his boyfriend and his dog.

But before he can worry too long, the twins pop up with identical knowing smirks on their faces. "Party pooper. You can't just lurk in the foyer all night," Jade scolds with a shake of her head.

"Yeah, Craig. This party is all for you; you can't dodge it." Jasmine winks. "Not that I don't completely understand the urge."

Jade loops her arm through his. "Come on, big brother. Someone brought an actual chocolate fountain and all kinds of stuff to dip in it. Pretty sure Chloe is trying to work out how she can steal it for the wedding."

Chocolate sounds good. *Food* sounds good—dinner service on the plane was much too long ago. And maybe he can find Alex, make sure he's all right, make sure he doesn't have a run-in with Duncan. His parents and sisters might be stellar examples of Oliver hospitality, but Craig is not about to consider, even for a second, that Duncan could be capable of that. "Yeah, that would be great." With a smile, Craig tugs his arm out of Jade's grip and strides into the family room, where he runs right smack into David—and a cup of hot chocolate. "Ouch!"

"Sorry. Sorry, Craig. Shit!" David's mouth drops open, and red blazes a splotchy trail from his neck up into his face. "I... I—I did-didn't see you there, I didn't mean to—" He yanks a fistful of paper napkins from the hand of a passing neighbor and ignores the man's protests as he dabs at the chocolate spreading across the front of Craig's favorite green sweater. "Fuck. I'm so sorry."

Always so cute when he's flustered. God only knows why this is the first thing to come to Craig's mind when his tall, dark, and handsome ex-boyfriend is frantically patting at his chest, but there it is. Could this night get any more bizarre and awkward? *No, Craig. Don't invite trouble.* He grabs David's hand and pushes it away. "Don't worry about it." The last thing Craig needs is for Alex to see him being patted down by a good-looking stranger. "Seriously."

But David tries again to blot the spreading stain. "It's going to soak in, Craig. We have to stop it now, or it'll never come out." A tiny frown creases David's brow right over his nose, a tiny frown Craig has seen so many times when David tried to work out a particularly vexing bit of schoolwork, or when he was arranging flowers after school, or when he was deciding whether or not to kiss Craig...

With a start, Craig pushes David back. Heat rushes to his cheeks at the surprise of that memory surfacing. "Honestly, David, it'll be fine." The awareness that he's got his hands on

David hits him, and he jerks away. "I'll have Mum clean it. Or I'll do it. It will get cleaned. Don't worry about it."

"No, really, I should—"

"David, honestly, it doesn't matter—"

"But it's just terrible—" David stops, takes a deep breath, and rubs at his stubbly chin. "Craig. Can we start this over?" His eyes light up. "Please. We are going to English ourselves right into the ground if we keep this up."

Laughter drains some of the embarrassment and awkwardness. "Yes. Yes, let's do that," Craig says. He snatches the napkins to blot at his chest himself. "Thank you for trying to help."

"You're welcome. Listen, Craig..." The old rueful smile on David's face is just as familiar as the frown, but stirs up fewer blush-worthy memories than the frown or the way he's rumpling his tousled brown hair. Craig tears his eyes away as David goes on. "Mum was too tired to come tonight, and I don't like leaving her on her own too long, so I'm afraid I have to get out of here. But I am glad I got to run into you, though perhaps not the part where I literally ran into you."

"Yeah. I follow." The sweater is a lost cause. Craig tugs it over his head and tosses it onto the piano bench. Fortunately, the chocolate didn't soak through the wool to his T-shirt. "I'm sorry you're leaving. I thought we could catch up." *And I thought I could look at you some more; oh, my sweet Lord, what is* wrong *with me?*

"Come to the shop tomorrow. Bring your fellow." David waves a vague hand in the direction of the buffet spread. "I met him over the chicken salad. He's nice. And he must be fairly sturdy to withstand the onslaught of your mother."

"He's incredible," Craig says, and no, he is *not* protesting just a wee bit much. "We're very happy together."

David's eyebrows go up; his smile is touched with confusion. "Yes. Right. I'm... sure you are."

"I... yeah." Back rushes the awkwardness. *Good job, Craig.*

"I'm going to go home now," David says, backing away slowly. His smile is a little *too* fixed; his nod is a little too deliberate. "I'm quite happy to have seen you, and I'll look forward to a visit from the two of you tomorrow, I hope?"

He's gone before Craig can get another word out. That's just as well, probably.

I have no idea what my problem is. Terminal idiocy?

Yes. He's stupid. And still hungry. "Food," he says aloud, ignoring the startled glances this earns him. "Food is good. Food prevents me from talking."

Now, that's a solid plan.

He's just picking up one of Mrs. Fitzpatrick's vol-au-vents when Chloe pops up next to him. "Ooh, bacon-wrapped prawns, excellent. I wondered if they were going to be able to talk Mrs. Jones into making them." In short order, Chloe has a paper plate piled high with the prawns and she commences to all but inhale them. "Oh, my God. Oh, yeah."

Craig regards his own sparsely inhabited plate. "Trust me when I say I'm not passing judgment," he says, adding a couple of mini sausage rolls and some boiled egg wedges to his assortment. "But isn't there a fairly ridiculous and vile tradition that brides eat nothing but lettuce leaves and the occasional half a cracker before their wedding?"

"To hell with *that.*" Chloe scoffs around a mouthful of bacon. "No, no, no wedding dieting, thank you." She waves a hand at her baggy jeans and three-sizes-too-big rugby shirt. "I just ran around like this for the last two months. This way, when I show up at my wedding wearing something that's properly fitted, it'll look like I lost half a stone, but I didn't have to do anything!" She stuffs another prawn into her mouth and chews for a bit. "Mind, I know that gossipy cow Melinda Connolly has been spreading it around that I'm pregnant, but whatever. She drank so many wheatgrass smoothies before her wedding, her dress was a tent! Anyway, how are you holding up?"

"Ah." Craig nibbles at a roll and cranes his neck, looking for Alex in the tight crush of people. He's forgotten to worry for an entire minute.

A fingertip poking the softness of his stomach calls his attention back to Chloe. "Stop worrying so much." She punctuates every other syllable with a sharp poke. "He's fine."

But Craig can't help it. He looks around until he spots Alex nodding and smiling while Moira passes him a never-ending stream of snacks. "Oh, Mum's feeding him." There's one thing he doesn't have to worry about, then.

"See? Fine." Chloe twines her fingers with his and tugs at his arm until he smiles. "Alex is great. I like him a lot, Craig. And I think he'll survive this week just fine, so relax, will you?"

Nerves shot, Craig glances around the room. "I can't."

"Craig?"

"Really, I can't." It's too much: this night, the awkward moment with David, Craig's worries about Alex, all that *and* a secret he's been keeping, a secret that's had him on edge all day, for months, really. It's a secret no one knows, and Craig finally has *got* to tell someone. And also get out of this tightly packed room, but mostly he has to tell someone.

Craig sets down his plate and grabs Chloe by the wrist. "Come with me, Cee. I have something to tell you."

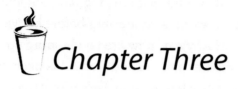 *Chapter Three*

CHLOE LAUGHS AS CRAIG HAULS HER INTO HIS MOTHER'S home office. "What are we doing in here? Why are you being so mysterious?"

Dropping Chloe's hand, Craig makes a beeline for his carry-on and hoists it onto a chair. "Patience. I told you, I have something to tell you." He keeps an eye on her as he rummages through the bag by touch alone. "But you cannot, *cannot*, squeal, or shriek, or do anything that will bring anyone in here, Chloe. And you can't tell anyone about it." He raises his free hand to forestall her protests. "No, not even Duncan." His fingers stumble upon what he's looking for, and his stomach churns. "Actually, especially not Duncan."

Chloe's eyes are saucer-wide. "Okay."

Craig squeezes his hand around the object in his bag, and the edges bite into his fingers. "Seriously, Cee. Not a word. You have to swear on your life."

"Cross my heart and hope to die, stick a needle in my eye," is the prompt, if childish, reply. A broad grin spreads across Chloe's face as she holds her hand up. "Swear to God."

"Okay. Seriously, though. Not a soul, Cee, not one word." Craig tosses the object to her. "Catch."

She plucks it out of the air and stares; her frown seems perplexed. "But what is it?" Even as the final word is escaping her mouth, it hits her. "Oh. Oh, my God. *Craig.*"

It's a box, just a small box covered in red leather and embossed in gold, a box that Chloe cracks open to reveal a burnished gold band nestled in charcoal-gray velvet. One hand flies to cover her mouth, cutting off the squeal that begins to slip loose. If her eyes were like saucers before, they're dinner plates now. "Mmmph!"

Craig all but loses it laughing as Chloe squeaks and bounces in place with her curls bobbing and her hand still clamped firmly over her mouth. The other hand, still holding the box, flaps like an excitable parakeet. "Oh, my God." The words are muffled by the barrier of her hand. "Oh, my God!"

"Nothing, not a hint or a whisper or so much as a peep to anyone," he reminds her, retrieving the box to tuck back into his bag. Chloe is emitting a whispery screech as she Snoopy-dances around the office. "Cee! I mean it, you promised!"

She stops in her tracks with an eye roll. "Yes, Craig. I heard you." She's next to him in a bound and flings her arms around him. "This is incredible! When are you going to ask?"

The question stills his hand in the middle of zipping the bag shut. "I don't know."

"You what?" Chloe hooks her chin over his shoulder. "What? No, come on. You must have a plan. This is you we're talking about."

"You're not wrong there. I did have a plan." He turns around in her arms. "Our anniversary was in August. I was going to ask then."

"And?"

"And he still wasn't quite over the arrival of your wedding invitation, so, I didn't." Craig places a hand over her mouth.

"Shh. Not your fault, we knew it was coming. It's just that he was already wound up about the wedding, so I didn't want to add, 'Hey, why don't I bring you to meet my family for the first time as my fiancé?' Too much pressure."

"Hmm." Chloe cocks her head. "For him, or for you?"

"For me," he admits, as everything that could have gone wrong with a proposal flashes through his head. "And of course, I didn't want to steal any thunder from you."

"Fair enough. I appreciate that." She frowns. "Why bring the ring, then?"

"I had to. Alex's cousin Samantha is going to be in our apartment this weekend checking on our plants and things. She's an inveterate snoop; I couldn't leave it for her to find." Craig tugs at a dreadlock. "I am going to ask him sometime, soon, if I can get past the fear that this week is going to be so awful and stressful that he'll decide I'm not worth the effort. That's why I'm..."

"Hovering?" Chloe winks and blows out a breath to flip back a curl dangling over her eye. "Being a helicopter boyfriend in a doomed effort to make sure everything goes absolutely perfectly and he doesn't run screaming?" She huffs. "Right, I'm not sure Alex is the one who needs watching over."

Craig opens his mouth to reply, but—"I don't know about that," Jasmine drawls from the doorway, catching them by surprise. She pushes up the sleeves of her messy sweater. "Duncan just got hold of him while you two were back here gossiping."

That's enough to make Craig start to bolt from the room, but Chloe snags a handful of his T-shirt. "Wait." She tilts her chin toward Jasmine. "You. How long were you there? What'd you hear?"

Jasmine sighs. "Jade and I already found the ring when we dumped the bags in here, so I knew before you did. Don't worry, we're not planning to tell anyone. There's more value in *keeping* a secret."

Craig nods. That explains their faces earlier. "Value? Fine. I'll untangle fairy lights for you or bake cookies or whatever—anything you want on the bright side of legality." With a jerk, he pulls his shirt free of Chloe's hand and glares at her. "Can I please go rescue my boyfriend from our brother now?"

"Better let him go, Cee." Jasmine inspects her fingernails. "Duncan opened the conversation with, 'God, you're a long streak of piss, eh?' and given that he's had four Stellas and a double whiskey, I'm thinking it'll just go downhill from there."

"Fuck! Who let him into the liquor cabinet?" Chloe doesn't wait for an answer. She's hightailing it down the corridor in a streak of wild curls and high panic before Craig can take his first step after her.

Here it is. Here's The Moment.

With effort, Craig follows Chloe at a much more leisurely pace. *Keep your head, Oliver.* His best trick for handling Duncan has always been to never let on that whatever is happening has gotten to him at all. As much as he wants to rush in and drag Alex away from whatever Duncan is saying, that would just let them in for a week of nonstop aggravation.

All Craig wants to do is see his best friend married to the worst of his siblings and then go home with his feathers unruffled and nebulous plans unshaken.

Right. Good luck with that.

"Y'r gonna come play rugby tomorrow," Duncan slurs just as Craig arrives in the living room. "Do a game every afternoon, five a side."

Alex wears the bland mask he puts on for shrill, impatient mothers-of-the-bride at the studio during pricing negotiations. Craig knows it like the back of his hand, along with the cool tone that goes with it. "Yeah, not sure there's going to be time for that, but thank you for the invitation."

"We *make* time, you got me?" Belligerence and alcohol combine to make the heavy Glasgow inflection in Duncan's accent lean hard toward incomprehensibility. "C'mon, whatsit, you can learn how to play rugby, easy as piss, or maybe y'r afraid to play a game without padding?" He shakes Chloe's tugging hand from his arm and leans closer, breathing in Alex's face. "Or're you like Craig, don't do real sports?"

"He swims. Swimming was in fact a real sport the last time I checked," Alex replies, still bland and smooth and cool and bored, though irritation radiates from him like quills on an agitated porcupine. "And no, I have no problem with sports that don't use padding. I played soccer in college."

"Soccer?" Duncan barks out a half laugh, half belch. It makes Alex flinch. Chloe rolls her eyes, and Moira's expression clearly says that she's two seconds and a dirty word from committing filicide. "Americans. It's football, y'hear? Y'r on my turf, you use the right words, okay—ow!"

Chloe, at last, has Duncan's ear in a grip that makes his eyes bulge. Craig has to look down and press his lips tightly together so that he doesn't laugh out loud. "That's it," Chloe says in a hiss, and she gives Duncan's ear a good enough yank that he has to follow or risk the possibility of losing it. "We're going home. You're being an idiot, and worse, *rude*."

"Cee, come on! Ow! I just—ow!—it's a joke, I'm not meaning—let go!"

Chloe smiles at Craig and ignores her fiancé. "Welcome home, Craig. I'd better get this one off to bed." With her free arm, she hugs Alex. "Lovely to have met you, Alex. Why don't I come get you tomorrow, and we'll go out to the farm?"

Alex's mask melts into a smile of anticipation. "Sure, great. I'll bring my camera?"

"Love it." She gives Craig a hug and a smile. "And you and I will do some test baking on Tuesday?"

"Wouldn't miss it for worlds," he says, and hopes fervently that Duncan won't be around.

"See you then." Still dragging a grumbling Duncan by the ear, Chloe makes the rounds to say goodbye to everyone before she vanishes out the door.

As soon as the front door clicks shut behind them, Craig is finished. Exhaustion hits him like a ton of bricks, and he notes with no surprise that the clock on the mantel shows that it's long past midnight. Though it's still early evening back in Seattle, Craig is completely done in.

"That's enough for us. It's been one hell of a day, Mum. I'd like to go to sleep, and Alex was tired when we *got* here." A sidelong glance at Alex, swaying on his feet, is all the proof Craig needs that it's time for the day to be over. "We'll go on up now. Sorry."

"That's all right, love, I think Duncan was the last excitement any of us could take." Moira stretches on tiptoe to kiss his cheek. "And look, Mrs. Fitzpatrick is already asleep." She gestures to where the blue-haired biddy in question is curled up and snoring in Stephen's big reading chair. "If I don't get everyone out now, they'll join her. Go on up, darling. Your room is all clean and ready for you. I'll have a nice breakfast in the morning, hmm?"

"Sounds great, Mum," Craig says, nearly ready to shove Mrs. Fitzpatrick out of the chair and curl up in her place. He takes Alex's hand. "Babe?"

Alex snaps to attention, blinking glazed-over gray eyes. "Bed?"

"Bed." Craig pulls Alex along by the hand. "Sleep. We'll have to drag our bags up to the loft. I'm sorry."

"If there's a bed at the end of the trip, I'd drag a sofa up the stairs by myself." For all that it's blurred with exhaustion, Alex's rejoinder is fervent and sincere. They gather their dog from Jasmine and their bags from the study in tired silence and climb the stairs, their footsteps and the muffled noise of the dying party behind them the only sounds.

Alex's thoughts are *loud*. Craig is sure what they must be about. And he fears it.

They're coming up the last flight of stairs to Craig's old bedroom when Alex speaks at last. "So," he says, voice loaded with trepidation. Craig was right to fear. "You and your brother really do not get along. Like, at all."

"Did you think I was exaggerating?" With some effort, Craig keeps his tone light.

"No. But it's one thing to hear about it and entirely another to see it with your own eyes." Though unmistakably tired and still unsteady on his feet, Alex stops in his tracks and parks his suitcase. His eyes are steady on Craig's as he tilts his head. "Now, he didn't make the best impression on me. But he was no worse than any guy in my frat in college; I can handle that. You, though?" He shakes his head. "You were furious, I could tell. I *know* you."

"Yeah, well." Craig shrugs.

"Yeah, well, nothing. I haven't..." Alex takes in a deep breath. "I wasn't attentive these last months the way I should have been. And I never asked you about Duncan. I think... I think we probably ought to talk about it now."

"Oh, all right." This, Craig can admit, he did not expect. He shoves his suitcase aside and lets the weight of his surprise and dread drop him to a sitting position on the stairs. "Okay."

It's difficult to know where to begin, to put any of it into words, now that it's truth time. There's always been that slight but persistent worry in the back of Craig's mind that maybe he's too paranoid about his brother. Maybe he was just too sensitive to the raucous teasing; maybe he should have tried harder to develop a thicker skin. The part of him that always looked up to his big brother and desperately sought Duncan's approval always raises these doubts.

But the part of him that endured taunts and being left behind, the resentful teenager who so often came home from school to find his room ransacked and his belongings hidden or stolen for ransom—that part always chimes in to counter that maybe he was right and Duncan always was the *worst*.

And then. Then there was that one day...

Oh, he's so tired.

"To be very fair," Craig begins at last, scrubbing a hand over his face, "I will remind you that Duncan and I are just about four years apart in age. He'd gotten awfully used to being an only child by the time I came along."

Alex sits next to him. Droopy, tired Fitz is tucked in his lap. "Okay. So not close."

"Never close, not at all." Craig sighs. "In fact, he was quite jealous of the new baby taking Mum's attention, from what she's told me. Right from the start. And he was still upset that they moved back here from Scotland when Dad finished his degree. Me and the move away from everything he'd ever known, I think they were linked in his mind for a long time."

"Got it." Alex nods. "So he was *always* a jerk about you."

"As much as small children are. I mean, he mostly just picked on me. When I started school, that's when it all really took off." Even now, the memories scratch at his heart. He had to walk to and from school exactly fifteen paces behind his brother. His packed lunches were always plundered for the snacks. If he tried to speak to Duncan at all in front of anyone except their parents, Duncan flatly ignored his existence. Craig can recite a litany of offenses as long as the street outside, and they all sting, even now.

Moira did her best to make them get along. But she'd been a very young mother, and boys do as boys choose, and Duncan chose to make Craig's life hell. And then he resented the attention that Moira gave Craig to make up for it.

It was a vicious cycle.

Explaining all of this to Alex is more draining than Craig expected. He'd almost forgotten the little voice in the background he has to work to ignore whenever he goes over all of this, the little voice that always asks what was so wrong with Craig that his own brother didn't like him.

"One day it all really blew up." Remembering it still makes his throat dry. Craig swallows hard. "I am still trying to be fair, so I will say that Duncan didn't mean to do it, and anyway, I shouldn't have been in the way."

He doesn't realize he's rubbing his left wrist until Alex lays a hand over his. "Craig?"

It's never been quite the same, his wrist. He can't knead bread dough for as long if his left hand takes the lead. The hand lags a little behind his right in terms of picking up heavy things. It aches a bit when it's about to rain—which means most fall and winter days, in Seattle. Craig clears his throat. "I was thirteen. One day, I was in the family room, working on a school project. I had my notes and things laid out across the rug. I mean, admittedly, I made a bit of a mess. I was in the way." He's never, ever been able to not accept some of the blame for what happened. But only some.

His throat is dry again; his tongue is almost numb. Craig swallows again and breathes deeply. "Duncan came in with his rugby buddies. They'd just won a big match; they were all high and excited on it. And they came rampaging into the house, heading for the kitchen, you know, like teenage boys do." His nerves set prickles of anxiety running just under the surface of his skin, and Craig tries to rub away the goosebumps. "Duncan didn't even see me. The other guys did, but he just... well. Basically, he ran right over me. With his cleats still on. Right over my left wrist."

Alex's mouth drops open. "Craig. My God. Broken?"

"Fractured. Cracked. It could have been worse. I mean, you saw how he's built." Though not quite as tall as Craig, Duncan was always much broader and brawnier, especially when they were teenagers. The impact of his full weight on Craig's wrist resulted in a lightning bolt of red, raw pain. "That wasn't the bad bit, though, not really. It wasn't even my first broken bone. No. The problem is that..." He blows out a long puff of air. "Duncan never apologized. Not even once."

And now Alex's eyes go very, very wide. "Excuse me?"

He sits up, almost stands, as if he's about to take off after Duncan and Chloe, exhaustion be damned. Craig puts a restraining hand on Alex's shoulder and uses his free hand to pluck Fitz from Alex's lap. "He didn't apologize, ever. In fact, he blamed me entirely for the incident, which was just delightful of him."

Still and silent, Alex sits for a long while. At last, he lets out a bitter little laugh and shakes his head. "I am suddenly very, very glad I was an only child."

"Not that that doesn't come with its own difficulties, my prickly hedgehog." Craig leans on Alex's shoulder and absently scratches a snoozy Fitz between his fuzzy ears. "But yeah. You did kind of miss out on a lot."

They sit in companionable, tired silence on the stairs. Fitz snores his wheezy puppy snore. "So what happened after that?" Alex finally asks.

"Duncan and I haven't spoken more than a handful of words since, for one thing, and only when we had to." Craig shrugs. "He went off to uni in Glasgow a year or so later, and we managed to avoid each other for that entire stretch of time. It helped that my parents set up the loft room for me; that got me away from everything. And it came in handy when they found out the twins were coming. They turned my old room into their nursery. So it all worked out."

"Maybe except for the part where you haven't really spoken," Alex points out with considerable gentleness.

"I don't really consider that to be a *problem*, as such." Craig hands Fitz to Alex and winces as he stretches his arms up. His back aches from sitting on the stairs. "My mother and Chloe do, but I only promised to behave this week. I didn't promise to reconcile." He's quite aware that neither woman will see it that way, but all he has to do is survive the week. "Not sure there'd be much point in doing so anyway. Duncan and I never had anything in common, and we're just not quite close enough in age. We've always been, more or less, strangers."

"There's also the fact that he's an actual asshole and you aren't, and if it's *me* saying someone's an asshole..." Alex's face is twisted into a scowl.

"It could have been worse," Craig replies, hoping he has enough energy to get up the stairs. "At least the one thing he always gave me a pass on was the gay thing. He never said a word about it, and I admit to a certain gratitude there."

"Hooray, basic human decency on a microcellular level." Alex's mouth puckers as if he's just sucked on a lemon. "You know what? Duncan does not deserve Chloe. What the hell does she see in him?"

"She's always adored him. I don't really get it, either." If he spends too much time thinking about it, Craig gets a wicked headache. "There have to be some redeeming characteristics there, apart from the basic goodness of never being prone to domestic violence or infidelity. And he is funny, good-looking, loyal, and kind to everyone apart from me. So... that's something."

"Whatever." It's clearly not enough for Alex. He bows his head and cuddles Fitz close to his chest. "We just have to get through the week without punching him, right? That ought to be easy enough."

Craig isn't so sure. "You think?" Not that he would really hit his brother, but the temptation, he suspects, is going to be fierce.

"I can hope." Alex tugs at his ear and offers Craig a lopsided smile. "I won't make you promise anything."

At this, Craig manages a laugh, if a very small and tired one. He leans against Alex again, and they sit shoulder to shoulder. Alex picks up Craig's hand and clasps it in both of his. His graceful fingers slip between Craig's to twine them together. He clears his throat. "So. Subject change. I met David." His cheeks flush pink. "He seems nice."

Craig chokes on a hysterical laugh, only just turning it into a cough. "Er. Yes. He is. Nice. Very nice."

Alex stares at him, and there has never been a time in their life together when he's more obviously questioned Craig's sanity. "Uh. You okay there?"

Nope. Craig has no more energy for this conversation, for this day. He leans hard on Alex's shoulder and sighs. "Just tired. Let's adjourn to bed, please. We don't really have to unpack a lot—" He'd rather unpack his carry-on without Alex around anyway. "—but I'd really, really just like to lie down. We can talk more in the morning."

"Yeah, that works." Alex puts a hand on the back of Craig's neck and tugs him in for a long, warm kiss. "Just so you're aware, your brother is an idiot," he mumbles against Craig's mouth. "You are the most generous—" Kiss. "—patient—" Another kiss, longer now. "—warm, interesting, talented, incredible person—" Alex punctuates each attribute with a kiss, which makes them laugh right into each other's mouths. "—who has ever been stupid enough to love me," Alex concludes, and, with a fond smile, he pulls away to sit back and look at Craig. His thumb traces Craig's cheekbone.

Craig covers Alex's hand with his. "It is an honor and a privilege," he gets out in a whisper, choked by all that he feels for this impossible, mercurial man. "I do love you very, very much, you know. Thank you for being here with me."

"I love the fuck out of you, too," Alex says, and Craig chuckles again, the laugh fading in the fierce light that burns in Alex's eyes. The conviction and sincerity there brands the sentiment onto Craig's heart and convinces him all over again that he wants to marry this man—is *going* to marry him. "And there was no way you were coming here without me, Craig, no matter how twitchy I got." Alex gets to his feet and pulls Craig up after him. "Bedtime," he says firmly, and Craig is not inclined to argue.

They haul their bags up the last few steps, and Craig reaches for the doorknob, mindful of how he'll need to give the tricky catch a jiggle, lift, and push all at once. The door wasn't installed quite correctly by his father, so there'd always been a knack to it. "Right. Home sweet temporary—"

He swings the door open and stops in his tracks, mouth agape.

It is thoroughly clean and ready, just as Moira said. Every surface gleams under the low light from the lamps; the floor and its throw rugs are immaculate; the desk is tidy; and the bed is piled high with pillows and turned down.

What Moira did not do, what it never occurred to Craig to ask her to do, was to take down the wall of posters that slants over his bed. The evidence of his lifelong obsession is more than a little embarrassing. It is the cherry on top of the very strange sundae that has been this entire evening.

Alex peers over his shoulder and takes in the sight. "Wow," he says, craning his head. "Is that an entire wall of Robbie Williams?"

 Chapter Four

AN ENGLISH SUNRISE HAS COME AND GONE, BIRDS ARE singing, morning has broken, and Alex has not slept a wink.

He lets out an enormous yawn and rolls onto his back to face the source of his insomnia. A good dozen Robbie Williamses smirk down at him from the attic ceiling-wall that slants over the bed. Alex has nothing against Robbie Williams; in fact, he has a vague appreciation for his music. He even has one of the guy's CDs. It's just that when there are more than several Robbies beaming their cocky grins down at you, then no matter how cozy the bed, how congenial the company... Alex finds it difficult to get comfortable enough to sleep.

Craig, of course, did sleep; his light snores were the perfect counterpoint to Fitz's wheezy ones all night long. He is now up, has been up, disgustingly chipper and alert as he sings along to the radio in the small attic bathroom. No change there, then. With a groan, Alex rolls over and burrows under the mountain of pillows.

"Morning, sunshine," Craig sings out as he emerges from the bathroom clad in nothing more than a white towel around his hips and a blue washcloth held to his jaw. "Cut myself a bit shaving. Kiss it better?"

Alex peeks with one eye from under the pillow and, despite the welcome sight of Craig clad in not much of anything at all, he glares. "Not before caffeine, *creampuff*."

"Then it's a good thing I can deliver on that." Craig tosses the washcloth to the bedside table, where it lands with a wet *plop*. In another instant, he's sitting on the bed with Alex's glasses in one hand and a red pottery mug of steaming tea in the other. "Up and at 'em, babe. Mum's downstairs making the biggest breakfast you have ever seen, and we have a long day ahead. I unpacked your toiletries bag; your contacts are in the loo by the sink if you want them instead of the glasses."

"In a minute." Alex struggles up to a sitting position and accepts both the tea and the glasses, taking care to apply them to his person in the correct order—that's a mistake he's only made once. He takes a long sip and sighs in gratitude. "You're an angel, Craig."

"Most nights you call me God. Bit of a downgrade." Craig winks and maneuvers around the tea mug to kiss Alex on the cheek. "Sorry I didn't have milk for the tea. I forgot."

"S'okay. Undiluted caffeine might be the better choice before we go downstairs to face the masses." Alex yawns again and takes a bigger gulp of his tea to hide his sudden surge of anxiety. "Have you already been down? Is that where this came from?"

"It's where the sugar came from, but otherwise..." Craig jerks his thumb over his shoulder to indicate the battered desk tucked under a window at the other end of the room. An electric kettle sits there next to a stack of old journals and magazines. "The kettle's a perk of being banished to the top floor of the house—along with the bathroom, the fireplace, and complete privacy. Didn't manage to successfully lobby for a mini-fridge, though. I expect Mum and Dad rightly concluded I'd never come downstairs again if they installed one of those."

He swipes Alex's mug and takes a sip. "There's also a handy sneak-out route through that window behind you, if you're up for shimmying down a rickety drainpipe."

"Three floors up? No thanks. I much prefer the quiet-stalk-down-the-stairs method." Alex snatches his mug back. "Get your own, I need all of this."

"Fine, greedy." Craig winks and ambles to the kettle with Fitz scrabbling at his heels. "Fitz and I slept like kings. How about you?"

Alex stares warily at the Wall O' Robbies as Craig disappears into the bathroom. "Okay, I guess."

"Liar." Water runs for a moment or two, and Craig emerges with the kettle in his hand and a skeptical look. "You tossed and turned all night. Is this trip getting to you so badly already?"

"Yes... no..." Alex rubs at his chin and sighs. "It's the staring, Craig. All those Robbies staring at us, all night long. Not blinking. I can't... no. I did not sleep."

Craig joins the array of Robbies, staring at Alex for a very long and, given that he has company, uncomfortable moment. "Are you judging? It sounds like you're judging."

"Only your choice of decoration, not the subject," Alex says, and it's as ridiculous out loud as it was in his head the instant before he said it.

Craig obviously agrees. "Do I need to remind you," he says as he crosses the room to plug the kettle back in, "that I am in possession of several photos of *your* untouched teenage bedroom, sent to me by your very own mother? A bedroom with not one but *four* walls solidly plastered with posters of Ben Affleck and Chris Evans?" One dark eyebrow arches nearly to a point.

"Posters, you idiot, I'm judging the *posters*, not your taste in men," Alex snaps as his face flushes ten shades of hot, red, and flustered. "I'm judging the fact that a dozen versions of Robbie Williams are leering at your bed like a gang of serial killers."

They glare each other down. Craig is the first to relent when the kettle boils. "Fine. I concede that the Wall of Robbies might take some getting used to."

It's Alex's turn to raise an eyebrow. "Getting *used* to? I may not sleep—"

"Ben. Affleck," Craig counters succinctly.

Alex *wants* to argue his point, and he can probably win by the simple expedient of pointing out that they're not sleeping in *his* room this week, but this has really gone on long enough. "Yeah. Okay."

Craig shuffles back to the bed with his steeping tea and lifts Fitz onto the duvet before he slides back under it. "New subject, please," he says as he gives Alex's shoulder a playful nudge. A soft smile curves his lips. "Or a return to the original one, at least. You didn't sleep well, but how are you otherwise?"

Alex considers as he runs his fingers over the decorative ridges of his tea mug. There is a lot to unpack, here. Yesterday was much more eventful than either of them expected, and his lack of sleep impedes him from making a full, fair assessment. "I think I need more time to adjust, but I don't feel like running away," he says at last, fairly secure with the notion of keeping things simple. "Your parents are nice. Your sisters are... ah... slightly frightening, in that teenage girl way, but I like them. I am reserving further judgment on your brother. Chloe may replace you as my favorite person."

"A reasonable assessment," Craig says with a nod. "Though I will have you know that Chloe may be able to offer you access to lambs, but she would have no idea how to make your favorite s'mores brownie pie."

"Which is why," Alex amends hastily, "she will never actually win."

"You're so easy." Craig grins, sets his mug on the nightstand, and then plucks Alex's mug away as well. With a gentle nudge, he's got Fitz out of the way and then he's pressing Alex back into the bed. His hand strokes down Alex's side and arm, where it tickles faintly across the skin before their fingers wind together and Craig is kissing Alex breathless. He gets a leg up and over to straddle Alex and rolls his hips forward. His tongue flicks over Alex's lower lip.

It's good, so good, so easy to fall into the familiar rhythm. Alex lets his hand come up and stroke the dreads that fall over the back of Craig's neck, lets it wind through the locks to grip Craig and pull him closer and—and then Alex opens his eyes, and it's over in an instant.

It takes a second for Craig to register the change in mood. He blinks as he pulls back to look at Alex. "Babe?"

Alex can only wave a limp hand at Robbie Number Two on the ceiling-wall. "He's... he's smirking at me."

With a sigh, Craig slumps onto Alex's chest. When he shakes his head, his dreads tickle Alex's neck. "I'm sorry. I'll take them down," he says into Alex's skin.

"No." Alex gives Craig's hand a squeeze and the top of his head a sheepish kiss. "I'll get used to them. And if I don't, we'll be home in a week anyway."

Craig crosses his arms over Alex's chest and props his chin on them. "I suppose it's just as well. Mum'll be yelling any moment now for breakfast and, if we don't answer in a hurry, she'll come looking." Another sigh, and he's pushing himself up and off the bed and walking back into the bathroom. "We should finish our tea and go downstairs."

"For the record, it was really good until I opened my eyes," Alex calls after him as he sits up. It *was* good. He glares at Smirking Robbie Number Five. "And also, for the record, I am completely blaming you," he informs the poster.

Obviously, this doesn't make him feel like an idiot *at all*. Obviously.

THEY'RE CLEAN, DRESSED, AND LARGELY IN GOOD ORDER fifteen minutes later when they present themselves and Fitz at the Olivers' enormous round breakfast table in the kitchen. Only Alex's slightly-less-than-artfully-tousled hair provides any indication that there might have been a brief, heated make-up tussle in the bathroom during the preparation process. He runs a hand over it in what he hopes is a surreptitious gesture, but sly grins from Jasmine and Jade are definite indicators that he can't fool everyone.

"I wasn't expecting you for a while yet," Moira says before she whirls to pull down an extra pair of bowls. She fills them with oatmeal and all but slings them down on the table in front of Craig and Alex as they sit. "Stephen's gone off to the school already, but you two could have slept in, it's only half past seven."

Craig lets go of his bowl, which was teetering in a wobbly little circle after it hit the placemat. He puts Fitz on the floor. "We're a bit turned around yet from the time change and the new place to sleep and all," he says, snatching a piece of buttered toast from Jade's hand. He answers her screech of protest with a cheeky wink. "Neither of us slept much."

The twins, dressed for school in identical blazers and tartan skirts, regard Craig and Alex with interest. "I wouldn't sleep a whole lot with Robbie Williams staring at me all night, either," Jasmine mumbles into her oatmeal, so low only Alex hears her.

He bites so hard on his bottom lip to hold in his laughter that he nearly breaks the skin.

Glasses of orange juice clink down on the table in front of them. "Mushrooms and tomato coming up, then I'll have the sausage and eggs out for you quick as I can," Moira says as she zips back to the stove. "Of course there's more porridge and toast if you'd like; ask for anything you want. Oh, Jazz, love, can you get the boys some tea or coffee if you have a minute? Alex, darling, if you don't like that orange juice, I have apple, or perhaps you'd prefer pear?"

Craig hops to his feet to guide his mother to a chair. "Mum. Stop. Sit. Porridge and toast are fine. We can get our own tea or juice or whatever. We're fine; stop fussing."

"As if I could, darling. I suspect you don't feed that young man of yours. Are you quite sure that you're my son?" An unlikely Donna Reed in skinny jeans and a Ramones T-shirt, Moira is out from under Craig's hands and back at the stove with a deft twist. Alex wishes he'd brought his camera downstairs; the women of this family are just begging to be photographed, to have all their spark and fire captured on film forever.

Craig and Moira are at the stove having a good-natured argument about breakfast—an argument that Moira, cracking eggs into a bowl with one hand while holding off her son with the other, is winning—when Chloe bursts into the kitchen and points at Alex. A brilliant smile sets her face alight. "There you are, man of the hour." She slides into Craig's seat and slips her arm through Alex's to give it a squeeze. "You'll be ready to go to my parents' farm after breakfast, right?"

"I'll just need to get my gear bag." He hands her his untouched orange juice and a slice of toast from the platter in the center of the table. Tired as he is, Chloe's seemingly bottomless energy crackles into him like electricity, and he finds himself more alert and curiously eager to visit a farm full of woolly sheep. "So, your parents raise what kind of sheep?"

"Eat." Moira sets a big plate of grilled tomatoes, sautéed button mushrooms, soft scrambled eggs, and sizzling sausage in front of him. "Chloe, I'll have a plate for you in a moment. Neither of you are leaving this table to go anywhere until both your plates are spotless."

Alex stares at his plate as the realization that Craig wasn't exaggerating at all sinks in. With the toast, and the juice, and the bowl of bananas and oranges that Moira is bringing to the table, this really is the largest breakfast he's ever seen— which is really saying something, since he grew up with his grandmother Hannelore serving him enormous German breakfasts every summer of his life. A glance at Moira's face tells him more clearly than words that, yes, he is expected to eat the lot.

A cold nose nudges his ankle: Fitz, bright-eyed and wagging his little tail like a flag. He's accompanied by the Oliver family spaniel—Norman? Newman? No, Newton—who, although larger and older, is in a similar puppy-like state of endearing entreaty. All right, then. When Moira drops off the fruit bowl and turns to refill her cup of coffee, it's the work of an instant for Alex to slice off two small bits of sausage and smuggle them under the table. It takes even less time for the bits to disappear and for Alex's hand to receive two sloppy licks of canine gratitude.

To his left, Craig does not seem to notice the sleight of hand. "I tried to talk Mum out of this," he says, looking up from his own mountainous plate. "But no one goes up against her in an argument and wins."

"Your father does," Moira sings as she settles into her chair with her fresh coffee. "Although I must say, I don't believe you'd find his methods particularly useful or even terribly *appropriate*."

"Mother, oh my God," Jasmine groans. She drops her spoon into her oatmeal. "I'm trying to eat here. We are *all* trying to eat here."

Moira's blue eyes sparkle with unmistakable mischief over the rim of her cup. "It is what it is," she says, putting the cup back down. In a flash the impish demeanor is gone, though, and she's all business. "Right, so the twins are off to school as soon as Frankie and her mother arrive. I take it Alex is going to the farm with Chloe today, so Craig, my love, that leaves you rather at a loose end, yes?" She smiles at her younger son. "I'm volunteering at the food bank after breakfast, and you're welcome to come along, but that's only a few hours. I'll be tied up the rest of the day with my latest manuscript—loads to revise and my agent *screaming* down my neck."

"The perils of being a bestselling author," Craig says with a chuckle as he forks up some eggs. His face is thoughtful as he chews and swallows. "Actually..." He slides a glance at Alex. "If you don't mind, babe, I thought I'd cycle to the flower shop and visit David. Catch up, like. He invited us both so he'd have a chance to meet you properly, but as you're tied up..."

"No, no, that's just fine." Alex manages a smile around a bite of sausage. It's harder to hide his twinges of jealousy at the mention of David's name now that he's *seen* David, now that he's *spoken* to him, now that he knows that David is nice, and selfless, and caring, *and* good-looking—really, really good-looking. Alex shifts in his seat. *Wait. Where the hell did that come from?*

He wills himself to be still and firms up his smile. "I don't mind at all. I hope you have a nice visit."

Alex ignores the knowing grin on Jasmine's face.

"Frankie's here!" Jade's happy outburst breaks the awkward silence around Alex. She bounces out of her seat, grabs her schoolbag, and moves with lightning speed around the table to give everyone a hug and a kiss. "Mum, we're all going to come back after school to rehearse some more. Is that all right?"

"Perfectly fine, darling. I'll look forward to hearing your lovely music while I work." Moira smiles and shoos her daughter out the door. Jasmine, of course, had already simply waved to everyone and disappeared to the waiting car ahead of her sister.

Chloe pokes him in the arm. "I wouldn't rush you, but I've got a pair of lambs on a schedule."

"Right, sorry." Alex bends to the task of his breakfast. He manages to shovel down two sausages, a slice of toast, and most of his eggs under Moira's gimlet gaze. "I'm sorry, Moira. There's no way I can finish it all."

"That's all right, love. I'll have all week to feed you properly. We'll get some weight on those bones before you leave here." She actually pats him on the head as she whisks his plate away. "You go on with Chloe."

Craig gives Alex a kiss. "Have fun, babe."

"Same for you," Alex gives Craig a long, hard kiss back before he slips the dogs a couple last bites of sausage and goes upstairs for his camera bag.

Chapter Five

"**I** CAN HEAR YOU THINKING," CHLOE SAYS AS SHE THROWS her enormous blue truck into park and shuts it off. "And I know what it must be about."

This is news of the most alarming sort to Alex, who spent the drive to the Pennant farm leaning against the door of the double-cab truck and considering the way David's eyes looked really green in the dim light of the Oliver living room last night. "Um," he says, frantically making a mental scramble for something, anything more eloquent. "Ah..."

"I will tell you everything about why I love Duncan this morning." Alex lets his long sigh of relief fog the truck window. "If you give me a little time, okay?" When he twists in his seat to look at her, her delicate face is solemn and worried, and she's twisting her engagement ring around her finger. "I just need to work up to it."

Memories of Duncan's drunken buffoonery crowd out Alex's musings about David and make his too-full stomach contract painfully. Because he likes Chloe so much, he wants to keep an open mind on the topic of her fiancé. At the same time, Alex would, without question or thought, take a bullet for Craig, so it's difficult to maintain objectivity.

"Anyway. Just give me a little bit to warm up to it," Chloe says. She pops off her seatbelt, opens the truck door, and swings to the ground. "Work to do; lambs await. Watch your step."

The warning comes too late as Alex pushes open his door and mimics her swing to the ground. His half-formed intentions of pushing her for answers vanish as he lands ankle-deep in a cold, mucky puddle that splashes filth up the legs of his jeans; all questions and concerns are lost in a single moment of freezing horror. "Oh, fuck."

It takes Chloe entirely too long to stop laughing.

He lets her tug him loose and lead him into a huge wooden barn that's redolent with the smells of sheep wool and sheep crap. She's briskly efficient as she manhandles him onto a bench and whips off his muddy boots and disgusting wet socks. Before he has a chance to take a deep breath—not that he's sure he wants to just yet—she has him in fresh socks and borrowed rubber boots, and he's following her down a corridor between sheep baa-ing idly from their straw-filled stalls.

"I'd stop to introduce you to them all," Chloe calls back to him, "but we really are very late, and Oscar and Bosie need their breakfast." She stops at a pen where two fluffy beige lambs are already making some very insistent noises at the sight of them. "Follow me. They won't bite." Alex is halfway over the railing when she adds, "Probably."

"Your timing with warnings really sucks," he tells her as he steps gingerly into the pen. "No mud here at least. That's good."

Chloe lets off a gale of merry giggles. "It's only accidental half the time. The rest of the time is strictly for my own amusement, and I'll never tell you which is which." The lambs crowd around her knees, and she scratches between their fuzzy ears. "I'll help you with these two, though. This one on my left is Oscar, and the one with the slightly lighter wool, that's Bosie. Their mother rejected them, so I'm Mummy now. And for today, so are you."

"Oscar and Bosie?" English literature was never Alex's strong point, but he took several film appreciation courses in college. *Wilde* was quite popular in his History of British Cinema class. "Seriously? Aren't they brothers?"

"They're sheep," comes Chloe's tart reply. "I don't expect it bothers them much."

She hands him a bottle full of some milky substance. "Here. You take Bosie. He's the more complacent one. Just pop the teat into his mouth, like so." She settles down on the floor of the pen, heedless of the dirt and straw and whatever else might be there, and cuddles Oscar close. In a flash, the bottle nipple is in the lamb's mouth, and he's feeding.

Alex holds his own bottle and looks at Bosie, who stares right back at him with expectation all over his fuzzy lamb face. "Just like that?"

"If you don't soon," she says, "I expect he'll climb you for it."

With a deep breath, Alex sits on the ground and waits for Bosie to tuck himself under Alex's arm. Before he can worry too much about what he's doing, Alex sticks the bottle nipple into the lamb's mouth and holds his breath.

The world doesn't end. Bosie doesn't keel over and die. The lamb tucks his legs beneath himself and sucks away at his bottle, occasionally blinking big, trusting brown eyes up at Alex. It's the most adorable thing *ever*, and Alex just melts. "Okay, so I get why you do the vet thing with farm animals," he says, giving Bosie a scratch under the chin. "They're so cute."

"This does sort of make up for spending far too much of my time with my arm shoved up the back ends of ewes and heifers," Chloe says with a wink. "And you don't *even* want to know what I have to do with rams and bulls sometimes."

Alex's head fills with mental images that will haunt him as much as Craig's Wall O' Robbies. Chloe takes one look at his face and the stall echoes with her peals of laughter.

When she's wiped tears of mirth from her cheeks, Chloe's face gets serious. "Okay. All right, then. I guess it's time to get this over with. Go ahead." She blows out a long breath that sets the curls around her face to dancing. "Ask me whatever."

"What. Now?" Alex looks around. "Here?"

"Where and when better? I have sheep shit within reach and no problem with throwing it at you if you get stupid." She points to a nearby pile of straw and other stuff Alex doesn't want to think too hard about. "So. Fire away."

But Alex has so many questions, where to begin? He must take too long trying to pick one, because Chloe lets fly an irritated sigh. "Okay. I'll start you off. The first major point, if Craig didn't already tell you, is that I had a crush on Duncan all through school."

Alex focuses hard on Bosie as the lamb slurps away. "He didn't call it a crush."

"He's being kind, in that case. Or oblivious." Chloe gets up to retrieve a pair of smaller bottles. "But it *was* a crush and nothing more than that. Just pull the empty bottle away, Alex; pull it out and get the new one right in there."

It takes a struggle—he had no idea lambs could bite so hard—but Alex manages the switch. "Okay, so you had a crush. And?"

"No, that's important. I wasn't blindly in love with Duncan my entire life, I wasn't ignorant of what was going on between him and Craig. In fact, I was there for all of it, and he certainly made it difficult for me to keep appreciating his very attractive outside when I knew how awful he could be inside." Chloe sets her jaw. "I was definitely there for the fallout from Duncan accidentally breaking Craig's wrist. You'll have heard about that?" At his nod, she goes on. "Even apart from everything he did to Craig, Duncan was just a *prick*. He was good at rugby and did well in school; he's hot and he knew it. That all made him the most insufferable prick in the village."

This has done nothing to alleviate Alex's confusion. "Okay, so given *all* of that, why the hell are you about to *marry* him?"

"Because hey, Alex. People change. Did you not get that memo?" She shoots him a dirty glare, and Alex scoots back when her free hand seems to twitch in the direction of a pile of unspeakable horror. "Duncan went to uni. He took off back to Scotland and he stayed there until about three years ago."

"Uh-huh." Alex nods, but still doesn't get it.

Chloe rolls her eyes to the heavens. "I am not about to erase or deny a genuinely awful past of terrible decisions, Alex." His name comes out like an epithet. "I've been a target of Duncan's shit myself, by the way. You really will never know the sheer irony of a half-Scottish man having the utter gall to make sheep-fucking jokes at *anyone*."

All Alex can do is continue to nod. "Yep."

"I had a *lot* of baggage to get past with Duncan. It took him *months* just to convince me to go out with him." Chloe tips her head back, and her slender throat moves as she swallows, hard. "He had to work to make me believe that someone so awful could really change for the better. But he put in the time and he showed me who he is now. So every day I'm with him, that's who I see." Her eyes, when her gaze meets Alex's, are bright with tears. "Do you believe people are capable of that kind of change, Alex?"

He wants to say no. Memories rise of Craig last night, and stretching back over the last few months—the tension, the unhappiness, the way Craig wouldn't talk about it. He hid behind his concern for Alex and a mountain of alcoholic desserts. It's all very fresh for Alex and, for Craig's sake, he'd love to refute any possibility of growth and change.

But he can't.

It could be me. It could so easily be me.

He inhales deeply, despite the acrid scents of the barn that fill his nostrils. "Little bit, yeah."

Chloe opens her mouth; her eyes are full of questions now. Before she can utter a single word, a voice like a thunderclap booms through the barn. "Cee?"

"Speak of the devil." Chloe bounds to her feet and she's up and over the pen railing in a heartbeat. "Back here, Duncan!"

Sure enough, in a moment or two, Duncan is at the pen and pushing a gray knit wool cap back on his forehead. "Hi, you two."

"Sweetheart!" Chloe bounces over, arms outstretched.

"Uh-uh. No, no, and no way in hell, Cee." Duncan backs up with extreme haste; his hands are out to fend her off. He's holding a large paper sack. "You know the rules: no hugs or kisses when you've been in the pen. I at least had the courtesy to shower off the cow placenta and put on fresh clothes before I came here."

"Didn't know when you were going to get here or I'd have washed up and got my nicest dress on, just for you." Chloe beams, unrepentant. "Cow placenta, eh? So you were at the MacKenzies', then."

Duncan makes a hideous face. "Got it in one. God, I hate a breech birth. The mess is disgusting, and you would not *believe* the noise the cow makes."

"Right, because I was never in my life around farm animals giving birth." Chloe casts a pointed gaze around the barn.

"Cows aren't like sheep, Cee, you know that. The mooing... it's like Lucifer's own choir of the damned." He gives a mock shudder before planting a kiss on the tip of Chloe's nose— the last unsmudged spot on her face, if not her person, Alex observes—before he turns to face Alex with a wary smile. "Hi. We, ah, met last night. You're Alex, and I am a total cock."

Alex snaps out of the startled, staring, open-mouth-stupid daze he fell into when Duncan turned up as a walking, talking, possible non-jerk of a human being. He scrambles to his feet. "Sorry?"

"No, that'll be my line," Duncan corrects. His smile grows more secure. "Sorry. Really, I am. I mean it; I was a complete shit last night. I came to apologize to you. I'd offer you a handshake of peace, but you didn't really get off a lot lighter than Chloe in the filth department."

Alex's jeans are spattered with mud and other, more unspeakable things. His sweatshirt and hands are equally gross. Duncan, by contrast, is immaculate in a blue sweater and white button-down over his blue jeans. Alex blushes. "Right."

"No matter. Listen, I'm on the run, I really just stopped by for the apology and to drop off some lunch." He holds up the paper bag. "I hope chicken tikka masala's all right. Wait, sorry, Alex, I didn't think to ask if you had food allergies?"

"No, that's... that's fine." Alex does not at all know what to do with the Duncan Oliver standing before him, neat and clean and sober, laughing, bringing them lunch, offering apologies that, near as Alex can tell, are sincere. "Craig's made it at home, sometimes."

"Probably his tastes a lot like this one. We've eaten at the local since we were small; he's surely able to duplicate it."

Duncan beams, and his smile is uncannily like that of his father and brother. "Right, you two clean up and tuck into that. I have to get back to the clinic. The Steiner girls are bringing me a stray kitten after school, and I have to check on the Smiths and their Irish wolfhounds. Did I tell you I had to tell them that both the dogs have bone cancer, Cee?"

Chloe's arms are crossed over her chest, and she has a perplexed frown on her face. "Wait. Duncan. Go back to the kitten? What kitten?"

"It's nothing, Cee. The girls flagged down my van this morning when I passed them on the way to school. I gave them a ride. They told me about this poor little kitten they found half-drowned and starving." He spreads his hands out and opens his eyes wide in an innocent, helpless manner that Alex recognizes as one of Craig's dirtier methods for winning an argument. "They figure the poor thing was abandoned. I told them bring it by, I'd have a look." He smiles, and again it's Craig and Stephen's smile, broad and bright in his dark face, and Alex has to look away while he deals with his confusion.

"Duncan." Chloe's tone is stern. "We can't have another cat. There's no room."

"It's a kitten, babe. It's bitty; you'll never notice it. We can find a home for it when it's big enough." Duncan dances out of the way when Chloe takes a swing at him and uses the chance to shove the bag of food into her arms. He backs away down the corridor before she can say anything else. "Honest, Cee, it'll be fine. See you later!"

"Duncan Joseph—ugh!" Chloe's hand meets her forehead with a smack. "Not again!"

Alex blinks. "Again? What? He does this regularly?"

"That's how we ended up with the two cats we already have. Not to mention all the barn cats here that my parents were generous enough to take in. There have never been enough mice around here to justify the cats they *already* had." Chloe shakes her head and follows in Duncan's path, lunch in hand. "But the neighborhood kids know that Duncan's heart is basically all marshmallow and they know that he never, ever turns away any stray baby animal. And we keep as many as we do because he gets so attached while he's nursing them back to health." She pinches the bridge of her nose. "Our landlady is going to have a *fit*. I don't need this right now!"

A large white van is pulling away, and Duncan's blue-sweater-clad arm waves a farewell out of the driver-side window. "Does he have multiple personalities or something?"

Chloe glares at him through her fingers. "We're not so far from the pen that I can't go back for a double handful of sheep shit, Alex."

"It's a serious question!" But he backs away just enough to get a running start just in case. He completely believes that she is capable of flinging poop at his head with alarming accuracy, but she has to catch him first. "Come on, Chloe. You said he changed, and I am trying to believe you, but I also know what went on between him and Craig. To go from that to the kitten-loving country vet with the heart of gold? Come on. That's a drastic fucking change."

"No," she snaps. "Last night when he drank himself stupid was a drastic fucking change. He doesn't drink, believe it or not. But he was so nervous about seeing Craig for the first time in so long that he got drunk and completely fucked everything, and I promise you, he knows it. Do you really think he wanted to make that kind of arse of himself? Do you think for one second I'd be about to *marry* him if he did act like that all the time?"

"No," Alex begins, and then he finds himself literally holding the bag when Chloe flings their lunch at him and begins to pace the barn corridor with her arms wrapped tightly around herself.

"I want you and Craig to see Duncan *now*, this Duncan, *my* Duncan," she says, taking deep breaths as she walks. "Craig and Duncan don't know each other at all. I mean, they never have, but they *should*. They're brothers. I want to help them reconcile."

Alex forms and discards a dozen incredulous responses. "Oh, boy."

Fire lights Chloe's eyes, and her jaw is set. "My Duncan is *good*, Alex. He loves his family, every one of them. Yes, Craig too. He rescues kittens; he watches *Coronation Street* with totally unwavering devotion. He brings me lunch. Did you know he runs half-marathons for charity? Or that he treats the sick pets of the local kids at no charge?" Tears trickle down her cheeks, and Alex tries not to cringe as she wipes them away with the grimy hem of her oversized green sweatshirt. "I love him. I love Craig. And it's my wedding, and they should be *brothers*..."

To Alex's horror, Chloe melts into a sobbing wreck, and he scrambles to put the bag of food down on a nearby bench before he gathers her into an awkward hug.

One day I am going to write a handbook on how to cope with wedding drama. "Okay, it's okay; it's going to be okay," he says, rubbing her back. It's a mantra he's broken out for every bride he photographed in the last year, including his own cousin. "Get it all out now; we'll fix everything."

Maybe not quite *everything*. He doesn't want to touch the business of reconciling Duncan and Craig with a ten-foot pole. It's nobody's business but Duncan's and Craig's, and if Craig's not inclined to pursue it, then Alex is in no way inclined to push him, no matter what Chloe wants.

In fact, what Alex wants to do more than anything else in the world right now is to steal Chloe's truck and drive back to the Oliver house so he can kidnap Craig and take him back to their peaceful life in Seattle. All that's stopping him is his lack of confidence in his ability to drive stick on the wrong side of the road.

In his arms, Chloe's sobs taper off into tiny sniffles, and she pulls back. "Oh, God. I am so sorry for just falling apart on you."

"You're getting married," he reminds her with a half-smile and a shrug. "I do work with a lot of brides. Never seen one who doesn't lose control at least once. It's universal."

Chloe's smile is watery and wobbly. "Thanks."

Alex releases her, and she works to get her breathing under control. "Jesus. You really do love him, don't you?"

"I really do," she confirms, locating the last clean spot on her dirty sweatshirt and using it to dab at her eyes. "And I love Craig, too. He's one of my greatest friends. In my opinion, it's time the two most important men in my life sort out their differences."

But it's not up to you, Alex wants to shout. *Even if it were, a week couldn't be enough time to do anything about it.*

He keeps his mouth shut. There is no way he wants to get involved in this familial drama any more than he already is. All Alex wants is to get himself and Craig through the week and then far, far away. To that end, the best time to bring up his concerns would appear to be approximately never.

"Let's go put this away; I'm not hungry yet." he says at last, picking up the bag. He slings an arm around Chloe's shoulders. "I'm still full of Moira's breakfast."

"Me, too." Chloe nods. She's still sniffling, but the worst of the storm seems to have passed. "You know I probably wouldn't have thrown sheep shit at you, right?"

"I don't, but I forgive you for the threats all the same." He tugs at a curl that's escaped her high updo and hopes that she can't tell his smile is mostly a put-on. "Listen, it's been an eventful twenty-four hours, and you are the bride-to-be. I don't blame you. But will the whole week be like the last day was?"

"It won't be, if you're very lucky." She beams a hopeful smile at him. "Do you feel lucky?"

"Oh," Alex says as his heart sinks into his borrowed boots. "Not in the slightest."

 *Chapter Six*

BY DAY, EVEN ON A GRAY FALL DAY LIKE TODAY, INGATESTONE is as picturesque as it ever was, with its green hedges and tall trees and friendly neighbors waving greetings to Craig as he bicycles by. There's a slight nip in the air—it is October, after all—but it's refreshing in its briskness, and he can spot the sun peeking out from behind puffy clouds. He's got one earbud in, and the sweet, guitar-laced tones of Nick Drake's "Northern Sky" accompany him as he pedals along.

It's a lovely day, and Craig is part of a lovely scene, and none of it quite manages to take his mind off the fact that his occasional bicycle commutes through Seattle have in no way prepared him for a lengthy tour of his home village.

My arse hasn't made this many complaints since that time Samantha dragged me to hot yoga without first checking the proficiency level called for. Ouch.

The journey isn't doing a whole lot to calm the just-under-the-skin agitation that drove Craig to take the scenic route to Morgan's Flowers, either. That agitation's been burning since Duncan's idiotic behavior last night, an agitation that Craig hopes, but sincerely doubts, that he's been able to hide from Alex. He's managed to hide it from his usually astute mother; but then, he has the advantage that, during their stint at the food bank, she was too preoccupied with thinking about the edits she needs to make to her manuscript to pay attention to Craig slamming boxes and cans around with more force than strictly necessary.

Craig had hoped that a night of sleep and the novelty of being home would allow his taut nerves to settle, but, if anything, he's even more wound up. *He didn't even say hello to me. Not a word, just right back to being the same old Duncan, only with a new target now. Lovely.*

He pulls the earbud out and tucks it into his jacket pocket without breaking his leisurely pedaling pace. Townspeople both known and strange to him wave as he cycles into Ingatestone's business district. Some smile; some shout a greeting. In Seattle, he is more likely to hear curses and honks and demands that he clear the road. He certainly never says anything to anyone unless he bumps into them by accident. But here in Ingatestone, it has always ever been thus: If you see someone out and about, you wave hello—even if you don't know or recognize them.

Some things never change.

The red-brick frontage of Morgan's Flowers is one example. Craig hops off the bike, ignoring the thrum of pain up his thighs and into his hind end as his sneakers hit the pavement. With a tilt of his head, he regards the shop at which he spent so many post-school afternoons with David. The door is, as it has always been, glossy forest green, and the picture window is dotted with precisely arranged flyers that announce sales. Everything is tidy and clean, and the swooping *Morgan's Flowers* legend in the window was clearly repainted recently. It is just as clear that David does not deviate so much as a centimeter from his father's design of curling white letters outlined in thin ribbons of gold paint.

No. Nothing changes here. That certainty simmers just under the surface and makes Craig's scalp itch and his teeth hurt, as if his skin doesn't quite fit.

He shoves it all down deep and chains his father's bicycle to the rack outside the shop door. With a whine, he limps over and pushes the door open; the same old brass shop bell clangs. "Hello?"

"Coming!" David emerges from the back room holding a huge vase of blue, purple, and white stalks of delphinium. He sets it on the shop counter and peers around. His eyes widen when he spots Craig. "Oh, hi. Not the Oliver I was expecting, though it's very nice that you're here."

Craig blinks and falls back a step into the doorway. "Uh, thanks? I mean, you did invite me just last night."

"Yes, but I wasn't—never mind." David shakes his head and comes around the counter for a quick hug. "Good Lord, I've no clue how I function in public or run a shop. Let's try again. Hello, Craig. Lovely to see you. The kettle's just boiled, would you like a cup of tea?"

"Much better. Yes, thank you. That would be great."

"No Alex?" David disappears into the back room of the shop. "Come back here so I don't have to shout, will you? It's warmer, and, besides, you can sit."

"No, I'm not sure I can," Craig mumbles as he makes his way past vases filled with arrangements composed of everything from marigold to dahlia, from fuchsia to phlox. Though in recent years the flowers Craig's handled have been made of sugar and fondant, and he deals more in whole-grain flour than hothouse flowers, the sensation of the delicate stems and velvety petals of his teenage years still lives in Craig's fingertips. They remember deadheading blossoms in the Morgans' greenhouse and wrapping wide lengths of white ribbon around the thick green stalks of calla lilies. He pushed countless pins through corsage stems and closed many, many lids of plastic clamshells over the delicate contents.

And his lips remember kissing David's in this very back room...

Why do I keep coming back to those memories?

"Craig?" David's voice is courteous, but curious, and, when Craig shakes himself out of his confused reverie, David is standing by the tea station in the back room with a bemused expression and a tea mug in each hand. "Did you hear me? I was asking if you brought Alex."

"Oh, ah, no. Sorry. Chloe grabbed him first thing at breakfast." He accepts the cup that David hands over. "He would have liked to come, he said."

"I would have liked to have met him more properly. Ah, well. We have time yet." David smiles, pulls a sugar basin from under the trailing vines of an English ivy, and sets it on a tea tray with a tiny milk pitcher and a plate of cookies. "So, how was your trip?"

"Um." Craig cocks his head. "It was... fine?"

"Sorry. Getting the small talk in now since I didn't get to have much of it with you last night." David brings the tray to the small table under the window. "How's the weather in Seattle? Did you sleep all right? Is Ingatestone as bizarre to you now as it was to me when I came back from Leeds?"

Craig bursts out laughing. "My flight was fine; the weather is gray; I slept like a rock; and, oh, my God, has this town always been so very small and unchanging?"

"I wondered the exact same thing. And it's like the setting for a zombie film after dark, isn't it?" David's shoulders shake with mirth as he sits. "Were you tempted to work out how fast you could find a cricket bat to defend yourself?"

"Never have I been so annoyed that none of us took up the sport." Craig leans in the doorway and tries as surreptitiously as possible to appreciate how David, wrapped in a green apron over his jeans and plaid button-down, has grown into a very appealing fellow. "Although there was a net bag of Duncan's rugby balls in the back of the van. I think in the event of a nocturnal undead rampage, we might have done all right chucking them at any attackers."

"So you learned how to accurately throw a ball, then?" David asks with a raised eyebrow.

"I'd make Alex do it," Craig concedes. "He's the one with experience in sports that require hand-eye coordination."

"Mm. Speaking of Alex." David stirs a spoonful of sugar into his tea.

"You can't have an opinion on him yet; you've hardly met him."

"Not that, although first impressions are favorable. No, I hear congratulations are possibly in order?" David's eyes dance with mischief, and he's got an all-too-familiar lopsided grin on his face. "True or false?"

Craig groans. "Chloe told you. I'll kill her."

"Technically," David says as he brushes his flop of dark hair out of his face, "no. She didn't. What she *did* do is call me at one o'clock this morning, demanded I turn on FaceTime, and then forced me to play an elaborate game of charades until I guessed at it."

That's fairly impressive. Craig can't even be sure he should be mad about it. "Damn it. I should have known she'd find a loophole."

"Honestly, yes, you should have. I am deeply disappointed in you, Craig." David makes a clucking noise. "I'll blame jet lag and stress for your lack of foresight. Now, come sit and drink that tea."

"Must I?" Craig resents the amusement on David's face as he eases himself into the other chair. "Sweet God, ouch."

"It's less than a mile from your parents' place to here." David chuckles and pours milk into his mug. "Life in the States has made you that soft?"

"I took the long way 'round, thanks. Thought I'd look at things, take my time." Craig fixes his own tea and shifts in his chair in a vain attempt to find a comfortable way to sit. "I just don't do as much bike riding as I thought I did."

David nods, eyes still bright and amused. "I know the feeling. I did a lot of bus riding and walking around in Leeds myself. When I got back here and found my old bike in the garage, I thought it'd be a piece of piss to take it up again, be environmentally friendly and all that." He lets out a rueful breath of laughter. "Not so much. Not at first. It did get easier, but as you're only here for the week, I suggest you have Duncan drive you around like he does the twins sometimes."

"No *thank* you." The objection bursts out more violently than Craig intended, and it startles David into setting down his tea. "A sore backside is far more preferable."

They sit in uncomfortable silence. David breaks it first. "Mm. So the rumors of an altercation last night are true. Are you all right?"

"Fine. I'm fine." Craig rubs his jaw, forcing away a protracted session of teeth grinding. "Let's not talk about it. Fratricide is both illegal and a mortal sin. I'd just as soon not be tempted."

"Ah, but the good news is neither of us are Catholic, so a sin is a sin is a sin is a sin, and in any case, all sins can eventually be absolved, regardless of one's religion." Chin in hand, David flashes a puckish grin. "Not that that does a whole lot for the illegality of it."

"Right. Prison not really being an ambition of mine…" Craig shrugs and picks up his tea. "I'll just avoid Duncan until, hmm, Sunday."

David's grin is replaced by astonishment. "Can you do that?"

"With some careful management." Craig wobbles his hand. He hasn't given a whole lot of thought to the idea until just now, but it has considerable merit. He is really only here for Chloe's and his mother's sake, after all. That means he has a vested interest in keeping the peace, which is easily managed if he avoids Duncan. And if *he* avoids Duncan, then maybe Alex can too, and they might manage to get through this trip unscathed.

Hmm. Yes. This idea is looking better by the second.

"Right. Okay." David can't seem to pick up his jaw. "Yeah, I don't actually think your mother is going to let you get away with that."

"My mother is consumed with both this wedding and her latest book. Besides, she gave up trying to make Duncan and me be friends a long time ago; you know that." Craig shrugs. *Chloe, on the other hand…*

"Okay, but, Chloe. This is not going to fly with her, and you know *that*," David shoots back as if he's able to read Craig's mind. "It's her wedding week. She's going to want everything to be perfect, all sunshine and rainbows. You will not be able to get around her."

"I'll work it out. As I said, careful management." It takes some doing, but Craig is able to arrange his face into the façade of calm he usually reserves for frantic mothers-of-the-bride and the people in charge of obtaining unreasonable quantities of muffins for conferences in equally unreasonably short amounts of time. "I do have a few decades of experience dealing with Chloe, after all."

"You have precisely *zero* experience dealing with *this* Chloe. By which I mean Wedding Chloe," David warns. "I'm afraid you may be expecting an impossible outcome."

"Optimism isn't a crime, thank you." Testy now, Craig plinks his fingers at the rim of his mug. "Topic change, please. Are you seeing anyone?"

"What? No, Craig, don't change the subject." A frown creases David's forehead. "You can't bury your head in the sand all week, come on. There's too much you don't know—"

"All I have to do is get *through* this week, damn it." Craig shoves his tea mug away as his fingers clench into fists. His mind presents a strong image of him confronting his brother with an entire lifetime of his frustrations and hurts. It's not a good image, and there's no way it could end well. He wants to avoid it for the sake of his mother and Chloe. "I have to get a cake baked, I have to get a kilt fitted, and I have to be in this wedding. I would like to get that accomplished without my oaf of a brother scaring off my boyfriend before I can propose!" He struggles to rein himself in. "If the best way to do that is to avoid the aforementioned oaf, then why *shouldn't* I do that, David?"

"I am trying to tell you why," David fires back, anger making his cheeks bloom red. "You haven't been home; you don't know how things—"

"Don't even start to try to tell me that things have changed! You said yourself they haven't!" Craig shoots to his feet, paces the tiny room, and flicks his fingers at clouds of Queen Anne's Lace. Tiny buds drift to the floor and over his sneakers. "And I saw with my own two eyes that Duncan hasn't changed. So

I've made my choice, David—the choice that best protects me and Alex."

He turns to see if David has any more arguments to make. But he never finds out, because just at that moment, just as David opens his mouth, the shop bell rings, and a voice calls, "Hello?"

It is immediately recognizable, of course. Craig stares at David. "My brother? Now? Are you bloody kidding me?"

"I did tell you that you weren't the Oliver I was expecting," David hisses. "Am I to assume you're not here?"

"Of course I'm not fucking here," Craig says through his teeth. "Go out there before he comes back here to see what the hell is going on."

"Fine." David starts toward the front of the shop, but pauses just before the doorway. "I will cover for you exactly *once* and that's it, understand?"

"Whatever, just go." If Craig's shooing gesture is a touch violent, then fine. He's earned at least a little agitation. Apart from that, he doesn't dare move, not an inch, not even to brush away the fern frond that's tickling his left ear. He hardly chances a breath.

"Hey, David, there you are." For a wonder, Duncan is friendly and almost human in his greeting. "I was on my way back to the clinic and I thought I saw my dad's bike chained up outside. Is Craig here? It can't be Dad. He's still at school, so I thought maybe..."

"Oh, no, no, he's not here." David's reply is just a smidge too hasty, and not quite smooth enough for Craig's comfort. Craig bites his bottom lip. He can only hope it's smooth enough for Duncan. He really, *really* cannot face his brother right now.

David clears his throat and carries on with the fib. "Maybe someone's at the chemist, and it's their bike?"

"Hmm. Maybe." A sigh from Duncan. "Too bad. I was hoping I'd get to apologize to Craig. I figure you heard about last night, yeah? I know Cee called you after she put me to bed."

"She mentioned that there was an altercation," David says with the utmost diplomacy. "Didn't really go into detail."

Duncan snorts, and Craig would almost believe it's a snort of the self-deprecating variety, were it not for the fact that it's *Duncan*. "Just as well. I don't exactly come off looking good at the end of it. Got nervous, got drunk, got stupid, in short. Not a word to Craig before Cee was dragging me home, *and* I made a tit of myself in front of the boyfriend."

Glass scrapes on the counter; David must have moved the big vase of delphiniums. "I see. No, that wouldn't be the best start to things, I would guess."

"Not so much. Though I did just drop off lunch for Cee and Alex, and I got to apologize to him. I was hoping to get Craig and Alex both in the same day, but, never mind then." Duncan sighs again. "Say, is this my order for Chloe?"

"It is. I finished it about twenty minutes ago, so your timing is perfect." The glass scrapes again. "Have a closer look. Is it to your liking?"

"It's perfect, like all your work." There's something in Duncan's voice that Craig wants to identify as admiration, but that can't be right, can it? Duncan never admires anything but his own accomplishments. "It's beautiful, David. Thanks so much. Chloe'll love it. Not a bad apology for being an idiot, right?"

"It always worked for my mother and father, or so I'm told." David chuckles. The cash register dings, and the drawer thunks out of its slot. "That's fourteen pounds forty, Duncan."

"Come on, David. That's nowhere near the real cost of this," Duncan chides. "You have to stop giving us discounts. How are you going to make a living?"

"Off of everyone else in town, of course." David's grin can be heard in his voice. "Besides, your mother makes up for it by feeding me every time she sees me. She invited me for dinner tonight, actually, but I can't go. Will you be there?"

There's a rustle and shuffle, like stalks of delphinium being settled against a shoulder. Craig holds his breath for Duncan's answer. *Please say no, please say no, please say no...*

"No, best not, I think," Duncan says, and Craig lets out his sigh of relief as quietly as he can. "Maybe if I thought for sure that I could catch Craig beforehand, have a talk and all... but nah. I don't want to make things awkward, and they would be right now. I'll just find him later."

Over my dead body, Craig resolves grimly. He is thankful despite his irritation, though, that David maneuvered the conversation to the dinner question. He hasn't even considered it. *Oh, I bet we have to dodge a fair few of those this week.*

"I suppose that's fair." David's tone, however, says he doesn't suppose that at all. "I hope you can find him to work it out. Seems a shame that this has all gone on for so long."

The words are uttered so tartly, with such a palpable slick of acidity, that Duncan is stunned into silence. "Right," he eventually says; his tone is mystified. "I have an orphaned kitten coming into the clinic soon, and I need to drop these off at the flat first. Oh, the MacKenzies gave me some manure for you when I went to help with their cow birth. I can drop it off at the greenhouse later if you want."

"That's fine, thanks—oh, no. Wait, Duncan, don't bring another stray kitten home; Chloe'll kill you," David calls, but the doorbell jingles and the crunch of tires on asphalt lets Craig know that his brother left, probably without acknowledging David's warning, but that's no surprise. God forbid Duncan let anything get in the way of what he thinks is best.

David bustles through the doorway into the back room. "There. I covered for you, though, for the record, you are being absolutely ridiculous. I take it you heard that Duncan wants to find you and apologize?"

"As if he's being sincere. You know better, he just wants to absolve himself to feel better about being a jackass." Craig finally flips the fern frond away from his ear and stalks to the table for his tea, which is now cold—another black mark in Duncan's ledger. "I am not interested in his fake remorse."

"I was just face-to-face with him, and I'm pretty sure it wasn't fake, Craig." David shakes his head and looks as annoyed as Craig. "Are you seriously going to be this stubborn all week? Why the hell did you agree to be part of this wedding if you were never going to meet Duncan halfway?"

"Wait, why am I the bad guy here? And with you of all people?" Betrayal twists in Craig's stomach. "I thought you'd understand. You were on the scene for basically everything he did to me; you *know* why..." He closes his eyes and takes in a deep breath. "No. Fuck it. This is not the conversation I came here to have."

"Craig..."

"I need to go." Craig brushes past David and makes his way out of the shop, his fists clenched tight. He'd hoped a bit of chat and flirting might soothe his nerves, but now he's more wound up than when he arrived at the shop. Outside, his agitation has him unlocking the bike with enough force to tear a fingernail to the quick. His legs and backside still ache, but Craig ignores all his hurts in favor of hopping onto the bicycle and speeding away as quickly as possible.

Fuck. This.

 *Chapter Seven*

CRAIG'S CALVES ACHE, AND HIS LUNGS BURN WITH EVERY breath he takes, but he doesn't slow down.

Out of the high street, past his house, pedaling harder and harder, Craig races toward the edge of town. He nearly wipes out making a violent left onto a tree-lined lane, then almost takes out a little old lady walking her dog. He ignores her shrieks of fright and goes on; the adrenaline from the near-miss just amps him up.

One final curve of the road and he spots his destination, marked by a line of the fragile, leafless skeletons of old hedges. He leaps from the bicycle while it's still in motion and hurls it to the grass. Behind the hedge-skeletons is a tiny pond, his old thinking place, and he breaks an angry path through the branches to get to it. That's accomplished as quickly as it was when he was a teenager. Craig pokes his sore finger into his mouth and wanders to the pond's edge.

"Damn—it—Craig—" David's remonstrating gasps are a shock, and Craig spins around, nearly toppling into the pond at the sight of his ex picking through the hedges. "You—stubborn—fuck."

"You *followed* me? What the—"

"Oh, shut up, Craig." David edges through the dead hedges to stand at Craig's side. "I wanted to make sure you were all right and I figured you'd come here."

Craig shoves his hands into his jacket pockets, taking care with his injured finger. "Predictable me, is that it? Just like this place, never changing."

David closes his eyes and rubs at his temples. "Damn it, Craig," he says again. "You are in for a long, hard week if you can't let that concept go. Seriously."

"If you came here to pick another fight—" Craig is cut off by an attitude-loaded eye roll, accompanied by what Craig would call a *presumptive* hand over his mouth.

It is an effort, but he does resist the childish urge to lick David's palm.

"I came here," David says with an excess of dignity, "to make sure you were all right or to see if I could help you on the way to being all right. Come on, Craig. Honestly, do you really want to spend the entire week dodging Duncan and annoying Chloe? Because you *will* annoy her; it won't take much."

Craig pries the hand from his mouth. "Again. Me, not the bad guy here. In fact, I am the guy who is trying to keep the peace. And yeah, I'm doing it in the way that suits me best. That's my right, David."

Silence stretches between them, broken by David's sigh. "You're right, of course. I'm sorry, Craig." He steps back and runs a hand through his hair. "I don't know what got into me."

"Chloe, I expect," Craig says with a wry grin. "You're forgiven. She can be quite persuasive. Believe me, I remember."

"That she is. Now, I don't really think she's *wrong*..." David holds up a hand to forestall Craig's objection. "I don't. But you aren't wrong, either. It is entirely your right to decide how

and when, or even *if* you're going to deal with your brother."
Abruptly, he drops to the grass and yanks Craig down to sit
next to him. "Come on. Let's just sit for a bit. Enjoy the peace
and quiet."

For all that the day is gray and chilly and there's more than a
bit of dampness on the ground that will do Craig's hindquarters
no favors later, it *is* peaceful at the pond, and the place works
its soothing magic on him as it always has. *I should bring Alex
here with his camera. He'll like it.*

Insects chirp and rustle in the grass as the conversation
falls away into companionable silence. The lump in Craig's
stomach loosens, but he's still a little wild under the skin, as
if he could burst out of it any moment now. Being home, even
if he were to concede that change is possible, is still confining.
It's as if he doesn't fit here anymore—and maybe he doesn't,
and maybe that's the whole problem.

"What are you thinking?" David asks.

"That you can't come home again," Craig replies. Cloudy
sunbeams play on the pond's surface. "More or less. You?"

"The old days." David lets out a soft laugh. "Remember the
owl runs we used to do before swim meets?"

"Oh, God. I managed to forget." Craig's laughter at the
memories is rambunctious as he throws his head back.
Christ, *how* could he have forgotten? A pack of teenage boys,
stripped to their team Speedos, racing through this very field
and hooting like owls in the dead middle of the night—that
should be an indelible memory. "We were absurd. But it did
seem to help, didn't it?"

"Meet jitters *were* fairly inconsequential once you spent a
few hours of the previous night acting like a complete idiot."
David's voice is dry as Chardonnay, but it isn't without humor.
"Whose idea was that, anyway?"

"It predated us. The swim team probably still does it." Craig loops his arms over his knees and clasps his hands. "It sure was a way to blow off steam."

"*Was* being the operative word, of course," David says, with a sidelong glance at Craig.

"Of course." But Craig... Craig has just had an idea. And it's *brilliant*.

"I don't like that look on your face," David says. "I know that look. No, Craig."

Craig jumps to his feet and grins at David. "No what, David?"

"No, Craig, you can't do an owl run in broad bloody daylight; that's a terrible idea." David yanks at the tail of Craig's jacket. "Sit back down, you twit. Let's have a nice, calming conversation and then we'll have a nice bicycle ride, and I'll leave you at your place, and we will never mention your temporary lapse of sanity to anyone."

"Oh, we are going to do that, and we are never going to talk about this to anyone, but this is happening, David." Craig pulls out of David's grip and whips his jacket off, dropping it to the ground. He is more convinced of the brilliance of his idea by the minute. "Just what the doctor ordered." With a soft *flumph*, his sweater and long-sleeved T-shirt land on top of the jacket, and gooseflesh crops up all over his skin when the cool, damp air hits it. A thrill of delight zips through Craig from toes to scalp.

"No doctor would order this; they'd order you to be locked up for thinking of it. I shouldn't be seeing this. You shouldn't be doing this." David has buried his face in his hands, and his voice is muffled. "Craig, for the love of God, you're an adult; please stop."

Craig kicks off his sneakers and strips off his jeans. After a moment of thought, he keeps his socks and boxer-briefs on. "God, that's invigorating."

"Yes, well, it's October; it would be at least that," David mutters. One horrified green eye peers up through his fingers for a split second before he squinches it shut again. "Oh, God. Craig, I am begging you to reconsider this. Put your clothes back on."

"You want me to loosen up. I need to blow off steam." Hands on his hips, Craig grins into the watery gray sky. "Beautiful day, time to get to it."

"Oh, God," is the last thing Craig hears before he takes off, whips off his wool cap, and flings it toward the sky.

The lingering aches in his legs and backside melt away as he stretches out into a good lope across the field. The farm to which the field belongs has long been unoccupied, but the field is kept mowed and tidy all the same. There are neither cowpats nor overly long glass to impede him. A stretch of clean field is all that lies between him and the tree that has always marked the turnaround point for the run. *Invigorating!* The word zings through his mind with a mad joy, and it's as though he could fly.

When he rounds the tree, its leafless limbs stretched gray toward the sky and a lazy, curious rock dove observing him from its perch, Craig spots David back at the other end of the field, waving his arms frantically. *What, does he want to join me now? Too late, I'm halfway back and not doing another lap.* One lap was more than enough. He is considerably calmer now and even strangely happy; the fires of aggravation under his skin are banked for the moment. Triumphant, Craig opens his mouth to let fly a wild hoot.

But then it's clear why David is waving. David is not interested in a run. David is warning Craig that they are no longer alone.

Huh. Craig slows down. *Don't I know that woman? That's Janey Fielding from school. What's she doing out here? Why is she dressed in a police uniform?*

Oh.

Two hours later, Craig trudges into the attic, past Fitz gnawing on a chew toy in his puppy bed, past Alex working at his laptop on the desk, and flings himself face-first across the bed. "Got arrested for streaking," he mumbles into the duvet. "Thought you ought to know."

A raucous burst of laughter from the laptop makes him jerk his head up to stare. "Connor," Alex says, clearly struggling not to laugh himself, "says hello."

"Fuck." Craig shoves his head under the pillows.

"I was just giving Alex here an update on the studio schedule this week," Connor says from the Skype window. His voice still brims with merriment. "His dad's coming by later to get a new headshot for his law firm's website; do I need to have him call you first?" Uproarious laughter fills the attic. "Yo, Craig, do you... do you need legal representation?"

"No, thanks," Craig mutters and pulls the pillows more tightly over his ears as Connor sputters and guffaws.

Alex lets a chuckle slip loose, but, to his credit, just the one. "Thanks for calling, Connor. I appreciate the update. Tell my dad I said hi."

"Sure, Al, no problem. Craig, hey, thanks for making my day." Connor is still laughing as the Skype call disconnects.

The laptop clicks shut, and, a few quiet steps later, the bed shifts and dips next to him. "So. Arrested for streaking. Craig, we've been here for *one day*."

"Shut up. It was a good idea at the time." Why, oh why won't the bed open up and swallow him whole? "Can we please just get on a plane and go home now?"

Alex lies down next to him and scooches his hip against Craig's until Craig straightens up and stops hogging the bed. "Bad plan. Chloe will kill you. I mean follow us back to the States and kill you—probably me too, for helping you."

"She's going to kill me anyway. My mother stopped me on the way up here. Apparently, while I was sitting in my underwear in a holding cell, Janey Fielding called her mother, who called *my* mother. At this rate, this is all the entire village will be talking about by Saturday." Craig pulls the pillow from his head and aims as plaintive a gaze as he can manage at his very beloved boyfriend. "Unless you help me out by doing something even more outrageous. Even just a *little* outrageous should do the job; you're American, and a little goes a long way on the gossip mill for Americans here."

"Yeah, I love you a lot, but I can't top you streaking." Alex kisses Craig's cheek. "And these days I'm not really into deliberately making myself look like an ass in public. Even for you." He kisses Craig more thoroughly and chuckles when Craig allows himself to grumble. "Aw, come on. I really do love you, Craig. But suck it up."

"Such a romantic," Craig mumbles and sticks his head back under the pillow.

Alex ignores the jibe in favor of allowing his fingertips to play up and down Craig's arm. "I have to know," he says as he shifts so that he can insinuate his fingers under the pillow to tickle Craig's ear. "What the hell brought this on? It's not like you. I mean, I understand the urge to run around nearly naked in public. God knows, I've done it too, but *you're* supposed to be the sane one."

Craig shakes off Alex's hand and pulls the pillow up so he can stare at his boyfriend. "Where, and when exactly, have you run around nearly naked in public?"

Alex's tongue makes a couple of revolutions in his cheek while he considers the question. "Reykjavik, Sacramento, Portland, Pamplona, Amsterdam, and, of course, Seattle." He offers a half-shrug and a grin. "I was in a fraternity, remember? We liked to travel in groups and we were all terrible influences on each other."

This is endlessly fascinating to Craig, and a fairly decent distraction from his own woes. "Pamplona? Really?"

"You know how they have the Running of the Bulls?" Alex asks.

Craig frowns. "Yeah…"

"My frat president thought a Running of the Balls would be a great way to wrap up our last night in Spain. Spring break my… junior year, I think." Alex goes back to tickling Craig's arm.

Craig tsks. "That's terrible. That's not even a pun."

"We were a few bottles into the Rioja when he came up with it," Alex says with another shrug. "Was funny at the time. Although to be fair, *balls* is still funny to me." He pauses. "You're dodging my question."

With a sigh that starts in the very soles of his feet and drags through his body to stomp him flat, Craig rolls onto his back. He turns his gaze out the window and over the back garden; he doesn't want to see Alex's face when he starts to explain. "I was with David—"

Sure enough, the very air that surrounds them goes still, and the bed jolts the tiniest bit as Alex's body goes rigid. "You did this... with David?"

"No, not like that. Listen." Craig gropes for Alex's hand, but as soon as he catches it, it's snatched away. Now he rolls over to face Alex, to witness the cool, still mask Alex's face has become. "No, I didn't do this with David. David happened to be there and, I can assure you, he wishes he wasn't."

Alex's throat works, and his eyes go a steely, stormy gray. "Was it his idea?"

"No, actually, he tried to talk me out of it." This time when Craig reaches for Alex's hand, it doesn't slip through his fingers. "Alex, this was all me. David was an innocent bystander." *Never mind my inconvenient attraction to him.* He wills Alex to relax, for that still mask to slip and soften into the face he loves. "It was stupid. I was visiting David at the shop, and Duncan came in."

That makes Alex perk up with something that might be interest. "Yeah? Did you talk to him?"

"No. I can't. Not yet." He lets his fingers play in and around Alex's and concentrates on the sight of their hands linked together. "I didn't want to. David thought I should, though, and he might have pushed a bit hard."

"Not so innocent, then." The interest vanishes, and Alex is aloof again, with his chin up and lips tight.

Craig untangles their hands and smooths back a lock of Alex's hair. "Stop. He meant well. But that doesn't make me any less angry at Duncan, much less ready to talk to him. So." He shrugs. "I took off in a huff. Ran out to this place we all used to go when we wanted to think. And David followed me to make sure I was all right."

"Which clearly you weren't," Alex says, and there might be a hint of a smile playing around his lips.

"Yes. No." Craig puffs out his cheeks in a sigh. "I lost my head a little, Alex. I don't know. I've been feeling like I wanted to crawl out of my skin since we got here yesterday."

Alex, no stranger to that, nods. "Got it."

"So, the whole streaking thing, David reminded me of it. We used to do it before swim meets—blow off steam, relax our nerves, shake out the jitters. He just wanted to make me laugh, though. He wasn't expecting me to actually take it up as a brilliant suggestion in the here and now." Craig hangs his head. "And there you go. That brings you up to speed."

"And gives me some excellent ammunition to retaliate with the next time *I* do something stupid," Alex says, and when Craig looks up, the storm clouds have cleared, and Alex is smiling again, a full and beautiful smile. "I almost can't wait for the next time I make an idiot out of myself, just so I can bring it up. I'm going to win all our arguments forever."

Craig raises an eyebrow. "Running of the Balls?"

"You weren't there; you can't prove a thing." Alex is pleased as punch. If it weren't at Craig's expense, he might appreciate the situation a little more.

"Enough." He rolls up to a sitting position and pulls Alex after him. "It's done. It's ridiculous. Janey Fielding finally got her revenge on me for a long-ago Easter prank involving paint-filled balloons and her new dress, and I will never hear the end of it." At Alex's smirk, Craig can only roll his eyes. "Okay. Moving on. Tell me about your morning with Chloe. Was it nice?"

The smirk twists into a wry smile, and Alex lets out a short laugh. "There was sheep shit involved. 'Nice' is dependent on how much fun you think dodging handfuls of that to be." He picks up Craig's hand and twines their fingers again. "I got some nice photos of her, though, once she washed most of the crap off. Decent lighting and judicious use of black and white photography hides a multitude of sins, thank God. It doesn't hurt that she's photogenic as hell."

"She always has been." Craig smiles. "What are the photos for? Are you making a scrapbook for her?"

"No, a slideshow. They're going to show it at the rehearsal dinner. We're going to mix old photos and new ones." Alex bites his lip. "That means I have to spend time with Duncan, you know. I have to get new photos of him."

Craig's first urge is to barricade himself and Alex into the attic and refuse to come out until after the wedding. He waits for it to pass. "I suppose you must. A wedding is for two people, after all."

"Yep." Resting their linked hands at his neck, Alex tilts his head so that his cheek lies on the back of Craig's hand and looks up from under his lashes. "He came by the farm today."

Right. "I did hear him mention that to David."

"He brought us lunch." Alex pauses, his face uncertain. "And he apologized to me for last night."

So it was true. *Doesn't mean he really meant it, though. Anyone can say they're sorry.* "That's uncommonly nice of him," Craig says aloud, trying his damnedest to stay neutral, to not pack up and run. "Then again, being the groom and all, he has a substantial interest in keeping the peace, I suppose. I would. Chloe can be a terror."

"You are not exaggerating even a little." Alex takes a deep breath and ruffles his hair. "Wasn't really expecting him to do it. He was a totally different person today. Which, well, alcohol does have..." He waves his hand as his cheeks turn pink. "Transformative effects. But apart from that, Chloe said he'd really changed. As a person, I mean."

"David did bring up that possibility." Craig pulls his hand loose so he can push himself across the bed and lean against the window. "Do you believe it?"

Alex shrugs. "He's your brother, not mine. What do I know? Although…" He frowns. "Apparently he really loves kittens, and people who like baby animals are usually all right, aren't they?"

Craig tries to imagine his surly, broad-shouldered brother cuddling a kitten, and his brain nearly sprains itself. "Maybe?"

What a day this has been. I'm supposed to live through six more just like it?

"We just have to get through the week," Alex says, echoing Craig's thoughts. "That's all. Hopefully, without punching your brother. Or getting arrested again. I feel I have to add that."

Craig groans, closes his eyes, and tips his head back against the window with a *thunk*. "I really am never going to hear the end of this."

"Probably not." Alex crawls across the bed to wrap his arms around Craig. "Oof. Someone needs a shower."

"Someone needs a *bath*," Craig corrects, wincing as his sore muscles reassert themselves. "Do you think I have time for a long soak and a nap before dinner? Maybe a massage?" He opens his eyes and does his best to be as pathetic, yet adorable, as he can. Alex is very susceptible to adorable. "You give the nicest massages, and my *everything* hurts."

Alex's gaze slides up the poster-plastered ceiling and his eyes narrow at a particularly smug-looking Robbie Williams. "Maybe."

Craig amps up the pathetic and bats his eyes for good measure. "I'll love you forever."

"Don't you already?" The tone is arch, but Craig's efforts pay off as Alex relents. "Yes, fine. Go run a hot bath. I will go find out from your mother when dinner is happening and see how much time I can buy us."

"You're a god among men," Craig informs him with a kiss.

"I do sort of feel like one today," Alex says with a thoughtful nod as he slides off the bed. Fitz uncurls himself from his puppy nest in the corner to follow Alex, and Craig is alone.

He moves slowly off the bed, wincing with every step. *I lost count of the bad ideas I had today. The bike ride is number one. Well. Half-naked in a jail cell…*

It's a toss-up.

He gets the water running and, with another wince, eases himself down to sit on the lid of the toilet. *Six more days.* If this day is any indication, though, he has no idea how they'll make it through unscathed—nagging friends, an incomprehensible brother, an inexplicably attractive ex-boyfriend, *and* a renewed talent for getting into trouble?

Craig saw a lot coming this week, but nothing exactly like this. And it's only Monday.

We're all going to die.

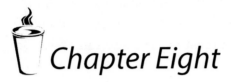

Chapter Eight

THE SMELL AWAKENS ALEX. *CINNAMON ROLLS*. HE'S SITTING up with his eyes still closed and swinging his legs over the side of the bed before it hits him.

He's alone.

Alex blinks at the empty side of the bed. Craig must have climbed over him to get out—which, fine, he's glad he apparently slept like a log for once—but a glance at the clock across the room shows that it's only seven-thirty in the morning. The expanse of bed by the window is cold when he rests his palm on it, so Craig's been up and gone for quite a while.

What?

Working very hard to ignore the olfactory siren song of fresh cinnamon pastry, Alex flops down to snuggle under the duvet again and listens to Fitz and Newton playing together in the back garden. He'd like to say it's not weird that Craig is up early on a day off, but that would be about as honest as saying he's gotten used to the Robbie shrine over his head.

Alex peeks out from the duvet to glare at the pride-of place-poster, a life-sized print that is the focal point of the entire wall. It's taken him a couple of days, but the constant presence of Craig's teenage infatuation has given Alex the key to unlock his understanding of the problems at hand. Or, problem, rather, but it's a big enough problem that Alex is counting it as several: Craig is behaving like a, well, a teenager—a secretive, occasionally sullen, and then inexplicably manic teenager, which is not, it must be said, anything Alex ever expected to see.

First there was the streaking incident on Monday, which Alex is *still* trying to wrap his head around. Then came Tuesday afternoon, when he walked into the Oliver kitchen to find Craig and Chloe in a real blowout of a frosting fight with scarlet and ivory buttercream splotching their paper caps, smeared all over their clothes, and covering so much of the kitchen that Moira turned nearly purple in rage.

Tuesday evening offered no break in the action. As Moira gave Craig and Chloe a dressing-down that had them cowering before her, she let it slip that Duncan was on his way to join them all for dinner. At that, Craig straightened up, tossed his frosting-coated cap aside, and informed the room that he and Alex had tickets to *Les Misérables* in the West End, so they'd have to give dinner a miss, sadly; he felt just *terrible* about it.

If looks could kill, Chloe's murderous glare would have struck down both of them right there in the kitchen.

Dinner was a decent, if less than romantic, stop at a kebab stand. *Les Mis*, never one of Alex's favorite musicals, was fine, but their last-minute cheap seats were awful. And for the whole train ride into London and back, Craig was hyper, talking a mile a minute about his plans for Chloe's cake, about his kilt fitting and how he didn't look as stupid as he thought he would, and so on and on and on, until Alex couldn't make heads or tails of any of it.

And through it all, three days running now, is this: It is seven-thirty in the morning and Craig is once again up bright and early when he doesn't have to be. He tried saying yesterday it was because of his mother, but Moira's been holed up in her office when she's not at the Pennant farm hashing out last-minute wedding details. No, Alex is perfectly aware of what this is, more aware than anyone else in the world might be. Craig is up early every day and late every night because he's too wound up to relax. It's a big, big red flag to Alex, who is used to Craig being so Zen, the Dalai Lama would be hard-pressed to out-mellow him.

He chews on his lower lip as he gets up and dresses while his laptop boots. This is not something it thrills him to have to do, but with them three days into this wedding nightmare and no sign of Craig returning to his regular self, Alex is in way, way over his head. He so badly needs to talk to someone that last night, while Craig was downstairs having a drink with his father, Alex paced the attic room talking to both Fitz *and* the Robbie Williams poster array.

Alex is freely willing to admit that he often lacks a healthy self-awareness, but even he knows that wasn't his finest hour.

He needs an actual person to listen to him, someone with qualifications *on* paper rather than someone whose only qualification is that they *are* paper. And so, late last night, Alex stopped pacing and sent a desperate email. *Please let there be a reply, please, please...*

To his utter relief, there's a new email in his inbox.

From: Veronique Laborteau
To: Alex Scheff
Re: Discussion

Alex –

Of course I'd be delighted to have a quick appointment with you. Skype is perfectly fine. I'm free at 9 a.m. my time for about an hour. Will that be sufficient?
   – Dr. Laborteau

Alex does the math. That's early evening. If he can find someone to occupy Craig, it should work. And he shouldn't have any trouble finding someone to help. At that time, he should have his pick of either twin, possibly Moira or Stephen, and maybe even Chloe if he can manage to get her to leave Duncan behind.

Scratch that, no chance. Chloe was too angry at Craig, and it had only cemented her batshit Bridezilla determination to force reconciliation between the Oliver brothers. Alex is still firmly in opposition to this stance, so Chloe is out.

Somewhat more reluctantly, he sets Stephen and Moira aside as well. Moira too, though to a much lesser degree than her future daughter-in-law, might be of the opinion that reconciliation is necessary. Plus, she'd be nosy in that motherly way about why Alex needs Craig to be occupied. It's understandable, but Alex doesn't want to worry her. And Stephen won't work because Alex can't be sure that Craig's father wasn't primed by Moira to ask about the Duncan thing.

That leaves him with Jasmine and Jade, and Alex is fine with that. Craig's sisters might be teenagers, but in the time Alex spent with them this week, they struck him as uncommonly levelheaded *and* capable of the sort of distracting mischief that would be useful. And they wouldn't ask too many questions up front. *Yes. They'll do nicely, unless something better comes along.* Alex nods, satisfied with his plans.

The scent of fresh cinnamon rolls can no longer be ignored, nor should it be, now that Alex has help on the way. He locks his laptop and goes downstairs to trade kisses for cinnamon rolls.

In the kitchen doorway, Alex comes to a dead stop because, while Craig is absolutely there, singing as he pulls a pan of rolls from the oven... he's not alone. David offers Alex a bashful grin from the breakfast table. "Alex. Hi. Morning. Nice to see you."

"Uh, yeah. Hi." Alex shakes off his confusion and resumes his amble into the kitchen to wrap his arms around Craig. "Hi, both of you."

"Hi, yourself, handsome." Craig leans back into the embrace without pausing in the act of drizzling white icing over the cinnamon rolls. "Glad the most reliable method of bribing you out of bed in the morning has yet to fail."

"It's a dirty trick, but I forgive you." Alex kisses Craig's cheek and sweeps away to the kitchen table, carrying Craig's fresh mug of coffee with him. He settles into a seat across from David. This will be the first time he's properly met the man whose inconveniently attractive face has intermittently invaded his thoughts for the last few days. Alex still hasn't quite worked out how he feels about David apart from his attraction, about David's clear role as part of the Oliver family, about his long history with Craig...

And about how he saw Craig nearly naked two days ago.

Be fair, that's really not his fault.

David smiles again, a bit more on the nervous side, and dimples that Alex finds adorable appear in his reddening cheeks. "Alex, listen, about the other day—"

"Thank you for trying to rescue Craig from himself," Alex says and smiles back. In the morning light, David's eyes are a brighter green than they were at the welcome party: bright green, like the green of leaves in late spring, and his eyelashes are unfairly long—

Alex blinks and snaps out of it. *Oh, my God, get a grip.*

As distracted as he is, Alex almost leaps a mile out of his seat when Craig comes from behind to give him a kiss and a cup of coffee of his own. "Craig! Hi!"

"Yeah, all right, Mr. Twitchy." Craig chuckles and nibbles along Alex's neck. "Milk and sugar for your coffee?"

"Yes. Thanks." Alex tries to will his jangling nerves into something along the lines of calm and he smiles again at David. He hopes it's a nice and normal smile. "So. Hi. Yeah. Thanks again for Monday; don't worry about it. How are you today? You came for breakfast?"

So much for normality. Silence descends, and Alex cannot look either his boyfriend or his new crush in the face.

Smooth.

"I, ah, yeah. I did. Craig invited me." When Alex looks up, David's smile is tentative and confused. "Though I admit, I believe he's bribing me as much as he is you. The difference is, I don't know what for yet."

"It's not a bribe! It's not; it's breakfast, that's all!" Craig's voice is a little too bright, very much *the gentleman doth protest too much* kind of bright, like his smile and his eyes when he swoops around the table to pick up David's empty plate. "Nothing more than that! More coffee, David?"

David answers Craig, but he keeps his eyes on Alex as he does, and he has one dark eyebrow raised. "That'd be great." When Craig turns to drop the plate in the sink, David lifts his eyebrow higher and points a thumb at Craig. The question is unmistakable: *What. The fuck?*

Alex widens his eyes and shakes his head as he shrugs. *No idea.*

At one time he thought that his desperate email to Dr. Laborteau might be a major overreaction, but no. It is not, not if David can also spot that something's up. Okay, then. Alex can only hope his therapist will have some guidance for him.

Across the table, David gives himself a full-body shake and beams a determined smile at Alex. "So, you two went to catch *Les Mis* last night? How was it?"

So they're going to pretend that everything is fine. All right. "We did, yes. It was pretty good. We got to meet some of the actors at the stage door." Craig was determined to ensure that they outlasted Duncan and Chloe's visit, and damn the fact that it was quite a chilly evening. "I'd only seen the movie, so this was kind of a treat." *Even if we were so far back we couldn't see anything.* "It was nice, if depressing."

"Yeah, that's not the most cheerful of musicals." The reappearance of David's dimples in a genuine smile makes Alex forget his worry about Craig. Then he's worrying about his crush again as David carries on. "Oh, but a good one is *School of Rock*; that's playing now too and it's great. Maybe you can catch it before you leave?"

"What a great idea!" Craig swoops in with the milk jug and sets it by Alex's hand. "We'll go tonight. I'll look into getting tickets for all of us. You'll come with, right, David?" He doesn't wait for an answer. In a graceful sweeping instant, he's picking up the plate of fresh cinnamon rolls from the stovetop and serving two to Alex before he glides to the kitchen door. "Eat up, babe. I'll take these to Mum; she's been working hard since before I got up. Then we'll hammer out details for tonight, okay?"

As Craig's apron strings flutter out of sight, David exchanges glances with Alex and sighs. His shoulders droop. "I knew it was a bribe."

Alex's temples throb. "Mm. What time are Chloe and Duncan due for dinner, then?"

"Six." David, whom Alex cannot help but notice is cute even when morose—possibly somehow even hotter *because* of his melancholy, like a hero in a Jane Austen movie—plops his elbow onto the table with a *thunk* and rests his head on his hand. "Stubborn as a fucking mule as usual, that's Craig."

It seems like a good idea to lay his heavy head on the table, so Alex does. "I'm not going to survive the week."

"You might. Duncan and Craig, on the other hand..." David lets out a whining groan. "Not so much. Chloe is officially on a rampage, despite everyone's best efforts to talk her out of it."

It's nice, down here on the table. The blue tablecloth is soft against Alex's cheek. Alex considers staying here forever. No wedding, no weird West End date night with David, no Oliverpocalypse with the charge led by Chloe. Just a nice, permanent nap on this table in this kitchen filled with the smell of freshly baked cinnamon rolls.

It sure beats the bathroom Alex usually locks himself into.

But no, this is not a permanent solution, no matter how fervent his wish. Alex hauls himself upright and grabs his coffee. "Listen," he says, flexing his fingers around the mug, no longer second-guessing his decisions. "I do actually need to get Craig out of the house tonight, but not with me. I was going to ask the twins to think of something, but maybe you can help? I just need an hour or so before dinner."

David looks thoughtful, then lifts his head and nods. "Yep. Done."

"What?" Alex blinks. "Just like that?"

"Yeah. Your timing is really good." David appears quite pleased with himself. "The twins asked me to take them to the cinema sometime this week. They're sick of wedding crap; they want a break. They can't drive themselves, and everyone else is too busy, so enter good old David, who has no problem helping, *but* would prefer not to chaperone a pair of teenage girls by himself." He spreads his hands wide. "Voilà. Problem solved. I'll drag Craig with me, piece of cake."

Alex frowns. *It can't be that easy.* "But how?"

"Easy." David shrugs. "If he says no, I'll remind him that he owes me big for getting Janey to let him off easy on Monday. Last resort, I'll get Moira to make him help me out. It's foolproof, Alex."

"So I take it you're not on the side of forcing Craig and Duncan to work their shit out?"

"I decided I am firmly on the side of whatever will get us all through this week alive." David is cool and collected as he sips his coffee. "Everyone but Chloe is on that side. No, actually, I think she's on that side too; she's just sure her way is better. Which, that's Chloe for you." Out come the dimples again.

Alex should not be finding him so attractive. It's getting mixed up with his jealousy to form a leaden knot in his stomach. *I have problems. So many problems.*

Craig chooses that moment to sail back into the kitchen, still wearing his much-too-bright smile. He drops into a chair and nudges Alex's arm. "So. Tonight? You, me, David?"

The caffeine that Alex has managed to ingest has not at all reached his brain fast enough to prevent a shockingly filthy mental image from springing to mind. He nearly chokes on a bite of cinnamon roll. "Ack," he squeaks and prays for death.

David comes to the rescue. "Actually, you, me, and the twins," he says with a firm nod. He gets Alex a glass of water.

"We're going to the movies, and I need you to help me out with chaperone duties."

Craig's mouth falls open. "What? No, wait, why can't we go into London?"

Alex's choking fit subsides after a few sips of water. "We should keep our budget in mind," he croaks. "Plus, I have work to do."

"And your sisters deserve a break. Come on." David flashes those unfairly cute dimples *again*, and now Alex almost wants to go with them. *Never mind the twins.* He tries desperately to drown his blushes in the water glass.

Next to him, Craig appears to be softening under the onslaught, but he does rally. "I don't know why *I* have to be with you."

David knocks down the argument with ease. "Because your sisters, being very different young ladies, will want to see different movies. I cannot be in two places at once. There has to be one of us with each of them. But you don't have to sit next to them. In fact, with Jade and Frankie, you're not going to want to anyway. 'Discreet PDA' is a foreign concept to those two."

Craig appears to go a bit green around the gills. "I'll go with Jazz."

"Nope. You have always hated slasher flicks." David's smile gives way to a smirk that can only be described as triumphant. "You'll be fine with Jade. Just never look directly at where she's sitting. Peripheral vision is your friend."

Craig turns to Alex. "You're sure you can't come?"

"I need to do some work on that slideshow for the wedding reception." Alex hopes he's sufficiently apologetic. "Sorry. But hey, you wanted to get out of the house anyway, right?"

"Well... yes." Craig slumps in his chair, defeated. "All right, David. You win. What time?"

"We'll leave here around four-thirty. It's twenty minutes to Romford, and we'll want dinner and a reasonably early show. It's still a school night for the girls, after all." David stands. "Right, I need to open the shop; we have some big orders today. See you later, Craig, Alex. Thanks for the breakfast bribe." With a wink and a surreptitious thumbs-up to Alex, he vanishes.

"It wasn't a bribe," Craig grumbles, still slumped in his chair. He's pouting, and the protest is halfhearted at best. "Really."

Alex takes pity on him. "I know," he says, with a pat on Craig's arm. He rests his head on Craig's shoulder and enjoys the comfort of the familiar, beloved presence while he considers his morning so far. He's got his appointment with Dr. Laborteau, who will surely have a solution to the insanity that's going on. He's got an accomplice, a disturbingly attractive accomplice, but an accomplice nonetheless, who's going to help Alex get Craig out of the house so he can keep said appointment. All of this is good.

Except that he has way, *way* too many hours to get through *before* then—hours of trying to be cool and collected and to somehow dispel his guilt about conspiring to discuss Craig behind his back.

Fortunately, Alex has one foolproof way to occupy those hours for a while, as long as he keeps his eyes closed and his wits about himself. As smoothly as he can manage, Alex turns to his left and surprises Craig with a long, sizzling kiss.

"Wanna go make out?" he asks when Craig pulls away, breathless.

Craig's nonverbal answer is a resounding *yes*.

 *Chapter Nine*

THEY'RE A COUPLE OF HOURS IN AND THINGS ARE GETTING *really* hot and heavy when Chloe bangs open the attic door, clad in a lime-green trench coat and tall black boots. "Hope you're not too busy, Alex. I need you and your camera." She peeks at them out of the corner of her eye as she breezes over to the mirror on the bedroom wall. "You're gonna need trousers. It's nippy out."

"Wh... now?" Alex grabs for the duvet and drags it over himself and Craig. "I mean... Hi?"

"I'll be in the loo until she leaves," Craig mutters. He climbs over Alex and snatches his T-shirt from a chair as he goes.

"Duncan's not here," Chloe calls after him, exasperated. "Oh, forget it. Yes, Alex, now, please. If that's all right." The tight brown spirals of her curls are swept into their usual tumbling updo; a few escape their confines to frame the smooth, fine-boned, brown oval of her face. Were it not for the crackling annoyance in her eyes, she'd look angelic. "We've got most of today with no appointments or predictable emergencies, and it's fairly sunny. It's kind of a miracle, really. I thought we could take advantage of that, and you could take some shots of Duncan and me at our favorite places?" She glances over her shoulder with wide, hopeful eyes. "Please? We'll do all the driving and we'll buy you lunch."

Alex does have to admit that his plan to make out with Craig has a much shorter expiration time than Chloe's proposed outing would. And it doesn't seem he'll get to put his hands on Craig again anytime soon. "Yeah. Sure, all right. Can you hand me my jeans?"

She does, politely not looking at him as he slides into them. "I'd ask Craig to come with us," she says as she wanders back to the mirror, "but he's being a *total fucking child.*"

The last half of her sentence is delivered in an eardrum-piercing shriek aimed directly at the bathroom door. Behind it, a cabinet door is slammed noisily shut. "Get off my *tits,* Bridezilla," Craig shouts back, in a voice that Alex has never heard him use. It is the angriest that Alex has ever heard him— and Alex was at the wedding for which Craig made a beautiful chocolate and raspberry cake, festooned with buttercream roses and edible gold flakes... only to have it crushed by a drunken, stumbling groomsman. Craig was frightening *then,* but it was nothing like this.

But Chloe only rolls her eyes at the insult and turns back to the mirror, while Alex sits frozen with one shoe on and one in his hand. "Craig and I are not currently on speaking terms," she says, as she adjusts a crystal butterfly barrette in her hair. "Which should make tomorrow interesting, given that he and I are supposed to bake my wedding cake while you're out and about with Duncan."

"Right," is all Alex can say to *that.* He shakes himself back into motion so he can get his other shoe on. "Okay."

Alex has been through weddings with difficult brides, irritating groomsmen, and frightening mothers and bridesmaids, but this wedding is the first one that's truly made him fear for his life or his sanity or both.

The good news is, once they're out of the house and Chloe has stopped muttering imprecations under her breath, the day is fun. Most of the happy couple's favorite places are outdoors and gorgeous, even on a slightly gray day. Duncan is well-behaved, funny, and self-deprecating when Alex snaps a shot of him leaning against a rugby goalpost.

"Make me look good, eh?" He tugs his flat wool cap over his forehead. "Chicks dig the bashful country vet thing."

Chloe skips over and smacks his arm but, since it's clear as a spring sky that Duncan is teasing her, the smack is playful. "Less of that, thanks, future husband."

"What, not allowed a bit of fun, future wife?" He grabs her arm when she doesn't dodge away fast enough and hauls her in for a silly, smacking kiss that Alex is delighted to catch on camera. "No flirting at all with the ladies that just love a fellow with a baby animal in his arms? You're killing me, Cee."

"Nope. Mine, all mine." Chloe beams a sunshine smile at Duncan that obviously melts his heart, and Alex is happy to commit this moment of genuine love and affection to film.

Duncan is, Alex has to admit, an affable fellow. Every moment Alex has spent in his company, Duncan has been nothing but friendly and gregarious, and he seems to like nothing more than to talk anyone's ear off about rugby, the wedding, and the scores of baby animals he's treated. In his wallet, he carries photos of Newton from puppyhood to now. There is an entire album on Duncan's phone dedicated to snaps of the half-drowned kitten he took in on Monday—an entire album in just three days! The kitten's name is Daisy and, according to Chloe, Duncan lets her sleep on his pillow.

Alex unloads his full storage card and tucks it safely away while Chloe and Duncan nuzzle each other like... bears. Puppies. Some kind of furry nuzzling animals, anyway. They have given him a lot to consider over the last few days. For one thing, the time he's spent with Chloe has convinced Alex that she has a solid bullshit detector. That has to mean, then, that Duncan is the real deal, a genuinely decent guy. Maybe he used to be a tyrannical, arrogant jerk, but now he isn't. Maybe.

But guilt twists in Alex's mind even considering it.

Duncan drops Alex off at the Oliver house at four-fifteen on the dot. "Best if we don't go in, I think," he says, with apologies in his eyes. He ducks his head to avoid Chloe's dirty glare. "Maybe it's not a good time, Cee," he mumbles. "Craig's made it pretty clear he doesn't want to see me yet. I'll let him work it out. Really. Alex, catch you tomorrow for the photos, yeah?"

"Yeah." Alex slides out of the van and hits the ground just as Chloe winds herself up into what promises to be a truly incandescent fury. Duncan waves and drives off with Chloe gesticulating wildly, pointing for him to return to the house. With a calm that Alex can't help but admire, Duncan does no such thing, and the van disappears down the street.

Upstairs, Craig is pulling a sweater over his head. "How'd it go?" he asks, his tone carefully neutral. Of course, he's only asking out of his innate sense of politeness and his love for Alex—and Chloe. No matter how angry Craig is with her, Alex is sure he still loves his childhood friend.

"It went all right." He drops his bag and fishes out the full memory cards. "Lots of material for the slideshow thing. Good stuff, I think."

"Naturally. With you behind the camera, they'll be brilliant. Even if one of the subjects does happen to be an enormous, rugby-playing ox." Craig grins and pulls Alex up for a kiss. He presses Alex backward until the edge of the desk bites into his thighs. "Mm. Thank you for earlier, by the way. Lovely way to spend a couple of hours with you."

"Oh, well, you're we—oh." When Craig's hand slides under the waistband of Alex's jeans and his fingers tickle the skin of Alex's stomach, Alex's brain shuts down. He forgets every word in every language he knows, and his awareness narrows to a warm mouth kissing along his jawline, to a hand that skims the cotton of his boxers with a promising little tease, to the firm, warm body that leans more and more insistently against his and pins him to the desk—

"Well, hello," Jasmine says from the doorway

Craig pulls back, lips pursed in irritation. "Damn it, Jazz."

"Sorry," she says as she saunters into the room, obviously not sorry in the slightest.

Frankie and Jade giggle as they slip in behind Jasmine, holding hands. "It's cute, Jazz." Frankie tosses her blonde curls. "Goals, honestly."

"Right?" Jade squeezes Frankie's hand. "*So* goals."

Jasmine rolls her eyes, clearly uninterested. "Okay, so, David's here. He sent us to make sure you didn't get distracted and forget that you were going with us tonight. And oh, look. You did."

"I didn't forget," Craig grumbles. "I just hoped he would." He leans around Alex to grab his wool cap from the desk.

Jade's eyes are wide and bright, sparkling with mischief. "I don't blame you, Craig. Alex looks nice today." She tilts her head and bats her eyelashes. "Very nice."

Coping with flirty teenage girls is not one of Alex's specialties. His face is a burning tomato, he is sure. "So, you're definitely your mother's daughter."

"Learned my best tricks from her." Jade winks, while Jasmine snickers and Frankie aims a sigh of exaggerated tolerance at her girlfriend.

"I can see I have a very long evening ahead of me. Okay. We're done here." Craig jams his beanie on. "Sure you won't come with, babe?"

"Sorry," Alex says, and unlike anyone else in this house today, he actually means it. He holds up his handful of memory cards. "Lots of work, and time is running out."

Craig sighs as the girls surround him and hustle him out of the room. "Worth a shot. Love you."

"Love you, too." Alex waits for the footsteps and cheerful bickering to get to the second floor before he flips his laptop open and gets to work. His hands are shaky and sweaty, his nerves are on fire, and his stomach is in knots, but he's got to do *something* to pass the time before his call with Dr. Laborteau or he will absolutely lose it.

All but the last of the cards is empty when his alarm goes off; the photos are sorted into folders labeled *Viable, Hopeless,* and *Blackmail Material.* Alex breathes deeply and flips to Skype. With unsteady fingers, he clicks on the entry for Dr. Laborteau.

After a couple of rings, his therapist fills the screen with her soothing presence. A bright smile lights her dark eyes as she pushes a lock of silver hair back behind her ear. "Hi, Alex! How's England?"

"It's bad; everything is so bad. Craig has gone over the edge. I can't deal with this," Alex bursts out, and his face immediately flushes with heat. He couldn't pretend to have a handle on things for a minute? He squeezes his eyes shut. "No. Wait. Sorry. Can I start this call again?"

When he opens his eyes, Dr. Laborteau is gazing at him with surprise written all over her face. She surveys him for an uncomfortable stretch of time before she speaks. "No," she says, slowly tilting her head. "No, I'd say that's exactly where you need to start, so let's go with it, okay? Let's just get right into it; let's start with the last thing and work backward from there." Her reassuring smile grows calmer by the moment, and Alex's lungs loosen so his breath moves more freely. "You say you can't deal with what's happening. How true is that, really?"

Alex allows his shoulders to drop. They are sore, as if they've been cramped around his ears for a month. "It could be truer," he admits. "I could be hiding in the bathroom all the time, or I could have gotten on a plane and come home already. Obviously neither of those things happened."

"And that's good, right?" Papers rustle as Dr. Laborteau pulls out a legal pad. "Have you kept up with your meds?"

"I have my Xanax, but I haven't needed it." The bottle sits untouched in his gear bag. "I'm not at that point yet. No panic attacks."

"Very good. Don't let that lull you too far into complacency, but that's good." She nods. "So far, so good. All things considered, Alex, I'd have to say that whatever's going on, you're coping with it. So now that we've settled that, why don't you fill me in? Using," she holds up her hand to stop him as he opens his mouth, "more words than, 'Craig has gone over the edge,' maybe."

Alex winces. "Okay. That might have been a little exaggerated."

One graceful silver eyebrow arches upward. "You don't say."

Sometimes, Dr. Laborteau's dry humor sets Alex's teeth on edge. He rubs at his jaw as his molars grind together. "It's been kind of a rough week."

Her smile doesn't falter. If anything, it twitches with a touch of amusement that Alex strongly resents. "Go on," Dr. Laborteau instructs him, folding her hands together on her desk.

Three deep breaths and a shake of his head clear a way for linear thought and allow him to begin. "So. You know we're here for Craig's brother's wedding. But I don't think I told you that they haven't spoken to each other in years..."

Dr. Laborteau doesn't know Craig personally, but she seems unsurprised by the litany of bizarre behavior that Alex unfurls in the course of his story: the streaking, the frosting fight, Craig and Duncan's avoidance of each other, the hasty dinner in London, Chloe's anger, her determination to have everything perfect on her wedding day.

By the time he's finished, they're halfway through their time, and Alex is out of breath. Plus, an incipient headache crackles at his temples. Alex tries to rub it away while Dr. Laborteau mulls over the information dump he's just laid on her.

Eventually Dr. Laborteau steeples her fingers in front of her face, and Alex would almost swear she might be doing so to conceal, of all things, a smile. "I've been waiting for this day to come," she says and bows her head a bit.

Alex blinks, sure that the lump-like sensation in his throat is his heart, which leapt there in a panic at the unexpected words. "What? What day?"

Dr. Laborteau's face, when she looks up, is carefully mild. "The day that Craig finally reveals himself to be as human, and therefore as flawed, as you see yourself to be."

She might as well have said the words in Czech, for all the sense they make to Alex. "No. What? No. That can't be right."

"Oh, but it can, and it's been a long time coming, Alex." Her mild demeanor melts into resolve as she lifts her chin to fix him with a piercing stare. "This is not to say that Craig is suddenly a bad person, if that's what you think I meant. No, I am not saying that. It's just that right now, he's not behaving in the most adult manner, and this is the first time you're really seeing anything like that from him. The good news is that your instinctive reaction seems to be to step up and take the place you normally concede to him."

Ha. Ha ha ha, no. "I'm the adult now? No one consulted me on this!" He's mostly joking, but there's some real panic that he can neither hide nor fight back. While he forces out a pathetic facsimile of a hearty chuckle, his hands under the desk are abruptly freezing cold, and his throat is closing. And the Xanax is just out of reach.

Dr. Laborteau's expression is almost... no. Not almost. It's an expression of outright pity, mixed with sympathetic amusement. "Alex, according to my records, you'll be twenty-eight next February. From a legal standpoint, you've been an adult for nearly ten years."

"No, it's..." He gropes around, unsure how to get what's in his head *out*. "Craig's always been the rational one. He's handled my issues like he was born to it. He runs his business; he writes; he keeps me sane. I don't know why all of a sudden he's just... crazy."

"I don't really like the casual use of the word crazy... in any case, Craig is stressed, Alex. He's experiencing a perfectly normal, if perhaps a little exaggerated, reaction to an amount and type of stress he doesn't usually encounter." Her calm smile returns briefly, before settling back into the resolve that gives Alex the willies. "Which is something I think will be good for you."

Alex stares at his laptop. "How, exactly? He's the rational one, I told you. If he loses it, we're fucked."

For the first time, a flicker of impatience travels across Dr. Laborteau's face. "This again brings us, as always, back to my firm opinion that you are just as adult and rational as Craig, and it's long past time for you to stop putting yourself in the backseat of this relationship." Not even a trace of a smile lightens her expression. "Craig has always seen you as an equal partner, so why haven't you?"

"I..." He frowns. She has an entire file of reasons that he's given her. "You know I..."

"I know a lot, yes," Dr. Laborteau says and wags a finger at her screen. "I know you think you're weak, and yet you chose to strike out on your own and open your studio. I know you told me that you let Craig make all the decisions, but, on the other hand, you told me he came to you for your opinion before he decided to buy into the bakery. You're saying to me that you can't handle what's going on now, Alex, but everything *else* you've told me since we started this call indicates the complete opposite. That we're *having* this call, that you sought out help, is notable." Now, at last, a half-smile tilts her mouth. "Alex. When you let your true nature have its head, you are every bit as rational and grown-up as Craig."

He still can't quite get there. "Yeah, but my anxiety, that's not curable."

"No, and I didn't say it was. But anxiety isn't what defines you as a person." Her compassion is nearly a tangible thing, and it is crystal-clear that she means every word. He can only stare as she goes on. "You can't help your panic attacks, Alex, but you can help how they and your other issues color your opinion of yourself. It's time you let that sink in. Because you want me to tell you how to make things go back to what you set as your baseline of 'normal,' Alex, but even if I wanted to..."

She spreads her hand wide and shrugs. "That genie is well and truly out of the bottle now, I'm afraid."

Twin thunderbolts of realization and understanding strike, and, in their wake, everything around and inside of Alex is calmer and more still than it's been in a very, very long time— maybe more than it's been in his entire life. True, his stomach is still home to an entire flock of butterflies, and his very scalp is tingling, but overall, he's still more or less calm. This is not the help he wanted to get, but it is the help he is going to get.

He meets Dr. Laborteau's gaze with a direct one of his own. "What do I do now?"

"What you've been doing, what you never thought was enough but is now more important than ever, Alex. Love Craig. Support him. Be there for him. Be yourself, because that's who he loves and needs." Something in her expression is unfamiliar, and it takes a second for him to place it: pride. It warms him from the inside out as she goes on. "You've been letting Craig take care of you for a long time. That's fine. You were hurt, and he seems to like to nurture and take care of things. But you, by nature, are not a person who is accustomed to being, or even much cares to be, taken care of under normal circumstances. It's time you remembered that."

Even Alex's hands in his lap are still now; at any other time they'd be twitching and white at the knuckles where he twists them. Tendrils of self-confidence, slow but inexorable, begin to grow and spread light through the dark places of Alex's mind. "I can try."

"I'm fairly certain that you can manage it." Dr. Laborteau props her hand on her chin, and her smile is in no way a calm, compassionate one. It's a full-fledged beam of pride and delight. "You do realize that this is quite a breakthrough for you, right? You worked hard to get here, Alex. This is a good thing. I know it's been a rough ride, and that this week hasn't been easy. I'd hazard, too, that it's going to get worse before it gets better..."

"Oh, I think you're right about that for sure," Alex replies, unable to keep the wry twist from his smile. After the mess with his ex, Jeff, Alex struggled hard with the resulting emotional PTSD and his doubt spirals and panic attacks. All of that had left him in such a dark place, it's good to have a moment when he remembers what it's like to be a functional human being. He loves Craig in a deep and frightening way, but, for the first time since they met, Alex might really be able to be a partner and not a burden. He might truly be the person Craig always tells him he sees. And that person just might be able to get them through this week.

"We could actually survive this," Alex says aloud. And for once, they don't seem like famous last words.

 *Chapter Ten*

"**I**T IS ELEVEN O'CLOCK AT NIGHT, CRAIG," DAVID SAYS. His hands grip the steering wheel. His gaze is straight ahead; his jaw is set. "I have a shop to open in the morning, so get out of my car."

"I just want to be sure they're gone." Craig cranes his neck and sticks his head out the car window to peer into the driveway of the Oliver home. "It's so dark. I can't tell."

David reaches for the keys in the ignition. "I can drive closer."

"No! I don't want to risk them spotting us." They're parked across and slightly down the street from the house. Craig is still not quite sure how he managed to talk David out of parking in the driveway. "I'm not going in until I'm sure Duncan and Chloe went home."

Bracing his elbows on the steering wheel, David buries his hands in his dark hair—a gesture that makes him resemble Alex to a startling degree—and groans through gritted teeth. "This is absurd, Craig. We have parked out here for thirty minutes. In that time, you could have texted or called anyone in that house for confirmation." He tilts his head to look past Craig. "Your boyfriend is probably waiting upstairs for you to come to bed and explain why you're two hours later than the twins getting home."

"No, I sent Jasmine to tell him you and I went to the pub," Craig says as he slumps and shoves his hands into the pockets of his padded vest.

David gazes heavenward. "Oh, I'm sure that went over a treat. Or did you not notice that your sister has all the tact of a stone wall? Right. This is stupid." He lunges across the car to tackle Craig against the door; his hands move fast as they grope through Craig's pockets. In seconds he's got Craig's phone in his hand and has located the entry for Alex in the contacts list. "You should probably put a passcode on this thing," he remarks, using his shoulder and free hand to keep Craig pinned against the door. "Alex? Hey, David here. Listen, have Duncan and Chloe gone? Yeah? Great. I'm going to send your boyfriend up in a moment, okay? Right. Glad we could chat. Bye." He thumbs the phone off and tosses it back into Craig's lap before he flops back into the driver's seat. "There. You can go in now."

"Jesus *fucking* Christ, David." Wincing, Craig peels himself from the car door. He's fairly certain he's going to have a long bruise right across his back. And it hurts; David rammed him with considerable force. "Was that necessary?"

"Yes." When David looks at Craig, his mouth is tight with irritation before he relents. "Look. It's late. I have enjoyed hanging out with you tonight. Thank you for helping me with your sisters. And thank you for buying my drinks at the pub."

"But?" Craig raises an eyebrow.

"But as one of your two oldest friends, I do not want to come off as choosing sides in your battle with the *other* of your two oldest friends and your brother." David smiles and gently punches Craig in the arm. "I love you and Chloe both. I'm not going to tell you to kiss and make up with Duncan; whatever you choose to do there is all on you. But this is definitely,

absolutely the last time I am going to help you dodge the issue."
He unbuckles Craig's seat belt and leans across to push the
passenger-side door open. "Now. Seriously. Get out of my
car."

Left with little choice, Craig follows orders. It is entirely
possible that if he doesn't, David will push Craig out of the
car and onto the street. "You're a bastard; you do know that?"

"Good night, Craig," David says. He waits for Craig to close
the car door and then drives off with a jaunty wave. Craig
considers his options and, in the last second before David
disappears, he responds with a rude gesture.

Then he sighs and turns it into a wave, because David is
only trying to help.

It's cold. Craig heads toward the house, where lights are
still on in the family room. His parents are probably having a
nightcap, so he will have to make small talk with them, and
he is tired. *How tired, though?* The gate to the back garden is
open. In theory, if he really wants to get out of talking to his
father and mother, he *could* crawl up the drainpipe and into
the attic window.

He actually has his phone out and is ready to text Alex and
ask for the window to be unlatched when he comes to his
senses. *I am not a scrawny fifteen-year-old anymore. That pipe is
old. Hitting the ground would probably hurt a lot.*

Into the house he goes then, and, sure enough, his parents
are on the big, green couch. Stephen is lounging with a highball
of whiskey in his hand, and Moira is tucked into the opposite
corner with a book and a large white mug of tea. Craig has no
doubt that the tea is laced with a healthy dollop of the same
whiskey. "Hi, Mum. Dad."

"Craig." Stephen raises his glass in a salute and smiles.
"Welcome home."

"Indeed." Moira's smile is less genial, more wistful. "So late. Alex went upstairs an hour ago, love."

Craig is thirty years old, and his mother can still reduce him to a shuffling, guilty mess. He tucks his hands into the back pockets of his jeans. "Yeah. Well."

"Have a drink with us." Moira's voice is soft, but that's an order, not a request.

"The whiskey's good," Stephen offers. "Glasses on the sideboard."

At least these days the parental lectures come with alcohol. Craig pours himself two fingers of Lagavulin and takes a seat on the padded piano bench. "So."

"God, son. Relax a little." Stephen shakes his head and chuckles. "It's a drink, not a firing squad. We haven't seen much of you since you got home. Not alone, anyway."

Heat flushes Craig's cheeks, and he squirms. "Right."

Moira's laughing into her tea mug. "Did you think we were going to lecture you about your patently obvious efforts to dodge your brother?"

Craig coughs.

"You're an adult. We do realize that." Stephen shrugs while he takes a hearty swig of his drink. His face is thoughtful, but his eyes are bright. "Even if Chloe doesn't."

The whiskey *is* good. Craig takes a couple of sips and allows them to roll around in his mouth while he tries to process the goings-on. After dealing with Chloe these last few days, his parents are an unexpected breath of fresh air. "She means well."

"Don't we all. But the road to hell, and all that." Moira sets her mug aside. "Craig, my love. All we wanted out of this week was to see you and to meet Alex." She exchanges glances with Stephen and then she laughs again, a little helplessly. "Oh, all right. I admit, we did think it would be nice if you and

Duncan kissed and made up. But we had a front row seat to all the rowing, after all. We weren't under any illusions that you *would*. And we certainly wouldn't presume to try to force you."

"Thanks." Somehow, he'd not fully registered he was carrying that burden until it was lifted away. Oh, not entirely. Chloe, after all, would keep pushing on him. But that it would only be Chloe is somehow better, more manageable. It leaves him free to be candid. "I mean, I was thinking I would try, to be honest. Right up until we got here, I was considering it. You do have to concede that Duncan fucked things up before I could get that far."

"Well, yes. But as I'm sure you heard by now, he 'had good reasons' for it." Moira's hands lift in honest-to-God air quotes. "Neither here nor there. Whatever will happen between the two of you is up *to* the two of you. We wanted you to know that *we* know that."

"And," Stephen adds, "we wanted to apologize to you. We never properly have."

After another sip or two of whiskey, Craig can manage a reply. Even then, it's not much of one. "You what?"

Moira sits up a bit straighter. "To apologize. Craig, we're sorry. We honestly didn't have any idea how to truly solve the problem of you and Duncan. We never have. It's no excuse that we were such young parents, and then suddenly our hands were full having two children with huge but distinct personalities. It's no excuse that when the twins came along, we were overwhelmed."

"You gave me my own room," he points out. "Somewhere to escape to."

"Somewhat after the fact, and as much for our sanity as yours," Moira says. "I always felt it an inadequate apology for what happened. We did what we could, Craig, but we didn't do our best. Things should never have gotten as awful as they did, and we are terribly, terribly sorry, my love."

Craig sits back against the piano, wishing he'd picked a cozy chair nearer to the sofa—and for another finger of whiskey. "Okay. Okay, then."

He hasn't any idea what to do with this, where to go from here. His parents don't seem to expect a response. They simply sit on the couch. Stephen moves a little closer to Moira, close enough to put a hand on her knee while he offers her an affectionate, intimate smile. The sight makes Craig's heart twist in his chest. His parents have been together since they were teenagers and they *still* love each other so much. They're such a tight partnership. It's what he has always wanted, and he smiles to himself, thinking of Alex upstairs and how sure he is that they'll have this, too.

"I'm thinking of asking Alex to marry me," he says casually, almost absentmindedly. In fact, he's hardly aware he's said it until his mother bolts across the room and hauls him to his feet for a hug.

"Oh, *Craig*." She steps back and reaches up to hold his face in her hands, and her blue eyes are like oceans, sparkling and swimming with tears. "Oh, my boy, my love."

His father moves more slowly, but his rib-cracking hug indicates equal enthusiasm, and Craig is glad that he didn't take off his puffy vest at the door. "Fantastic news, son."

The warmth in his stomach isn't entirely due to the whiskey. Craig squirms, pleased and bashful. The more he says his intentions aloud, the more real and wonderful they become. "I don't know when. I just wanted you two to know. Please, don't say anything to anyone."

"Of course we won't." Moira is holding his face in her hands again, and it keeps him still while she beams her happiness at him. "Not a word. Thank God you told us this week, though. No one will question why we're so happy. They'll just mark it up to wedding planning delirium."

He laughs. "That's not why I told you now."

"It'll do." Stephen squeezes harder, and Craig can't hold back his groan. His back still protests from the abuse he got from David. His father lets go. "Sorry, son."

"No, it's fine," Craig lies as he blinks back tears of pain. "I'm happy, too."

Moira releases him at last, but not before she stands on her tiptoes to kiss his cheek. "As parents, we don't play favorites, strictly speaking," she says with her huge smile. "But if we did, you'd certainly be our favorite right now."

Craig ducks his head. "Thanks."

"Now. Go on upstairs to that lovely fellow of yours," his mother instructs, shoving him bodily toward the hallway. "He's been waiting for an age."

He doesn't need to be told twice. Emotion that wells from his toes up sends Craig drifting upstairs almost on a cloud; only the ache in his back keeps him from taking flight.

In the attic, Alex is curled up in the bed around Fitz; both of them snore gently. Craig sheds his clothes and slides in behind them. A twinge of guilt twists his stomach as his cool skin hits the cozy warmth of Alex's. Alex stirs and awakens from his light doze. "Mm?"

"Hi, babe. Sorry I'm so late."

"'S'all right. Figured you were outwaiting Chloe." Alex lifts Fitz with one hand and sets the snoozing bundle of fur on the upper corner of the bed. With a twist, he's facing Craig, bobbing his dozy head so that their foreheads touch, and he nuzzles Craig with his nose. "Mm. You smell like really good whiskey."

"Mum and Dad offered; I accepted." Craig pulls Alex closer, gathering him in. "How was dinner?"

"Fine. No big. I showed Duncan and Chloe some of the photos I got this morning; they're happy." Alex is at his slightly loose and loopy stage of half-sleep, a jumbled bundle of cuddly warmth in Craig's arms, as sweet as he gets only in this particular state, a sweetness that only Craig ever gets to see. "Did you like the movie? Jade said you covered your face a lot."

"I did enjoy the movie, more than I enjoyed watching my baby sister make out with her girlfriend. Let's not discuss that." His hands slide down; they glide over Alex's skin, making Alex chuckle and squirm. "I miss you. I missed you for the last two days."

"Here I am." Alex gasps as Craig pulls him even closer, until there's nothing between them except the cotton of Alex's boxers. "And here you are."

"Can you ignore the posters for a night?" Craig asks against Alex's mouth.

"Oh, fuck the posters," Alex breathes, and he's not half asleep anymore, and then he's also not wearing his boxers anymore, and Craig's very puzzling emotional roller-coaster of an evening takes a welcome swing upward.

 *Chapter Eleven*

Alex opens his eyes. Alone again. At this point, it's not even a surprise.

He rolls his head to look at the nightstand and sees a mug of tea on a little electric warmer. A big yellow sticky note clings to the outside of the mug. Alex picks it off to read while he drinks.

Babe—
You know wedding cake baking can't begin too early, and it's already Thursday. I'm with Chloe at her parents' place, since they have a bigger kitchen. I'll be there most of today. If you need to reach me, the Pennants' phone number is on the list taped to the wall by the kitchen phone. Have a great day, see you at dinner.
—C.

Alex tosses the note onto the nightstand, and hauls himself to his feet as he yawns into his mug. He does vaguely remember Craig leaving; a faint memory of a kiss on his forehead lingers around the edges of his consciousness. Stronger, though, are the entirely pleasant memories from last night. Alex smirks at the largest Robbie poster. "How'd you like *that*?" he asks, a split second before he feels as stupid as he ever has.

On the bed, Fitz yaps to be let down, and Alex obliges. "You need out?" A responding yap and puppy-dodge around his ankles is all the confirmation he needs. "Okay. Hang tight a sec."

Since he'll be out with Duncan for most of the day, Alex carries his tea to his bag to take a quick inventory. Freshly emptied memory cards, check. Trusty digital Canon and backup, check. Spare box of granola bars and water bottle in case they go too long, check. Lenses, flashes, light meter, spare battery packs for everything, check, check, and check.

His hand hovers over a little plastic bottle. Xanax, check.

Dr. Laborteau's confidence in Alex sits off-kilter on his shoulders. He likes it, mostly. It's already fueling his own confidence; it gives him more trust that he can get through this week. But it still takes getting used to. He's only been sitting with it for half a day, and several of those hours, he spent asleep... or otherwise occupied. Today he has to keep adjusting, keep repeating affirmations, keep reminding himself that once upon a time, not so long ago, he was kind of a badass. A jerk, but a badass. He can get along without the jerk part just fine, but he does have to keep the bad in badass, since nobody likes an ass.

Alex taps the lid of the pill bottle. He'll leave that where it is.

He gets dressed and picks up Fitz to see what kind of breakfast they can put together. For once, it should be quiet in the kitchen. Noisy clomping on the second floor followed by the slam-bang of the front door is his clue that the twins are gone. Craig, of course, is with Chloe. Moira should be locked in her office with her book, and Stephen, who is off for the rest of the week, is probably running around doing wedding errands.

So it's a surprise when Alex wanders into the kitchen and finds Craig's parents...

Well, they're making out. That is what they are doing. "Oh, wow."

"Alex! Oh, God, darling." Moira giggles into Stephen's chest, then peeks at Alex with nary a blush. "Sorry, love. We, ah, forgot that the house wasn't totally empty."

"Craig hasn't brought a boyfriend home in a very long time," Stephen adds, with a broad grin. "We're a bit out of practice accounting for everyone."

Alex puts Fitz on the floor and takes his time moving to the back door to let the dog into the back garden. Even if Moira isn't blushing, *he* is, and he needs time to cool off. "It's all right. I'll just let Fitz out."

"Good. Newton's out back already; he'll welcome the company." Moira extracts herself from her husband's embrace and sweeps around the kitchen, pulling down skillets and plates as she goes. "Stephen, start a fresh pot of coffee. Alex, have a seat when you're ready. I'll have a proper breakfast for you in a wink."

"You really don't have to," he begins, but his heart isn't in it. She'll only ignore his protests. With any luck, his photo shoot with Duncan will involve a good amount of walking and he can work off some of the sausage and eggs. "I mean..."

Moira tosses a package of sausage on the countertop and crosses over to cup Alex's face in her hands. "Alex, darling. Yes, you are perfectly capable of feeding yourself and you are not starving to death. But I am a Scottish mother of four children, two of whom are still teenagers and the other two were very large, athletic boys. I do not know how else to feed people. Hmm?" She pats his cheek and spins around to grab a tea towel. "Now, Stephen, hurry it up with that coffee and sit yourself down as well. Don't think I haven't noticed you dodging breakfast this week."

"Yes, dear." Stephen's tone is mild, but his dark eyes twinkle as he takes a seat next to Alex. "My younger son is very much his mother's child," he stage-whispers to Alex with a conspiratorial smile and a wink. "It was never a doubt in my mind that you would be a perfectly adequately fed individual."

"Didn't I just say I'm aware he's not starving, Stephen Oliver?" Moira's tea towel flicks out and catches Stephen's arm with a snap that makes him yelp. "Oh! Sorry, love, that wasn't meant to land quite so hard."

She gives him a kiss of apology, one intense enough to make Alex fidget. They've been together for over thirty years; they met when they were seventeen and nineteen. Craig told him the story. And they *still* act like teenagers in love, in their honeymoon phase. Time does not appear to have scratched the surface of their obvious affection for each other, let alone made a dent in it.

He considers this as Stephen grabs Moira around the waist, pulls her into his lap, and laughs while she shrieks and kicks her bare feet. What will he and Craig be like in thirty years? Graying at the temples, a bit slower to get out of bed in the morning? Will Craig still make pancakes every Sunday morning? Will Alex still enjoy watching him do it?

And kids, what—

Alex nearly swallows his tongue. *Kids? Kids?! I'm thinking of kids?*

"Alex!" Moira is out of Stephen's lap in a flash. "What is it? Do you need water? Stephen, get the boy a glass of water."

"I'm okay," Alex gurgles, aware that his strangled speech belies the statement. He takes in a slow, deep breath, presses his palms to his cheeks, and wills his heart to calm the fuck down. "Really."

Moira lifts an eyebrow and gives his shoulder a pat. "If you say so." She kisses his cheek and steps back to the breakfast makings on the counter. "Now. Let's try this breakfast thing again, shall we?" Her hands move quickly to crack eggs, fry sausage, and slide a tray full of buttered bread slices under the grill in the oven. "What are your plans, Alex?"

His mind is still reeling from the very idea of raising children with Craig, of being with him in thirty years' time. *Did she read my mind?* "I don't have plans; who said I have plans," he blurts, keeping his eyes fixed on the tablecloth. His fingers tap an agitated tattoo. "Plans?"

Their astonished gazes tickle his skin before he looks up to meet them. "For the day, love," Moira says slowly; a bowl of beaten eggs dangles in her hand. "I... thought you were going to go around with Duncan."

"For pictures," Stephen adds just as slowly and with great care. He cocks his head to regard Alex as if he's encountered an exotic animal for the first time.

And if Alex had the mental faculties to do so, he might be able to name a dozen dumb animals he feels like right now. A stunned chimp, maybe. A fish that leapt out of its bowl. A very tired horse. "Oh."

"Ah, so you acknowledge you have a plan." Moira winks to take the sting out of her words. "That we poor old ailing adults aren't going prematurely senile."

"No! No. No, yes, I mean, I'll be taking photos of Duncan today." Maybe he should have stayed upstairs until the afternoon. It would have caused less damage. "He's coming by in the late afternoon."

"Good. I'll keep you out of trouble this morning myself. You can come help me at the food bank." Moira casts a smile over her shoulder. "The girls are just dying to meet the gorgeous American who's stolen my boy's heart. They'll not know what to make of you, you handsome thing."

The way Craig's mother flirts with him is both adorable and disturbing, and it puts Alex even farther off balance. "But... your book," he says, wishing he could string a few more words together and sound a bit more like an adult.

"I'll work on it tonight. Don't you worry about me; I've been doing this longer than you've been alive." She leaves the stove to give him a kiss, then turns to give her husband one as well. "You'll come along, Stephen. We never have enough helping hands. Now, come here, will you? You're better at cooking sausages, and we both know it."

Stephen obediently follows Moira to the stove and leaves Alex agog at what just happened and what he's been dragged into—what *family* he's found himself in. Stephen and Moira chuckle and nudge each other's shoulders while they put breakfast together, not quite like the coordinated dance he and Craig perform when they're making breakfast in their tiny kitchen, but not entirely unlike it, either.

They're happy. Comfortable. Clearly in love. And that? That is a lot like him and Craig.

And of course, that leads him right back to pondering the potential future that's just hit him over the head. Now that the shock has worn off, that future could be very worth pondering...

"I thought I was in better shape." Alex groans as he eases himself out of the Olivers' minivan. "I walk my dog; I haul camera equipment around."

Stephen isn't moving any more quickly than Alex as he winces his way out of the van's front seat. "Ah, but that mostly benefits your legs. It's the arms that need help lifting boxes of canned goods." With a grimace, he rotates his arm. "Think I'll take Chloe up on her offer to do those yoga videos with her."

"I need to start going to the Y to swim with Craig more often. His shift at the food bank didn't hurt him *this* much." There's a particularly persistent cramp between Alex's shoulder blades that is crying for a massage. Too bad that's something he won't be getting any time soon. "I'm going to crawl upstairs and have a long, hot shower before Duncan gets here."

"Good idea." Moira is moving with considerably more briskness than either of the men. "I'll knock up a plate of sandwiches for you and bring them upstairs." She hustles into the house, whistling cheerfully.

"As long as you don't bring them right into the bathroom," Alex calls after her, but she's already out of sight.

Stephen gives him a gentle pat on the arm. "Lock the door, just in case."

Alex cannot be sure if Stephen is joking or not, but, when he gets upstairs, he does lock the bathroom door all the same.

He does not lock the bedroom door, so he gets a surprise when he emerges from the bathroom post-shower to find not only the plate of sandwiches, but Duncan sitting in the desk chair and munching on one of them.

"Mum sent me with lunch," Duncan says, waving what's left of the sandwich with a cheerful nonchalance. "Don't worry, there are plenty left. They're ham and cheese."

"Cool." Alex nods. "Okay. Should I make tea?"

"No. Mum sent a couple bottles of water." Duncan hands one over, along with one of the sandwiches.

Alex starts in on his lunch. "So, where do you want to go today? For your photos."

Duncan uses his sandwich to send a vague wave toward the window. "There's a lake. It's not far from here."

Lakes are picturesque. Alex approves. He gets up and checks his gear bag. "Is there good light? Will I need a flash, do you think?"

"Sorry, no idea." Duncan shakes his head. "It's surrounded by a pretty heavily wooded area. Light does get through the canopy, and the ground cover grows pretty well. Does that help you at all?"

Alex's fingers trace his equipment. "That's fine. I always take a flash, just in case. Light might get through those treetops, but it could be inconsistent." It might make for some interesting light patterns, though. Maybe he can get some nice nature shots. Alex zips the bag closed and hoists it over his shoulder. "Should we go?"

"Yeah, all right." Duncan gets to his feet and picks up the plate. "I told Mum she didn't need to make so many sandwiches. I'll drop the plate off and meet you out front?"

"That's a plan." Alex grabs his jacket and strides out.

Outside, the afternoon is cool and breezy. Alex leans against the doorway to wait for Duncan.

A tap on his shoulder startles him. It's David, who squeezes past him out of the house. "David. Hi. Flower delivery?"

"Yep. Corsages, sprays for the twins to pin in their hair." David fits an earbud into an ear and descends the porch steps to unchain his bicycle from the railings. "You going out with Duncan?"

"Yeah. Some lake or something. You know it?"

Something—concern? disturbance? irritation?—flits across David's face. "I do. We all used to sneak in there. People still do; it's a party place sometimes." He hesitates; the coils of his bike lock go still in his hands. "Be careful, will you? It's full of badger setts and giant roots and things, and if you fall into the lake, God knows what you could catch. It's scummy. Ah, and you'll need to climb two fences to get into the area, so I hope you're up for that."

Alex frowns, not totally on board with this excursion all of a sudden. The lake setting might be picturesque, but nature has never really been his bag. Also, fences? "Huh. You want to come with? Keep me out of trouble?" *Keep me company? Stop it, Alex.*

David's mouth tightens. "I'd actually love to. But unfortunately, I have to get back to the shop to work on some of the standing arrangements for Saturday." He lets out a short grumble. "Otherwise I would come along."

That's that, then. "Busy day for you."

"Isn't it just." David stuffs the coiled bike lock into his backpack and slings it over his shoulders. His mouth is still tight as he turns to walk his bicycle toward the street. "Sorry, Alex. Be careful in there, all right? You have your phone?"

Alex fishes it out from his hip pocket. "Right here."

"If anything goes wrong at all," David says, his face grim, "and I do mean *at all*, call me. Immediately."

"What could possibly go wrong?"

"Nothing, I'm sure. I'm being paranoid. But just in case." David hops onto his bike. "Remember, call me *immediately*."

"Hey!" But David is gone with his annoyance and grim expression and uselessly cryptic warnings, and now Alex *really* doesn't want to do this.

He's still trying to work out how to get out of it politely when Duncan turns up. "Hey-o. Sorry. Mum got to talking, wedding stuff, God."

"No problem." Alex twists the strap of his bag between his fingers. "Hey, if you need to stay and work some stuff out with her, we can do this tomorrow." *Or never. Never is starting to look like a good life choice.*

"Nah, nah, no. I need to *not* talk about the wedding or do wedding stuff for a while!" Duncan pauses, and his mouth twitches as he thinks about what he just said. "I mean, shit, I guess we're technically doing wedding stuff right now, aren't we? Whatever." He takes Alex by the arm and strides across the lawn toward the road. "What we're doing doesn't involve kilts or ring bearers or what our first dance is going to be. Funny story there, though. I've been telling everyone we're dancing to "Hi Ho, Silver Lining" just to be a cock. Ever heard it?" When Alex shakes his head, Duncan shrugs and keeps walking. "It's an old one, anyway. Right! How are you at fence climbing? We have to get over a couple to get to the lake."

So there's no escaping. *Spectacular.*

As Duncan promised, it's not far to the lake. However, just as he also promised and David confirmed, they have to scale two fences to get into the wooded area that surrounds it. And for an awful lot of their journey here, Alex felt the distinct back-of-the-neck tingling sensation of being watched. Or followed. It does not make him feel better.

"I'm kind of dubious about the legality of this," he begins as he reaches up to hoist himself over the second fence.

"I'm not," Duncan replies breezily. "It's completely illegal. We are trespassing. No need to be dubious, Alex. We are in the wrong."

Comforting.

He hits the ground and follows Duncan to a break in the wild hedges that surround the wooded area like another sort of fence.

"It's usually kids who come through here, so the passage isn't very big," Duncan says, pushing at some of the greenery and breaking off sticks and twigs. "This'll be slow going, but we can get through if we crouch. Hey, can you come help me with this?"

Now more than ever all of Alex's instincts are screaming for him to run, and they are at war with his deep-seated need to not rock the boat with Craig's family. *I could hop the fence now. He wouldn't chase me. He'd just think I'm weird.*

And yet, he does nothing. Alex suppresses a sigh of exasperation at himself and walks over to help his boyfriend's estranged brother trespass on private property.

The two of them working together open the break in the hedge wide enough to let Duncan in to make a wider path, with Alex, bent nearly double, following behind. The hedge is thick, claustrophobically so, but Duncan pushes through, breaking out an alarmingly large pocketknife to saw through a few of the more troublesome branches. He looks back at Alex. "You never know when you'll need a huge knife, being a country vet," he volunteers with a wink and a grin so cheerful it's almost a *Psycho* level of menacing.

"I bet," Alex manages to cough out.

But his nervy edge and paranoia fall away when he emerges at last from the hedge and straightens, taking in his surroundings. "Holy shit."

"It's pretty great, eh?" Duncan asks, hands on his hips and a tremendously pleased smile on his face.

The lake isn't visible yet, but only because the distance between it and them is filled with huge trees, oak and yew and types Alex can't begin to identify. Many of them are so large and old, it would take three people joining hands to encircle them. Fading ivy crawls up the trunks toward branches that have lost enough of their leaves to allow the sun to stream through breaks in the faint cloud cover.

It is straight out of *Lord of the Rings*.

"This is straight out of *Lord of the Rings*," Alex says.

Duncan chuckles. "Something like, yeah."

Alex's fingers are already at the zipper of his gear bag. "Mind if I take a few shots of this first?" he asks, locating his Canon and the appropriate lens by touch. His eyes dart from tree to tree as he fits the lens on. "To get an idea of the light and surroundings?"

Duncan waves a hand. "Sure, go ahead. Hey, do *you* mind if I step away for a second? Visit the facilities, like? I'll be quick."

"Take your time." Alex already has his camera powered on and lifts it to his face. He's enchanted by the gorgeousness around him. "I just want a few shots."

"No problem." Duncan's footsteps crunch away behind him, but Alex is already engrossed in his task.

There's no wildlife in sight—birds, he hears chirping birds, and the occasional rustle of what might be a squirrel. He just can't *see* any of them. And that's fine, because he is absolutely captivated by the luminescent fingers of sunshine that beam through the branches, filtered by the clouds and dappling the leaf-covered forest floor with the most fascinating patterns.

It takes him a few minutes to pull himself back to the world, and he frowns. If Duncan is still peeing, he rivals Austin Powers in stream-length. Austin Powers *and* that one guy Tom Hanks played in *A League of Their Own*. Combined.

It is an epic pee.

If that is what is happening.

It is dead silent in the woods, the eerie silence that horror movies promised Alex is a harbinger of doom. There is nothing so much as a bird chirp to lighten the air now, let alone the sound of a large man relieving his bladder. And in this silence, Alex would surely hear that whether he wanted to or not.

He does not want this silence to mean what he is increasingly afraid it means. *Don't be an asshole after all, Duncan. Come on.*

Alex pushes down his rising nervousness and takes the lens off his camera to nestle it into its pocket in his bag. He powers down the Canon and stows it into its own space. The careful tending of his equipment is habitual, but right now it also keeps his hands occupied and his mind from going in circles. Slowly, Alex zips the bag shut. When he can't put it off anymore, he wipes his hands on his jeans and takes stock of his situation.

He wandered farther into the wooded area as he snapped photos. He thinks. Maybe he just moved westward? Alex turns in a cautious circle, trying to distinguish one tree from another and failing entirely. For the first time in his life, he regrets not joining the Boy Scouts or Camp Fire USA or whatever social group might have given him more in the way of survival skills than flute lessons and soccer did. He has to get out of here. Somehow. *Start at the beginning.*

"Duncan?" he calls out, and oh, how he hates the way his voice wants to choke itself off in his throat. He shakes his head and takes as deep a breath as he can. He tries again. "Duncan?"

Silence but for a startled bird rattling out of a clutch of branches overhead, then nothing again. If Alex harbored any hope that Craig's brother wasn't ditching him here, well, it took off with that bird. *Goddamn it.*

David's words flash to the front of Alex's memory. *If anything goes wrong at all, call me. Immediately.* Okay. Alex would definitely qualify being stuck in an unfamiliar wooded area that is growing increasingly creepy as *something going wrong.* Yes. Good. He has a plan. Digging into his pocket,

Alex locates his phone. He has a solution. He has a step two. He has a—complete lack of signal. "Are you kidding me?" he asks his phone, giving it a shake as if that will make the *No Service* notice magically transform into five full signal bars. "Motherfucker. *Fuck*."

Only rapidly stuffing the phone back into his pocket prevents him from hurling it across the forest. Only rapidly stuffing his fist against his mouth prevents him from yelling his useless rage into the sky.

Right about now, Alex Scheff is ninety-eight percent certain he is capable of murder. And that is new. He closes his eyes to clear his mind. He doesn't have much in the way of options.

It is a bad idea to go walking off into the woods, even he knows that. He will undoubtedly get lost among all the unfamiliar trees that look so much alike. But maybe he can scratch crosses or something into the tree bark, like in the movies, and he has his own pocketknife, if not as large a one as Duncan's. That at least will tell him if he's passing the same group of trees more than once, maybe. It's a start.

The wooded area is fenced. It is finite. If Alex is slow and careful, he'll come to the fence or the lake at *some* point. He can walk around the lake and keep going until he finds a fence. He doesn't have to go out the way he got in, he just has to get out. This is not the complete disaster his anxiety thinks it is.

It's not the best idea, but it's what he's got.

Alex turns, starts to take a long confident step, and hooks his right ankle under the humped root of a massive oak tree. Pain roars through his leg like wildfire as he falls to the ground with a primal howl of agony.

The world lights up with a thousand golden fireworks, and then it goes black.

 Chapter Twelve

WHEN HE COMES TO, ALEX IS AT FIRST SIMPLY GRATIFIED that no bear mysteriously materialized in this enclosed forest and ate him.

Then the reality of his situation hits, and he can't breathe, he can't breathe, he can't breathe, he cannot *breathe*; he is injured and trapped and lost and he is going to die and he can't *breathe*; and his chest aches from contracting so tightly, and his ankle *hurts*, and he is going to *die* and he will never see Craig again and—

Craig. Alex seizes on the thought of his boyfriend, the man he loves. He grabs on to the thought of Craig's sunshine smile and easy laugh. He latches on to memories of being in bed, of skin on skin and gentle touches. He holds on to a butterfly kiss on his temple from just this morning as if it's a lifeline and, right now, it is.

It is nearly as agonizing as the pain in his ankle, but Alex corrals his rising panic attack with the coping skills he's learned from Dr. Laborteau. He grits his teeth as he forces himself to concentrate on the best thing in his life, the one thing guaranteed to pull him back from the brink. *Count good moments backward from ten*, Dr. Laborteau's voice says in his head, and he starts.

Ten. Waking to Craig in the kitchen as he makes pancakes and sings along to a blues CD on the radio their first morning together.

Nine. Craig on their bed, taking a nap with Fitz curled up and snoring on his broad chest.

Eight. Craig pulling open the door on the day Alex decided he couldn't live without him, looking exhausted and hurt and sad and still the most wonderful sight Alex ever laid eyes on.

Seven. Craig slipping granola bars under the bathroom door the night of Alex and Connor's studio opening, making sure Alex didn't starve while he worked up the nerve to go to his own party.

Six. Craig giving Alex a kiss every morning, waking him out of a grumpy sleep-stupor with tickling kisses to the back of his neck and a wandering hand...

Five. Craig underneath him, under his hands and lips and love, and laughs interspersed with gasps and sighs.

Four. Craig at Sucre Coeur, in his element, covered in flour and frosting, with a smile that encompasses the world.

Three. Craig with Connor's daughter Kira, making her giggle while she tosses back her soft dark curls and claps her little starfish-shaped hands to his cheeks.

Two. The image of future-Craig, gray at his temples and in his goatee, his smile unfaded, the love in his dark eyes as bright as ever.

One. Craig. Just Craig.

Alex's chest loosens at last, and he can pull in deep, slow breaths. *In. Out. In. Out.* Air fills his lungs, but this isn't the end of his panic attack. It's better, way better, but it's not over. Alex continues to breathe to hold the panic at bay and takes stock.

The pain in his ankle is a fiery, throbbing protest, and the skin stretches and goes hot as it swells. A really bad sprain, he's pretty sure. Thanks to soccer, he's got a survival skill he never wanted to use: He is intimately familiar with the shrieking pain of a broken bone. The good news is that this does not hurt *nearly* as much as the broken ankle he suffered in his senior year of college. But he's not going to be able to walk on it, which means he can't get out of here.

That is not comforting. That brings the panic back to the surface. Alex gropes for his bag and zips it open. He fumbles out the pill bottle and in seconds he's got a little peach pill in his hand. He swallows it dry. *Fuck, fuck, fuck!*

The reality of his situation is all too clear and not at all relaxing; he is stranded in an area he does not know. His phone does not get service in this godforsaken place. He is injured. And in about fifteen minutes, he's going to be mellow as hell, but he has to get through that fifteen minutes first.

Then Alex hears the noisy crunch of leaves being crushed behind him, and he cranes his head to see who or what it is. "Duncan? You asshole. Is that you? That had better be you." If it is, Alex is not at all sure he will wait for them to get out of here before he murders Duncan. No, he does not particularly care about the unwisdom of that course of action.

Not that it matters. There's no answer. His mouth goes dry.

Night is approaching, a few hours off yet, but still, approaching *at some time.* And there is a very loud rustling behind him and to his right. It could be anything. It could be a police officer. It could be an angry farmer with a big shotgun. It could be... Alex swallows. It could be what it sounds like as it gets closer, which, quite improbably, is a panicked animal stumbling through the woods at high speed. Now his throat closes.

This is where he is going to die.

Alex pushes himself around to face the galloping stampede. His hands tighten around the rough diameter of a fallen tree branch.

The stumbling creature bursts into his line of sight from behind a large tree and reveals itself to be—David. He skids to a stop. His flop of dark hair almost, but not quite, conceals the alarm in his green eyes as he bends over and tries to catch his breath. Alex blinks, trying to make sense of this. "David?"

"In the flesh." David slips into the dell where Alex landed, picks through the leaves until he arrives at Alex's side, and drops to the ground, slinging his backpack down beside him. "Fucking hell. I ran all *over* this place to find you. I was starting to think you fell into the lake and drowned and I have *no* idea how to explain that to Craig."

Alex can only stare. "I don't understand anything that's happening," he says, aware even as the words emerge that they are lame and pathetic.

David, to his surprise, fumbles a pack of cigarettes and a lighter out of the pocket of his leather jacket. "I rather wish I *didn't* understand, myself," he says as he passes the pack over. He waits for Alex to light up and takes back the lighter. "Smoking in a wooded area is probably a really bad idea, actually. Fuck it. Needs must."

"It's not like today has been full of *good* ideas." Alex clears away a pile of leaves and digs out a little hole in the dirt to use as an ashtray. "We'll just have to be extra careful."

"Like you were careful watching where you were going?" David uses his cigarette to point at the giant loop of tree root that tripped Alex. "I assume that's what happened, anyway. Right?"

Alex looks at the tree root, then back at David. It occurs to him that there is something distinctly convenient about Craig's ex showing up now, not long after Duncan abandoned him. Isn't there? He ignores David's question and goes on the offense. "Were you in on this?"

As he expected, the non sequitur throws David off. "What?"

"Were. You. In. On. This?" Alex repeats, fighting to keep his voice calm. "This joke of Duncan's. Not that I find it funny, but I assume he did mean it as a joke."

David tilts his head and eyes Alex warily as he ashes his cigarette. "He did, but he's an idiot... are you hurt? If you're hurt, I should go find someone to help us."

"Don't change the subject, and don't you dare go anywhere." It comes out more sharply than he intended, and Alex has to look down and breathe in some calm before he can continue more rationally. "I mean. Please. I prefer that you not leave me alone just yet. And I want to know what's going on."

David only looks away as he takes a deep drag on his cigarette. His unhappy squirms do convince Alex that he wasn't in on Duncan's plan, but, given David's vague warnings earlier, Alex is not at all convinced that he didn't know ahead of time that something was going to happen. He rolls onto his side to grab David's foot and give it a shake. "Hey. What is this? Why are you here right after Duncan ditched me? I thought you had stuff to do at the shop; that's why you abandoned me with him."

David's eyes darken as he turns his gaze back to Alex. "You're not going to like it."

"Yes, because I'm having *such* a good time right now." Alex raises an eyebrow. "We're not going anywhere for a while. You might as well fill me in."

David looks as if he'd rather be absolutely anywhere else doing anything else, but tough shit. So would Alex. He keeps his stare leveled at David until David rolls his eyes and sighs. "Fine. No, I didn't really know ahead of time, but when you said you two were coming here, I had a bad feeling about it. Duncan has..." David hesitates. "He has a bad habit of playing very dirty tricks on anyone his siblings bring home. Always has, me included. I haven't been able to eat guacamole since I was fourteen."

"Tricks?" Alex laughs bitterly. "Some trick this turned out to be."

"I hoped Duncan wouldn't be so *stupid*. But I knew there was a chance. I couldn't shake the bad feeling so I doubled back and followed you two." His eyes widen, and he scoots back a little. Alex understands why when he sees that he's still got a hand on David's foot and he's squeezing.

He doesn't want to know what his own face must look like. The blood has already rushed to it and is burning in his cheeks.

David pulls his foot free and scoots farther away. He drops his cigarette and scuffs it out. "Still. Duncan *is* an idiot, Alex, but I'm sure he never intended for you to get hurt, only a little lost."

"*Only a little lost,*" comes out in a breathless snarl as the fingers of Alex's free hand convulse around a handful of crumbled leaves and loose earth. He remembers the look on David's face, back at the house: the trepidation, the conflict.

"You *knew*." The two little words emerge in a near-roar of frustration. "You knew and you let it happen. Goddamn it, goddamn it, god*damn* it. You couldn't have warned me?"

One hand covers his with a gentle squeeze. "I'm sorry," David says, his gaze steady on Alex's face. "I'm so sorry, Alex. I wanted to be wrong. I hoped I would be."

Alex pulls his hand free and rolls over onto his back. "You could have warned me."

Above his head, David runs a hand through his hair. "Wasn't sure how. I wasn't exactly sure what Duncan would *do*. And I didn't want to cause trouble if he *wasn't* planning anything and get you wound up for no reason. It's no excuse, of course. I really am sorry." He sighs. "Craig's going to be furious."

That much is irrefutable. Alex can only hope to defuse his boyfriend's anger quickly. "We'll figure something out."

Hmm. He feels pretty good right now, all of a sudden. The Xanax is finally kicking in, and another fit of temper is unlikely. That's something.

David lights another cigarette. "We should call someone to help get you out of here. I'd say not Craig, but we're not going to have a lot of choices."

Alex's brain has begun to melt and his body to relax, and his ability to care has wandered off on its own. "We can't call. Or can you? My phone isn't getting a signal." And that does not bother him as much as it did. Hooray for modern medicine.

David digs his phone out. "No. No signal. I'll have to walk until I get one." He gazes at Alex soberly. "I'll have to leave you. At least for a minute."

Alex flaps a loose hand. He really does not care. "It's fine."

Confusion flits across David's face. "Really?"

Alex fumbles through his bag for the little bottle and holds it up. "This just started to work. Thank *God*."

David leans closer to look at the bottle, and his eyebrows shoot up. "I see."

"I wasn't going to tell you guys..." A yawn overtakes Alex, and his hand drops to the ground and lets the bottle roll out of it. "Thought I had it handled... was a just-in-case thing... didn't see this coming." A nap would be nice, so nice.

David picks up the bottle and tucks it back into Alex's bag before he stands up. "I'll be back."

"M'kay."

He crunches off, leaving Alex to lie on his back and stare at the patterns of light and shadow overhead. Alex doesn't like to take the Xanax. A whole tablet comes too close to knocking him out. He took it more in the early days of therapy, when picking over his memories brought panic attacks just about every day, but since then he's only rarely felt the need for it. In fact, he hasn't taken even half of one since the day they got the wedding invitation.

And now, in hindsight, he's going to be of no use at all in his own rescue effort. Normally this would annoy him, but right now all he can do is muster up a vague chuckle at his own stupidity. At least he's not freaking out at David anymore.

A crunch of leaves heralds David's return. "Help is on the way."

"Awesome." Alex wishes he had a pillow. A pillow would be great right now.

David sits and lifts Alex's head to rest on his knee. "I'm not trying anything funny," he warns. "It's just too chilly for me to take my jacket off and let you use it as a pillow. This is strictly me being nice."

"Oh, no, this *is* nice." Alex manages to resist the urge to roll over and fall asleep. His boyfriend's ex-boyfriend is most certainly *not* a pillow. "I was just thinking I w..." He yawns. "Wanted a pillow."

"Yeah, I gather it's not one of those things a photographer usually keeps in his bag." David hesitates. "Is Xanax?"

Alex lets out a little chuckle and wobbles his head back and forth in a loose approximation of shaking it. "Only the ones with an anxiety diagnosis and a history of panic attacks."

Over his head, there's a swift little intake of air, and, when Alex focuses on David, the other man's mouth is tight with anger. "Fucking Duncan," he says. "He shouldn't have—"

"He didn't know." Only the throbbing fire in his ankle keeps Alex semi-alert. He still has to concentrate to make sure he's speaking in coherent sentences, if not terribly quickly. "I mean, no, he shouldn't have. But he didn't know. I didn't... didn't want you all to know. Craig treats me like I'm made out of glass as it is."

"Got it. I won't tell." David leans back on his hands, slowly, so as to not jostle Alex's head. "I'm sorry again, Alex. Really."

Alex pats David's knee. "Thanks for coming after me."

David opens his mouth; his eyes are dark. But whatever he's about to say, he shakes his head and appears to change his mind. "Listen, Alex. I should check your ankle. You yelled pretty loud when you went down."

Alex pouts. "But I'll have to sit up."

A chuckle. "Sorry. But we should assess the damage before help gets here and we have to move you." Gently, he helps Alex sit up. "Okay. I'm going to pull you over to sit against this tree... good. You're doing a fantastic job." He snags his backpack. "Good thing I carry a first aid kit. Let's get that shoe off."

"We have to?" Alex sucks a deep breath in through his teeth as David eases his sneaker off. "Ow. Ow."

"Sorry." David peels Alex's sock away and grimaces. "Oh, this does not look good."

You do. Oh, no. Now was so not the time for Alex's inconvenient crush to resurge. "Um. Yeah. Doesn't really feel so good either."

David smiles at Alex, and it is ridiculous how cute he is, damn it. Those *dimples.* Unfair. "I would imagine not. This is a nasty sprain. I've got an Ace bandage in my kit." He puts down Alex's ankle and rummages in his bag.

"You have a nice smile," Alex informs him and then he immediately wishes the earth would open and swallow him whole. That's another reason he detests Xanax, he remembers, as David fumbles and drops the Ace bandage. Xanax kills filters.

"Okay," David mumbles as he picks up the bandage and removes bits of leaf from it with exceptional care. "Thanks?"

"I don't mean anything by it," Alex says. His face has to be flushed as red as the cranberry-colored wool sweater David is wearing, which, it must be said, is doing him about a thousand wonderful favors. "I mean, I'm sorry. I took a higher dosage of Xanax than usual; I have no filter. You do have a great smile, but I love Craig."

David begins to wrap Alex's ankle; his hands are careful. "And Craig loves you. He's been a little weirdly flirtatious this week, but he loves you very much."

That's interesting news. "Has he?" Too interesting. Alex has to beat back the equally interesting mental images that just spring to mind.

"I might just be imagining things, though." David's face, too, matches his sweater. "Right. Listen. Speaking of Craig."

He looks as though he's about to vomit. Alex's heart sinks. "Oh, no."

"Yeah. He'll be on his way. Like I said, not much choice in the matter." David clips the bandage closed and stands to shove his hands into his pockets. "My vehicle's back at the shop. I didn't stop to get it, I just turned around on my bike to follow you. Anyway, in my opinion, it's a little weird to follow people in a big white van." He ducks his head. "Sorry. Point is, we need manpower to get you over the fences and a truck to get you back to the house, and I thought we'd all probably murder Duncan, so I called Chloe. And Craig is with Chloe, and... well."

"Shit." Alex flops into the leaves. Craig is *definitely* going to explode when he sees Alex like this. Alex halfway hoped to get back to the house, get cleaned up, and somehow sort out his ankle without bothering Craig. No luck there, then.

Or, hey, it might be good. After all, an explosion is what this week has been building up to. The boil between Craig and Duncan has to be lanced sometime. Why not now?

All the same, Alex's stomach sinks at the gloomy agreement on David's face. It's as if they agree that Armageddon is coming and there is not one thing they can do to stop it. "This is going to be so bad," David says with a groan.

"Subject change," Alex says, not wanting to think about it. "Let's go back to you and me and Craig for a second. Much nicer to consider."

David's face is in full bloom when Alex lifts his head to look at him; a charming, patchy flush of red has spread all along the pale column of his neck and into his face. "What... what about us?"

"I'm attractive; you're attractive; Craig's attractive; we're all attractive." Alex waves his hands as if he's conducting an invisible symphony. "Mmm. Attractive."

David's laugh is light and low. "I suppose... but Alex, you must know I'd never come between you and Craig. I do find you both quite attractive, yes. And of course Craig and I have a history, but I wouldn't ever try to do anything."

"I'd never do anything to hurt Craig. I'd never leave him. I love him." His filter is still useless, clearly. "But you're *very* cute."

If David goes any redder, he'll be able to top a Christmas tree. "Well. I mean. Ah... thank you?"

"You are *welcome*." Afraid of where his wayward tongue might take him, Alex clamps down on anything further.

David gathers himself together with a brush of his hands. "Right. Craig and Chloe should be outside the fence any minute now. It would help if I could get you back through the hedge tunnel. I should be able to help you limp that far, if you're up for it." He tilts his head. "How do you feel?"

Tilting his head, Alex eyeballs the forest canopy. "Like Chicken Little."

"Pardon?" David's brow creases in a frown.

Alex sighs and pushes himself upright. "Oh, I just have this weird feeling that the sky is about to fall on all of us, that's all."

 *Chapter Thirteen*

IT IS EXACTLY AS DIFFICULT AS CRAIG EXPECTED IT WOULD be to bake a wedding cake with Chloe when she refuses to speak to him.

Oh, they're managing, mostly. If he asks for something, she finds it for him. She follows his directions with surgical precision, so they already have one layer of orange vanilla cake cooling and another nearly done in the oven. Craig is working on the third layer out of five now. In fact, it's almost *efficient* to have an assistant who doesn't talk. Things get done—and without the frosting fight that made his mother shriek that he was not too old to be grounded. That is a bonus.

But Craig still maintains that Chloe's reasons for the silent treatment are childish. And besides that, just because Chloe isn't speaking or hurling frosting doesn't mean she can't convey her displeasure in other irksome, and occasionally painful, ways. So, after she slaps the bottle of orange extract into his hand with unnecessary force for the third time, he calls for détente.

"If you'd just apologize for your constant conspiring to put my brother and me in a room together without my permission or knowledge, I would *happily* forgive you," he says, with what he considers to be a more than sufficient magnanimity, as he gently mixes the extract into a bowl of milk, sugar, and egg whites. This statement is guaranteed to get under Chloe's skin. That's fine. His palm still stings from the bottle slap; she deserves a little needling.

The silence stretches on, broken only by the ding of the timer and the oven door being opened and closed. There's a rattle as the cake tin is placed on the rack. Then, only Chloe's harsh breathing.

Craig sets the bowl of liquid ingredients aside and reaches for a larger bowl and the cake flour. *Three... two... one...*

"Me! Me apologize to you!" Chloe stomps across the kitchen to hit him over the head with a tea towel. Craig winces but carries on with sifting the cake flour into the bowl while letting her rage away. "I am *not* the one behaving like a child."

"I am peacefully baking your wedding cake. You are assaulting me and screeching like a banshee," he points out, his voice calculated to be calm to the precise degree that will infuriate her further. He sifts in the salt and baking powder. "Could I have the butter, please?"

"Get it yourself; stick it up your arse," she sputters, nevertheless crossing back to the counter to pick up two sticks of butter. "Just because you're behaving at the moment doesn't mean you haven't been a complete shit this entire week!"

He turns around just in time to catch the butter sticks she hurls at his chest. "Okay. I am absolutely not going to listen to you when you're throwing dairy products at me. I'm sorry I even tried to start this conversation." Setting the sticks down by the mixing bowls, Craig points at the two finished layers of cake. "And I can leave, thank you. Good luck serving a two-layer wedding cake to all your guests. Without champagne buttercream frosting. Does the Sainsbury's Basics range include frosting options?" He whips his improvised tea towel apron out of his jeans, hurls it at her, and turns as if to go. *Three... two... one...*

He makes it as far as the back door before Chloe explodes. "Ugh! Fine! You manipulative, blackmailing idiot! I fucking apologize!"

"Say it like you mean it," Craig can't resist adding and he dodges the return trip of his towel. "And stop throwing things at me!"

"Stop pretending you're a martyred saint!" Chloe shoots back, and Craig pauses in his volley when he sees her eyes shine with tears. "I just wanted everything to be perfect..."

Craig struggles with conflicting urges to strangle and hug her and crosses the kitchen to go with the latter when her tears begin to roll. The weeping is only partly genuine, but it's also only partly exaggerated, and besides, he's never been able to fend off the guilt that wells up at the sight of Chloe's tears, even if he *is* completely justified in his feelings. "Cee. Cee, Cee, Cee."

"It sounds condescending when you do that," comes the weepy, muffled admonition from the vicinity of his neck.

"It's not meant to." He sighs. That is on the guilty side of a lie, but to admit it would just invite more things to be hurled at him, and all Craig wants is peace. "Look, Cee. We've got to get on the same page here. Yes, I am aware that you want all fences mended and Duncan and me skipping off into the sunset."

A sniffle. "It would be nice."

Craig takes a deep breath. "But I would like to remind you yet again of all the very shitty things he's done to me. The very shitty way he treated me most of my life. He injured me, Cee. He didn't mean to, but that's what happened. And he never apologized."

Her hair tickles his neck as she nods. "I do remember."

"So you tell me." Every time this comes up, it's like cutting the wounds open again. Craig finds it hard to breathe, to resist allowing his anger to curdle into a sour lump in his stomach. "Chloe, that is a lot of hurt you want me to forgive, and I don't know that I'm up to it in less than a week. Especially given the hash of things Duncan made my first night home. You had years to get used to this new Duncan. He's never so much as emailed me."

"I know and I don't..." Chloe lifts her head, and red rims her brown eyes, which are glassy with tears. "I don't expect forgiveness, Craig, honestly. I was just... I know I'm terrible, I do. But I hoped the two of you would at least talk. I love you both so much and I *know* Duncan wants to at least try to make amends... You're just both so difficult."

"Not without reason on my part, I remind you again," he says, dry as a cracker. "No, I see where you're coming from, Cee. And okay, yes. I have been trying to work up the nerve to have a deep conversation with Duncan. But it truly is not easy." He tucks a stray curl behind her ear and smiles, waiting to get a watery smile in return before he goes on. "You have to let me work it out on my own, Chloe. Trying to force me into it just makes me want to run in the other direction."

She sighs. "It certainly does. Very effective in that."

Craig diverts his urge to strangle her into squeezing her hands. "I can offer this. I promise I will smile and be civil on your wedding day, Chloe. Just for you. Not that I didn't plan that anyway, but I will make a very extra special effort."

Her smile widens. "That's all I ask."

Then why have you been pushing for more all week? he doesn't ask, and he stifles his pique before he gives in to his more murderous instincts. "Then I will do my best."

Chloe nods. "Thank you, Craig. For what it's worth, I'm sorry I've been such a beast."

"It's your wedding week," he reminds her, albeit with far more grace than he actually feels. "Believe me, as amazingly irritating as this all has been, I have seen worse. Far worse. Before you take off for Spain, remind me to tell you the full story of the wedding that hired Alex and me as a package deal. The only people who even remotely liked each other in the party were the flower girl and ring bearer."

"Not even the bride and groom?"

"Not by the time the final photo shoot rolled around." He yanks her makeshift towel apron out of her jeans and taps her on the nose with it, leaving a puff of flour behind. "Everyone in tears, the bride's Vera Wang with a new hem of yellow frosting, the groom speaking to no one and the maid of honor hauled off for public disturbance... at least you still *want* to marry my brother, as ill-advised as I personally think it is."

Deftly, she ducks out of his arms with a sly grin that doesn't exactly fill Craig with joy. "Right. Avoiding that topic in the interests of maintaining peace?"

Uh-oh.

"Let's talk about *your* wedding plans!" She takes back her towel and tucks it into place, smiling at him all the while. "Hmm?"

No. No, there's not one thing about that question that he likes, not even a little. "Don't quite get what you mean," he lies. Of course, he knows exactly what she means. He's been tense while waiting for her to find an opportunity to bring it up again and damn if he didn't just hand it to her himself. Still. Four days, one almost had to admire her restraint.

But he doesn't *want* to think about it. The ring has been a pulsing beacon from its new hiding place, fraying his nerves with its very presence as everything goes pear-shaped.

"You do too," Chloe retorts, her eyes narrowed. "Assuming you find a good time to propose and Alex accepts, you'll have your own wedding to plan. Any luck figuring out when you'll pop The Big Question?"

"Ah, well, I had in mind perhaps the thirty-fifth of Septembruary, at the High Noon of Absolutely Never." This is a conversation Craig wants to have even less than any with or about Duncan. Proposing to Alex seemed like such a no-brainer when he first picked up the ring. Even when he was making sure it was still securely hidden in his bag, he had nothing but confidence in his decision.

Then they came here. And everything went madder than Craig could have expected. He winces. How can he even consider proposing after this?

Craig crosses back to his bowls of ingredients. He rests his full weight on the counter, and the sigh that comes out of him could send a paper boat across a pond. The guilt that propels it could sink the boat. "Chloe."

"No, no, no," she says as she scampers over to stand next him. With pursed lips, she sticks a finger in front of his face and waves it around. "No second thoughts. You bought the ring; he's lovely, no second thoughts."

Craig laughs in disbelief. "I'm not having second thoughts about *him*, Cee." Not even remotely. Almost two years they've been inseparable now, and Craig loves Alex so much it could steal his breath and he'd count the loss as negligible. "Never about him."

Chloe manages an entire ten seconds of staring before she raises her hands and asks, "So, what then?"

He snorts and gives her a sidelong glance. "You spent Tuesday night combing buttercream out of your hair and you have to ask?"

"It did end up being a great conditioning treatment..." When he doesn't laugh at the joke, Chloe pokes him in the side. "No, seriously, Craig, come on. What of it? So it's been a little off the rails this week."

"Exactly, that's exactly it." Craig counts his breaths. "Totally off the rails, not a little, though thank you for that courteous understatement. Chloe, he did not sign on for this nonsense."

"Everyone signs on for that in relationships," she tells him firmly. "And if they can't deal with it, they can run. Alex is still here."

"It's not fair to him," he mumbles.

"It's not for you to decide that."

Wasn't it? Or should it have been? At the very least, Craig could have been a little more diligent with his warnings, a bit more thorough. But no, he thrust the man of his dreams into this dysfunctional crapshoot with virtually no preparation. Craig can excuse it all with *he never really asked* and *it's not his problem to deal with* all he likes, but the real truth is that Craig came back here for Chloe, not Duncan, while fostering a desperate hope that he wouldn't have to address the Duncan thing at all while he was here—which is the worst thing.

It's not that the week has been out of control, though it has; it's that *Craig* has been. As entirely legitimate as his emotions toward his brother are, in coping with them he has perhaps behaved unreasonably. In some ways. And that, unpleasantly, is what has given him pause on his own matrimonial front.

Pause? Better to say full stop.

"Stop being a horse's arse." Chloe whips him across the backside with her towel, and the sting startles Craig out of his mope. "If he couldn't deal with the insanity of the Olivers, he'd be back home already, I am sure. Or maybe he can't deal, but he loves you enough to pretend he can. What do I know?" She nudges his arm until he looks at her and answers her smile with something he hopes resembles one. "I've only known him a few days. Still, he hasn't run."

"No. He hasn't." Craig flexes his fingers against the countertop to brace himself for the admission he's embarrassed as hell to make. "Maybe he should have done, though. From me."

Alex has been the more rational of the two of them this week, when he's had every right to spend sixteen hours of each day here locked in a bathroom. Instead, he's spent most of his time with the Olivers. They all like him, and he hasn't been very anxious at all since just after their arrival; whereas Craig has been having frosting fights, getting arrested for streaking, and hijacking his ex-boyfriend to avoid running into his brother for even thirty seconds.

If there's an Oliver that Alex should be running from, it's Craig.

But he hasn't.

"He hasn't run from you either, you big pillock." Chloe echoes his thoughts with one of her patented around-the-world eye rolls. "Though I do agree with you that he has grounds to do so." When he continues to dither, she straight up punches him in the arm. "Craig! For the love of God, you stripped nearly naked in front of your ex-boyfriend and got yourself arrested for the trouble! And Alex is still here! What does that say to you?"

Put that way, she has a point. And a wicked right hook. Craig rubs at the sore spot on his bicep. "That he loves me," he admits with considerable reluctance. He picks up the softened butter sticks and mixes them with the rest of the wet ingredients. "He really must. Because justified or not, I have been something of an idiot."

"You are a prize of extremely dubious value, but yes, I expect he actually does," Chloe says as she greases the next cake pan. "Stubborn, pigheaded thing that you are and all. You certainly are your brother's brother. And your mother's son. Don't for one moment think I don't know where it came from. I haven't decided what I fear more about my eventual motherhood, the potential for twins or the Cunningham stubbornness from your mother's side…"

Startled by the comparison, Craig tunes Chloe out and pauses in the middle of blending his wet and dry ingredients. He stands blinking like a Christmas tree and stares out the kitchen window, seeing nothing. *Oh, my God.*

It is true that difficulty in admitting he might be in the wrong, even a little, is a distinct genetic trait in his family. Well, within a small, select group: not the twins and certainly not his father. No, this week has shown that within the Oliver family as it is shaped today, that elite club of stubborn, bullheaded idiots is populated strictly by Moira, Duncan… and Craig.

Hmm. He and Duncan might have more in common than he thought, which is to say, they might have anything at all in common, really. Craig holds back the urge to regurgitate his breakfast into his half-mixed cake batter. He shakes his head and then shakes it again, but he can't dislodge the thought now that it's there, buzzing around in his brain like a gigantic, disgusting housefly. He and Duncan share the one trait that's made it impossible for them to even say hello to each other all week. And now that Craig is aware of it, he can't continue to hope that the problem between himself and his brother will just vanish. The costs are much too high; the repercussions this week *alone* are an astounding litany of shame.

Craig's quarrel with Duncan stuck Alex in the middle of a family conflict that isn't his, irritated David, annoyed the Olivers, and kept Chloe in a nearly constant flood of tears and thwarted peacemaking attempts. Not that Chloe doesn't deserve to stew in it all for a bit still, given her one-track mind and breathtaking issues with obtaining consent, but Craig has to admit that, in the end, even she meant well. Her goal was to achieve peace, even if it wasn't her job to do so in the first place.

As crucifying as it is, as sour as the realization tastes in his mouth, Craig and Duncan are the ones with the power to end this. And, oh, it *is* crucifying.

Craig takes a deep breath and forces himself to resume stirring. "Listen, Cee," he begins; his thoughts are still nebulous and forming even as he opens his mouth.

Out in the family room, the phone rings and cuts him off. "Hold that thought," Chloe says with a breathless smile. She spins on her heel and sprints away. "Hello? Oh... hey."

Okay. He can always try again when she's finished. Craig cocks an ear toward the family room to listen in. *It's not really being nosy if Chloe has a phone voice like a foghorn, is it?*

"Sorry. What?" Chloe's voice leaps a good half-octave upward in just two words. "Say that again?"

Hmm. That doesn't sound good.

"Right. Okay. Right. Um, shit." The cake batter is smooth and ready to be poured into the prepared tin, but Craig can sense Chloe's agitation from a room away, and she's pacing the floor. He keeps stirring and listening to her. "Christ al-bloody-mighty. Fuck. All right. Stay there, we'll be there in a bit."

The phone clunks as it falls into the cradle. Chloe muffles a scream into the palms of her hands. *Oh, okay, yeah, this is really bad.*

Sharp beeps follow as Chloe snatches the phone back up and dials. *"Duncan Joseph Oliver,"* she hisses, and while Craig doesn't make a habit of wanting to be his brother at *all*, in this moment there is nothing he has ever wanted *less*. Whatever is going on, Duncan fucked up but good.

Hmm. His spoon stills. Duncan, who is supposed to be with Alex today, fucked up. That... that is not only not good, it is very bad. Unease uncoils at the base of Craig's spine and snakes its way along his nerves.

"I do not know what has possessed you to do what you did, Duncan, but this..." A pause, like the calm before a storm. "You know *exactly* what you did! *Exactly!* And guess what, Duncan, just guess what's happened now." Another seething pause, and Craig clutches at the spoon in his hand. "No. No, it has *not* all gone well, and everything is not fine. No, it's gone all sorts of tits up and there is now a line for who will want to kill you first."

Craig gives up bothering to pretend to stir.

"Guess what? He's hurt. Yes, Duncan. Hurt, as in injured, yes. We're going to get him now." Craig's heart stops as Chloe rages on at his brother. "Pull yourself together and get to the house. We'll meet you there. No, you can't come with us to come get him. I'll kill you myself if I see you right now! Meet us at the house!"

Ice has settled in a ball in the pit of Craig's stomach. He traces his spoon through the cake batter and tells himself to be calm. Maybe it's not Alex who is hurt. Maybe there's a slim chance that Duncan didn't do the most completely stupid thing just when Craig was about to give him the chance to speak...

It almost works, almost, until Chloe smashes the phone into its cradle with enough force to break it. Plastic cracks, and Chloe lets fly a muffled curse. Dread rampages through his thoughts. "Chloe?"

When she appears in the doorway, his spoon hits the floor and spatters droplets of cake batter all over his shoes. Chloe's mouth is compressed in a way that he remembers as a warning sign, the sign that means she is going to blow her top and someone is going to lose their head. The curls on one side of her head have been pulled out of her updo to form a cloud, as if she's maybe wound her fingers into it and tugged in frustration. Her eyes are dark, and tears fall down her cheeks in a slow trickle. They are genuine tears, this time, of this there is no doubt.

She is positively terrifying, and the lump in Craig's stomach is giving him heartburn. "Chloe."

"The wedding's off," she informs him with a hysterical cackle. "Sorry, but I'm going to have to kill my fiancé, and there's just no room in the chapel schedule for a wedding *and* a funeral."

 *Chapter Fourteen*

"**S**AY IT. JUST BLOODY SAY IT." CHLOE GRINDS THE GEARS of the truck and spins the steering wheel in a violent reversal out of the drive that leaves mud and gravel spewing from the tires in their wake. "Go on! Yes, yes, you told me so!"

But Craig isn't sure he can say much of anything; he's sitting shocked and senseless in the passenger seat. He's still trying to wrap his head around what Chloe told him as she switched off the oven, grabbed her keys and purse, and shoved him out the door.

Alex really is hurt.

It really is Duncan's fault.

"They're not far. Duncan just took him to the lake." Chloe pushes the truck to speeds it was never meant to achieve and hurls it around the turnoff to the lake in a squeal of black rubber. "But he can't walk, David says. I have some ideas for how we can get him out, though."

Craig still can't speak, can't even nod his head. He is frozen; his fingers are in a white-knuckle grip around the door handle as he tries and fails to make sense of what's happened.

His brother failed him, but worse—he, Craig, failed *Alex*. He didn't remember Duncan's penchant for playing pranks on his siblings' significant others and he *should* have, he so should

have. Chloe should have as well; she came in for her fair share
of pranks when they were in school herself. But Craig really,
really should have remembered and he should never have been
okay with Alex going off alone with his brother.

Although really, Duncan should have known that Alex would
have to be completely off-limits.

He did know. Craig knows it like his own name. *He just didn't
care.*

He could strangle Duncan. Cheerfully and with no regrets,
he could absolutely do it. And amends of any kind are *certainly*
off the table now.

Craig keeps his mind on that, firmly on that, because if he
starts in on how he got too wrapped up in himself to keep Alex
safe, he really will go completely mad.

Chloe pulls the truck up at the end of the road, as close as
they can get to the lake. Craig is out of the truck in a flash.
Adrenaline and anger boost him over the barrier in a hurry, and
the second, chain-link, fence is even easier to climb. Swinging
over the top of it without looking, Craig drops to the ground
and nearly lands right on top of David.

"Craig! Watch it!"

"Sorry." His breath catches in his throat as he searches.
"Alex?"

"Baaabe," a voice burbles from the vicinity of his knees, and
Craig looks down. On the ground, one foot in a sneaker and
the other in a bandage, his face so chalk-white that his freckles
stand out in stark relief, Alex sits and smiles a tiny, lopsided
facsimile of a smile and waves. "Hi."

Craig is at his side in a flash. "Oh, my God, babe." His heart
is pounding with the speed of a hummingbird and the power
of cannonball strikes. He touches Alex's hair, his face, his
shoulder. "My God."

"I'm fine. Fiiiinne." Alex waves at his ankle. "It's not broken. I'm not dead; I'm fine. Have you seriously been flirting with David this week? I don't blame you. He's cute."

Craig pulls back to stare. "Come again?"

"Nothing." But Alex is blushing, and so is David. What the hell did he miss in a handful of hours?

Today is really turning into quite the clusterfuck.

Chloe drops over the chain-link fence before Craig can assemble enough coherent thought to chase down the David question. "Okay, so, this fence? No problem," she says and holds up a large pair of heavy-duty wire cutters. "I keep these in the back of the truck. We'll cut through this fence and come back later to patch it."

David points his chin toward the larger wooden fence. "And the fortress over there?"

"I stand on the cross braces to hang over the top and pull Alex up; you and Craig push him from below," Chloe says. "Won't be easy, or anything approaching an entertaining afternoon activity, but with some careful maneuvering, it should work. I did it one time when Janey Fielding was tripping on magic mushroom tea. I'm pretty good at it."

David is still frowning. "Yeah, but how does he get *down* once we get him *up*?"

"He swings over, Craig and you and I all drop down, and then we help him the rest of the way." Chloe shrugs. "Lemon squeezy."

All right, then. She does seem to have it all well in hand. Craig tries to keep his brow smooth and untroubled. *Pity any of this is needed in the first place.*

Chloe kneels next to Alex and brushes his hair back from his forehead. "I'm sorry, Alex. My fiancé is an idiot."

"So I heard." Alex still has on his lopsided, slightly plastic smile, and he swings an arm around Chloe's neck for an awkward hug. "You're too good for him."

"It's true," Chloe agrees with a little sniffle. "I am definitely second-guessing my life choices right now."

Alex leans close. "You could marry *me*. Or Craig, if you really want an Oliver. We could take you..." He lets his free hand waft through the air. "Faaar away from here. Craig makes great spaghetti. And pancakes. Are you sold yet? You met our dog, right? He's so awesome."

Chloe giggles through her sniffles, and Craig stares at his boyfriend. "Are you stoned?"

"Oh, yeah," Alex confirms with an emphatic nod and a big dopey smile. "Can we take Chloe home with us?"

David sidles up alongside Craig while Craig tries to come up with *any* good answer to Alex's question. "He took a Xanax," David whispers, and, oh, now everything is very clear. "Said he didn't want everyone to know. It seems to have hit him pretty hard, Craig. Is it a high dose?"

That means Alex had a panic attack. *Another tick in the "Kill Duncan" column. What court would convict me?* He keeps his tone mild, though, as he replies. "No, he just doesn't take it often, so if he takes a whole pill it's like someone who doesn't drink doing a bunch of tequila slammers. So he says." Craig shakes his head; Alex is bonelessly placid, nothing like his usual high-strung, whipcord-quick self. "How is everyone else *not* going to guess something is going on?"

"Chloe is busy committing vandalism, so really, it's only me who's noticed," David reminds him, waving a hand at where Chloe is now taking her clippers to the fence. His mouth twists and puckers as though he's just sucked on a lemon. "Listen, Craig. I respect you and Alex, and I didn't mean to tell him that I noticed you flirting with me, and I didn't know he was going to tell me he thought I was cute."

Oh, this again. Craig squirms. "Yeah, okay, what's going on there?"

"Not sure. But now we all know we've been ogling each other all week." David's face is beetroot-colored. It matches his sweater nearly exactly, but he's holding his head up with dignity.

"Craig," Chloe calls as she pulls wide the hole she's made in the fence. "I almost have this open. Can you two get him to his feet?"

There's no more time for the exploration of awkward disclosures. All Craig can concentrate on is getting Alex out of this enclosure in one piece.

They manage, not perfectly, but they do it. The now broken-open chain-link fence is a snap to get through. The wooden fence is, as they all expected, more of a challenge. Alex's yelps of pain as he whacks his tender ankle more than once, along with his gritted teeth and shining eyes when they finally get him down to the ground again, they will fuel Craig's anger for a long time.

Now it seems the height of absurdity that Craig thought of forgiving Duncan, even for a second.

"We should take him to hospital," David says as they load Alex into the back seat of the truck. "Get that properly checked out."

"I just want to get to the house," Alex says, his voice tired and soft. "We can go to the hospital later. Tomorrow. Right now I want a bath, and tea, and… just, please. Get me to the house."

"As you wish." David hands over Alex's bag and closes the door. "We'll be there in less than five minutes. Less than three, even."

Silence fills the truck and Craig holds Alex tight, as if Alex could be taken away any moment. There was no chance that he would have *lost* Alex, not really. The wooded area is small; a sprained ankle is not life-threatening. Even if David hadn't followed him, eventually it would have occurred to *someone* that Alex was missing. Then Duncan would be forced to confess, and they would retrieve him.

But it *feels* as if he could have lost Alex today. That terror sits in Craig's chest like charred wood, and it hurts. It makes him want to get back to the house, pack their things, and *leave*. He squeezes tighter.

"Sorry I told David he was cute," Alex mumbles, shifting and snuggling farther into Craig's arms.

"What?"

"I do think he's cute, but I wouldn't do anything about it. I love you."

Craig can't help but chuckle, but it's a sad chuckle, a tired one, all he can muster. "I love you, too. I love you so much, Alex. I'm sorry about my stupid brother."

"He didn't mean it," Alex mumbles.

"I don't care." It's hard to talk around the lump in his throat. "I shouldn't have brought you here, Alex. I'm sorry I talked you into it. We can go home first thing tomorrow."

"No." Alex yawns. "It's okay. I don't want to go home, Craig. We can't afford to change our tickets, anyway."

"We can," Craig begins, but Alex is already rolling his head back and forth.

"No," he says, and there's surprising concrete in that short word. "No more hiding from this, Craig. You're better than that." And he melts back into snuggly pliability while Craig presses his lips into a tight line.

I don't want to be better than that.

He opens his mouth to say as much, but is interrupted by Chloe calling, "We're here," and they have to get Alex into the house.

Into the house, where Duncan is, if he followed Chloe's directions. Craig's skin crawls. *Here we go.*

It's a full house in the living room: Moira standing with Stephen and the twins sitting, tense, on the sofa. But Craig's eyes go straight to Duncan when he and David get through the door, and only Craig's position under Alex's arm keeps him from anything more proactive than a snarled, "You son of a bitch."

Moira raises a hand and imposes herself between her sons; she's a powerhouse of authority though they're each a good head taller than her. Her chin lifts and sets, and the look in her steely blue eyes says she will brook no nonsense. "Craig, let's be calm. You have every right to be angry."

"You're damn right I do, Mum!" He has to force himself to loosen his jaw, to stop grinding his teeth long enough to get words through them. "I do; Alex sure as hell does. Of all the things you could do to me, Duncan, attacking my partner is the lowest."

"It wasn't an attack!" Duncan protests, jumping up from his seat on the piano bench. "I wouldn't! It was supposed to be a joke, Craig, that's all."

Is it possible for one's eyes to pop out of one's head? Craig's are definitely making a one hundred percent effort. "Does this look in any way *funny* to you?"

Duncan swallows as his eyes pass over the tableau of David and Craig holding a rather limp Alex upright. "Of course it doesn't, Craig, but I didn't mean—"

"What you meant doesn't matter! What happened is what matters!" Craig only vaguely notices his mother as she ducks away, conceding the ground to the pair of them. The room is still, apart from the tension that crackles between him and his brother. He wishes it were real electricity, that he could shock sense and guilt into Duncan. "He could have been stuck there all night, lost, whether he got hurt or not."

Duncan shakes his head. "No, I'd have gone back later, or a patrol would have gone by, something."

"Oh, that's better, is it?" Craig's laugh erupts, bitter and hot with rage. "Getting my boyfriend arrested for trespassing is an *improvement*?" He wants to laugh again at the look of slow-dawning comprehension that creeps across Duncan's face. "Oh, that never occurred to you, did it? You're thick; you're so thick."

Again, Duncan shakes his head. "I didn't mean—"

"You never do." Craig clings to Alex, as if he's being supported as much as he's doing any supporting. Alex's waist, solid under his arm, their hands linked where Alex's arm crosses his shoulder, these things keep Craig tethered, but it's tenuous. He is so angry, and that anger is spilling out faster and faster. "You know what you never do? You never apologize."

Duncan's face compresses into anger, and his fists clench. "Hey, now."

"You never say you're sorry," Craig continues, and he takes one shaky, furious breath after another. He laughs again, and the sound is brittle to the point of breaking. "Not you, never you. Not even now. All you've said since we got here is that you never meant to do it."

Duncan lifts his chin. "Well, I didn't."

Still no apology. Craig's gossamer-thin control evaporates. "You never understand the harm you do." He ducks out from under Alex's arm; Chloe takes his place. As he stalks over to Duncan, Craig's mind plays the dozens of scenarios that have plagued him since he first saw Alex on the ground, ashen and in pain. "What's worse is that you don't care. You have never cared. And it wasn't enough to treat *me* like crap my entire life, you hurt the one person I love more than anything else in the world. That is low, even for you that's low, and that I cannot let slide."

Duncan backs away, alarm in his eyes. "Craig, listen, let me, I am sorry, really—"

It's laughable. "Too little, too late. Doesn't matter anymore." Craig flexes his fingers. He's taking a perverse pleasure in the wariness on his brother's face.

"No, you don't get it, I'm *sorry,* Craig, I didn't *mean*—"

"I don't care." Craig is smiling; it's a nasty parody of his usual cheer and he knows it. "It. Doesn't. Matter."

Moira steps forward. "Craig, darling, please."

"No, Mum." As gently as he can, he brushes past her. His eyes are fixed on Duncan—Duncan, who has stopped in his retreat, who is now standing straight, shoulders back and chin set. "This has been a long time coming." Craig tilts his chin and closes the distance between himself and Duncan. At arm's length now, this is as close as he's been to his brother in years. "A long time coming," he repeats, and he breathes in deeply.

Without another word, Craig pulls back and swings, landing a hard, direct hit on Duncan's cheekbone that sends him reeling.

 *Chapter Fifteen*

"**W**HAT WAS THAT?" ALEX ASKS FOR THE FOURTH TIME
in as many minutes. He's looking down as if he could see, from
the second floor, where everyone is milling around the living
room. Some will be helping Duncan; some will be trying to
work out what to do next. Craig left them all to it, turning in
the shocked and silent aftermath to grab his boyfriend and
haul him upstairs to their room. It took a little time for the
silence to collapse into mayhem, and they were just about all
the way upstairs before that happened, thank God.

"I punched my brother," Craig says, having considered and
discarded a dozen flip responses. "I hope I got him in the eye.
He deserves a good black eye that he didn't get playing rugby."

"Was that strictly necessary, though?" They're at the stairs
to the attic, too narrow and steep for them to go up side by
side. Alex solves the problem by bracing his hands on the wall
railings and hoisting himself up, one stair at a time. "I mean,
punching, pretty sure that's nothing I ever expected from you,
and the wedding is more or less right on top of us."

"Oh, fuck the wedding." It comes out in a snap Craig is
too exasperated to be guilty about. He holds Alex's waist for
balance while Alex swings himself up the stairs. "And yes, thank
you, it was necessary. It was something I should have done

quite a few years ago, really. Might have stopped half this mess in its tracks."

Alex opens the door and hobbles into their room. "Well," he says with a worried look, as he rumples his hair.

"Too late now. Don't worry about it, just get out of those clothes. You wanted a bath, I believe?" There is a desperate need to change the subject, if only for a minute. Craig pulls the bottle of Lagavulin and a highball glass out of his desk. He sets them down with a clank, meddles with the taps in the bathroom, and runs water, soothing and warm, into the ancient claw-foot tub. "You asked for tea, but I'll do you one better. Come on, babe. Strip."

It is a testament to Alex's exhaustion and the Xanax that he doesn't even whip back a ribald comment, but simply sheds his layers of clothing, limps into the bathroom, and slides into the tub without so much as a murmur. Craig leaves him to recline and pours out a generous measure of whiskey to bring to the bathroom. "Drink up."

"Mm." Eyes closed, Alex reaches for the glass and takes a sip. As it hits his tongue, he sits up straight and wide-eyed. "Damn, wow. That is good stuff."

"Best in Dad's liquor cabinet. I pinched it the other day. You can thank him later." He makes a move to go out to the bedroom, but Alex's hand snags him by the leg of his jeans.

"Stay," Alex says and gives a light tug. "Get in with me."

Craig estimates the size of the tub. "Bit crowded."

"I don't care. It's been a hell of a day. Please?"

They never get to take baths at home, having only a shower and, admittedly, Craig would not mind keeping close to Alex for a while longer. There's still a frisson of panic along his nerves over the events of the last few hours. "Yeah, give me a minute, though? We need more towels, and I want to put some music on, something nice and calm so I don't nick one of your pills."

He plugs his phone into the speakers and turns it on before he sneaks down to the second-floor linen cupboard. Quiet as a mouse and keeping one ear out for any noise from the family room, Craig pulls out towels. He can hear only murmurs, nothing he can really decipher. Craig is turning away from the cupboard when something catches his eye.

He fishes the bright blue oversized bedsheet from the back of the middle shelf, adds it to his pile, and heads back upstairs.

"What took so long?" Alex asks when Craig finally hustles into the bathroom and begins to peel off his clothing. "I had to run more hot water."

"I had to move slowly, be quiet and all." Craig tosses his shirt to the floor, removes his jeans, and kicks off his sneakers at the same time. "If they hear me moving around outside the bedroom, they'll try to make me go downstairs for a family discussion, and I am not up for that."

It isn't a lie, but it does embroider the truth—for a good cause, though, maybe the very best cause. Craig hides a smile as he strips the rest of the way.

Craig slips in behind Alex with his knees bent and they manage the fit, only just. Alex rests his injured ankle on a towel draped over the side of the tub and leans back against Craig's chest. Long, companionable moments go by with them passing the glass of whiskey back and forth as the hot water draws the tension from their bodies.

"Oh, right," Alex says after a little while. "Alcohol is contraindicated with Xanax."

Craig could hit himself and does, a small but solid smack to the forehead. "Damn it. So it is."

"It's okay. I only had a few small sips. Take the rest." Alex hands the glass back. "You need it more than I do."

That is perhaps true. "I won't turn it down." Craig breathes in the scent of the drink, allowing the fumes to fill his nose. It would be nice if they could go right to his brain, winding in and calming his burning thoughts. He takes another sip to try to melt the lump in his throat. "Alex... I am so sorry about my brother," he says, his words halting and guilty. "I knew he was a fucking cock, but this? God."

"Shh." Alex takes Craig's hand and kisses it, with a little bite for emphasis. "I've done a lot worse, myself."

Craig pulls his hand back. "Alex."

"No, seriously. This is probably karma for every stupid, hurtful thing I ever did." Alex shrugs as if he really doesn't care, which Craig cannot understand for the life of him. "Honestly, it was a joke, Craig. I believe Duncan when he says that. It just... it went wrong."

"Joke? Went wrong?" Craig needs a much bigger gulp of whiskey to tackle this. The whiskey burns his throat and grows harsher as he inhales. "You are *injured*. You had a panic attack. What if David didn't follow you? You'd still be there, alone, hurt. I can't even think about it."

One eyebrow up, Alex twists his head back to look at Craig. The Xanax stupor has cleared somewhat. "Do you really believe I'd still be stuck there? I'm not that useless, Craig. I had a plan before I tripped over a tree root."

Shame bows Craig's head even as heat rushes to his face. "No, of course not. I just mean—"

"I know." Alex settles back. "Look. I appreciate you being furious on my behalf. I'm just saying it's not really necessary, Craig. Seriously."

"Next thing I know, you'll be telling me to make it up with him," Craig replies with a bitter laugh.

Alex is silent for too long, much, much too long—long enough that Craig suspects he's not going to like what he hears next. Sure enough... "I'm not thinking it's a *bad* idea, to be honest."

Sometimes, Craig reflects, it really does not pay to be right. His eyes once again make their best effort to escape his head as he stares at Alex. "You must be joking. You should have been able to go with Duncan without worrying about nearly breaking your neck." It's a heated statement, and he's so angry he nearly spits out the words. "It was fucking ridiculous of him to pull this."

Alex's damp shoulder moves against Craig's skin in a shrug. "I won't argue with you there."

"Then how can you ask me to do it?"

"I'm not. It's your call," Alex says. "Entirely yours. I completely understand you being pissed off with him, and it's your *right* to be. But I could be mad, too, and... God, Craig." He inhales with an audible shudder. "I've had enough of holding on to anger in my life, that's all. I was so furious with Jeff, and that did so much damage in only a year. I can't imagine what it must be like to carry that around for a lifetime."

It's a few words, just a few, but they deflate Craig as effectively as a pin to a balloon. Of course Alex would be familiar with the difficulties of letting go. Craig is a complete fool for having forgotten that.

"It just festers," Alex says, quietly. "No one deserves to sit with that and feel it burning, turning into poison. I'd do anything for you not to."

Craig allows another drop of whiskey to roll over his tongue and slide down his throat to join the melting anger in his stomach. "It's not easy. Letting go, that is."

Alex nods. "That's why it's just a suggestion."

The problem is that it's a *good* suggestion, a suggestion unmotivated by selfishness, presented by the one person in the world who has more than a good idea of how Craig felt all this time. The logic, in this setting, from this person, is beautiful in its simplicity.

Maybe it's not fair. Maybe it lets Duncan off the hook much too easily.

But maybe it's a weight Craig can put down at last. He presses the cool, heavy glass to his forehead. Where his brain should be is the sensation of a rubber band that has just snapped; relief floods through him. "Oh."

A hand squeezes his knee with gentle affection. "I'll support you either way," Alex says, calm but firm.

Craig cocks his head to survey his boyfriend. There's a new relaxation in Alex, something still and quiet that takes the place of the constant anxiety Craig's used to. "You're rather Zen about all this."

Alex waves his hand. "Good drugs."

"No," Craig says. "You were pretty Zen for a lot of this week, whereas I acted like a prize idiot the entire time."

"Maybe a little," Alex confirms and cranes his head back so that Craig can see his teasing smirk. "That's okay, though. I'll marry you anyway."

The words hang in the air, and the conversation is quite thoroughly derailed. Craig blinks, unsure of what just happened. Surely he's not losing his hearing at thirty?

"Come again?"

Alex's eyes go wide and his face is the color of a summer tomato. "Oh, no. I said that out loud."

Craig still isn't sure he heard it correctly. It's the last thing he expected, ever, but especially now of all times. He can't help but laugh. "Said what out loud, exactly?"

"That I'll marry you anyway." And as Craig stares in astonishment, it's clear that Alex means it, that it's true. True and real and, oh, dear God. "And, um, I will. If you want to."

Craig can't even begin to find words. Water drips from the tub faucet. The music in the bedroom plays on, faint and sweetly mellow. Alex is in his arms, holding his breath, and his eyes—so bright, so clear and gray, so surprised and pleased with himself—speak volumes.

Craig's entire world narrows to those two small words as important as any book on earth. *Marry me.* Even though they've been on his mind for months, they're still heavy; they hang in the air with all the substance of life. *Marry me.* It's everything he's wanted and never known when to bring up.

And no wonder. In the end, this question was never his to ask.

Everything else is entirely forgotten, and he has to swallow twice before he can even attempt to speak. "We're naked," he wheezes on a laugh. "Oh, my God, you're proposing, and we're naked, we're in the bath."

"Yeah, we are." Alex's laugh is magic, a thing of joy and delight. "You know, it seems appropriate?"

"It does; it really, really does." In fact it's perfect, exactly perfect. Unexpected and wonderful and perfect. "Is it because of Duncan and Chloe and the whole..." Craig gestures with his whiskey glass. "Just general sort of wedding atmosphere of the week?"

"It's because I love you." Alex rolls over, a little awkwardly as he accommodates his long legs and injury. Water splashes over the side of the tub. He lies on Craig's chest and pins him. "Because when I have a panic attack, you're my top ten reasons to grit my teeth and ride it out. Because you gave a sad bastard a cookie and invited him home for tea. Because you believe in me, because you'll punch your brother for me, because you love me." He stops. "I mean, you are not without problems, but—"

"Excuse me," Craig protests, but it is halfhearted. His anger at Duncan may yet be justified, but he's still the one who got arrested. He can't really fight the assessment.

Alex hasn't taken his eyes from Craig. "I didn't mean to just come out with a proposal, but I won't take it back. I watched you with your family all week. I have all these thoughts about us together in the future, Craig, and they scare the crap out of me, but... I want that. With you. Sex and pancakes and, God, I even started thinking about *kids*. We could have kids."

The water is shaking—no, Craig is trembling, and the water trembles with him. "Alex."

He stops, just stops, because what can he say? There are no words, no thoughts, nothing at all that Craig can express in this moment. He sits still but for his shivers with the whiskey glass dangling precariously from his fingers as he tries to sort through his emotions, because all he can do right now is feel.

"You really do want to marry me," he whispers, going back to the simplest, most important thing of all. "You seriously want us to get married."

Alex's pause for thought is a blatant put-on. In less than a second, he's nodding. "I seriously do."

The angle is awkward and the water is almost cold, but Craig sets aside the whiskey glass and takes Alex's face in his hands. He tastes the lingering flavor of whiskey on Alex's lips and breath; he memorizes the droplets of water that slip and fall between his fingers. "But what about David?" he breathes as he leans back, a laugh almost splitting his chest open at the look on Alex's face. "Would I be interrupting a new and torrid love affair?"

"You're ruining the moment," Alex mutters with a wet slap to Craig's bicep before he moves in for another kiss. "Anyway, I'm not the one making googly eyes at him over breakfast."

"We could see if he's interested, maybe later, a few years from now." Craig's hands slide over Alex's slick skin, and his mouth sucks in Alex's sharp exhalation of laughter. "I don't think he'd mind, and the traditional fifth anniversary gift *is* wood..."

"Shut up; you're an idiot," is all Craig hears before Alex grabs the sides of the tub and surges forward to cover Craig's mouth with his.

They make their way out of the tub, maneuvering so that they don't have to spend more than a second or two not kissing as they towel each other dry. Toweling dry, of course, comes with no small amount of surreptitious fondling and low moans, soft touches, and gentle laughs.

Alex pulls his mouth away when they get out to the bedroom and he takes in what Craig has done. "Oh, my God. You covered the Wall O' Robbies. That's what took you so long."

Quite proud of himself for this one, Craig grins at the blue bedsheet that covers his poster wall. "It is. I did."

Alex chortles. "Strangely," he says, "I got used to it. But this is fine." He fumbles to pull Craig close and drag him into the bed.

There's no more room for conversation.

Yes, Craig spells with the tip of his tongue, a feather-light touch down Alex's throat. *Yes*, he breathes into the skin of Alex's chest, warm against each rib. *Yes*, his fingers press into the muscles of Alex's thighs, leaving behind the faint pink marks of his fingertips and shallow crescents from his fingernails.

Craig pours his affirmation and acceptance into every movement, each kiss, each touch, into the slow push and thrust of himself inside of Alex.

They move together; they rise and fall; they hold and stroke; and their fingers tangle together in a white-knuckled grip of desperation. Alex's hand wraps around the back of Craig's neck and pulls him into a jerky, gasping kiss; their lips bump and brush past each other in the hectic riot of movement. *Yes,* Craig thinks and allows it to be carried out of his mouth on a wave of broken, wordless gasps that Alex sucks into his lungs.

Craig handles Alex with care, holds the skin and bones and blood and sweat of the rest of his life in his hands and burns every second of *now* into his memory, every laugh and breath and moan and the single, surprising tear that slips from the corner of Alex's eye.

Yes, says every cell in Craig's body when he falls over the edge and brings Alex with him.

It rushes through his veins and electrifies his nerves as they come down; it pulses into his fingertips as he reluctantly pulls free. But he doesn't stop touching, trailing his fingers over Alex's chest and stomach. *I love you.* At first it's a whisper of thought, and then he just says it. "I love you."

"I love you." Alex's eyes are anxious, though, as he lifts his head to look at Craig. "Although, you haven't *actually* answered my question..."

Craig leans forward to kiss Alex, long and sweet, and not at all for the last time in their lives. He rolls onto his stomach and fishes between the layers of his bed for the little box hidden there, the little box he's half-fancied Alex might sense through the mattress as in *The Princess and the Pea.* Craig wraps his fingers around the box, pulls it out, and shifts to face the man he's about to spend the rest of his life with.

"My answer," he says, as he pries open the box and falls in love all over again when Alex's mouth drops open, "is yes."

 Chapter Sixteen

"CONGRATULATIONS," IS DUNCAN'S FIRST WORD TO them when they arrive hand in hand in the living room. Alex panics a little at first—Jesus, did they have someone listening at the attic door? But no. From his hunched-over pose on the sofa, Duncan is looking directly at Craig with his one visible eye. The other eye is concealed behind a package of frozen spinach. "You landed a good one, little brother."

He takes the spinach down and indeed, Craig does seem to have landed a good one. Duncan's left cheekbone is visibly puffy in comparison to his right, and it is surely going to bloom into a large bruise, frozen spinach or no. Alex winces. "Oh, God."

"Eh, didn't really get me in the eye; didn't knock out any teeth. It works out." The spinach is put back in place. "Definitely going to bruise, though. Chloe says she's going to make me wear something called Dermablend. We're going into London tomorrow to get it."

"Where is Chloe?" Alex looks around the living room, realizing quickly why no one came to get them. Only the three of them are left in the house. "Where did everyone go?"

Duncan shrugs. "Went to get dinner. We're to fend for ourselves." Steady and calm, he keeps his eye on Craig. "And talk."

The expression on Craig's face clears up any question Alex ever had about what a trapped animal might look like. His hand shakes in Alex's. "Oh."

"They would have waited for you," Duncan says, directing his one-eyed attention to Alex now. "But I owe you an apology, too, and I figured you wouldn't leave Craig alone with me."

That's an undeniable truth. "Yeah." Alex squeezes Craig's hand, hoping to still the trembling. "That's true."

"I don't blame you." Duncan gets to his feet, very slowly and with care, as if he doesn't want to startle them. He waves at the kitchen with his free hand. "Spag bol?"

And unaccountably, this is what gets Craig to relax. "Spag bol," he says, with a nod of agreement, and something that almost resembles a smile softens the anxious lines etched into his face.

Alex will take it.

A few minutes later he's installed in one of the kitchen chairs with Newton and Fitz at his feet and a glass of red wine in his hand that, to hell with contraindications, he's going to drink. At the stove, Craig and Duncan perform a dance of spice bottle passing and can opening that can only be described as a work of art. Alex is impressed. "So. The two of you can work together."

"Please. This is old hat." Duncan hands Craig two cans of tomatoes. "We had to get dinner for ourselves all the time when Mum was working on a book. Spaghetti Bolognese is the one dish we got really good at."

"Which is why I make it all the time at home." Craig tosses a wink over his shoulder as he pops the cans open. "I can do this in my sleep."

"Dinnertime was about the *only* time I wasn't pulling shit on Craig. I mean, I wanted to eat, right? One bad move and he'd burn everything on purpose. We'd have to start over *and* deal with Mum shouting about wasted food. It wasn't worth it." He nudges Craig aside, very gently, and shakes oregano into the pan with the ground beef and tomatoes. "Dinner was peacetime. Always."

Craig moves away. "I'm really not ready for you to touch me yet."

"That's fair." Duncan backs off. "Chili paste?"

Alex is fascinated. "This family is like watching a soap opera."

"Don't knock soap operas," Duncan protests. "I love *Coronation Street*."

Goddamn it. I said that out loud. Maybe I should reconsider the red wine. Alex sighs.

"He took something earlier," Craig says to his pan of sauce. "He won't have an inner monologue again until it wears off completely."

Alex glares as Duncan eyeballs him. "No, I get that," Duncan says with a judicious smile and a firm nod. "I'm like that when I drink. As you know! So, not a big deal. I mean, I don't want to know about my kid brother's sex life, so maybe we can keep the conversation away from that?"

Craig splashes red wine into the pan of sauce with what looks to Alex to be a little more force than is needed. Ruby droplets spatter the top of Moira's immaculate white enamel stovetop. "You're a pig, Duncan."

"Yes." Duncan's grin is almost infectious. Craig is clearly having a hard time not grinning back. "But are you telling me you want to hear about *my* sex life?"

Alex sits back with his glass of red wine raised to hide the fact that he's nearly swallowed his tongue. They're just such *brothers*. No matter what happened between them, the essential bond is still there. He swears he can see it, but that's probably the mixed alcohol and drugs talking.

It's there though, through all the dinner prep, through refilling wine glasses, through cooking the pasta, through stirring the sauce and throwing together a salad. The conversation is affectionate on Duncan's side, cautious on Craig's. There haven't been any apologies yet, but they are communicating.

Craig pokes his brother in the side with the butt end of a wooden spoon, and Alex takes that as a sign that Craig might be ready to talk at last.

Duncan lays out the plates and scoops pasta. Craig comes by with the saucepan and ladles out great dollops of rich, hearty tomato sauce. The salad bowl is set out, a block of cheese and a grater are found, and, once the wine glasses are topped up, there's nothing to hold them back from the long-avoided conversation—except that nobody wants to be the one to start it.

Alex waits. It's not his conversation to have, and he's blurted out quite enough in the way of awkward shit today. An irrepressible urge to fill the air with small talk bubbles up, and he solves the problem the only way he knows how: one swallow of wine, followed by a mouthful of pasta.

Whoa. "Good pasta."

"Thanks," Duncan and Craig say in stereo. Alex sighs. So much for that brilliant tactic. He is definitely going to ask his doctor for a new medication.

This most irksome of side effects is helpful for once, since it seems to break the silence and kick-start the Oliver brothers into action. Duncan inhales. "Craig."

"Duncan," Craig begins at the same time, only to shake his head and let out a breathless laugh wired by nerves. "Sorry. Go ahead."

"I know the polite thing to do would be to say, no, you first," Duncan says, "but all things considered, I expect that my part of this is going to take longer, so I better go first."

Alex holds his breath as Craig considers this. "Okay, sure," he says at last.

"I... am sorry, Craig. Very sorry." Duncan's fork catches the light and bounces it away again as he twirls his spaghetti. Noodles and sauce mound around the tines, and then he shakes it all loose and starts again. "I apologize to both of you. I mean, let's start with today, right? It was a shit thing. I didn't mean for you to get hurt, Alex, but it was a shit thing just to start with, and I'm sorry."

"You really, really don't always know when you push a joke too far, or play it on the wrong person." Craig's voice is brittle as cracked glass. He doesn't twirl his pasta, doesn't even try to eat it. He stabs at his salad instead, impaling the same lettuce leaf over and over until the plate's floral pattern is visible through the sad, limp green. Clearly, being ready to talk does not automatically mean being happy about it. "You've always been so extreme with the shit things, but your apologies just don't go quite as far... well. I suppose you'd have to have a reliable track record of *making* apologies in the first place for me to have a decent point of reference."

Duncan nods. "I deserve that. You're right. I go too far. I don't think. And I have absolutely not apologized enough to you for anything."

"You haven't apologized to me for anything *at all*," Craig corrects as he harpoons a slice of tomato.

Alex is careful to say nothing; he makes his best effort to not even think anything. A small, selfish part of him wishes the rest of the family *had* waited for him before they left for dinner. It would be okay to get his apology later, because this, right now, after all the wary camaraderie before dinner... this is uncomfortable in the extreme.

But Craig needs him. This is exactly why Alex was left behind. And a larger part of him is glad, glad that he can press his knee against Craig's under the table, glad that he can drop his fork and cover Craig's hand with his and stop the terrible salad murder. He is glad that they can face this together, that he can be here for Craig.

Duncan's eyes are on them, and he smiles. "Craig's lucky to have you, Alex. Really fucking lucky. I am sorry to have been so disrespectful to you and that I got you hurt. As I said, it was a shit thing. It was a stupid thing to do."

"In the grand scheme of things, I got off light. And that I got hurt was really more my fault than anything else." All Alex can do is shrug. Forgiveness in this instance, for himself, that's easy. What else is there to say? "I would really prefer that you never do anything like that to me again, but apology accepted."

"No, I will never do anything like that to you or to anyone else ever again." Relief shines in Duncan's eyes, but as his gaze shifts to Craig, he goes back to twirling pasta.

Craig's knee against Alex's is jittering like he's had too much coffee, and his arms are crossed tight across his chest. "Okay. You have demonstrated that you are in fact capable of apologies. It fixes nothing."

"I know that, Craig; do you really believe I don't?" Duncan drops his fork with a clatter that makes them all jump. His fingers flex as if he wants to pluck the words he needs out of thin air. "More than anything else in the world, I wish apologies could fix what I did, because I *am* sorry for everything, Craig, sorry and then some. I wish I didn't break your wrist. I would love to be able to undo the really terrible way I treated you; I've wanted that for a long time."

"You never called." Craig's mouth tightens, and Alex puts a hand on his knee, willing relaxation, calm, peace. "You never called or emailed or anything. Not a word."

"Because I just couldn't, Craig. I couldn't fix it." It's a plea and an apology and a desperate hope. "I was at a loss for what to say. I always knew an apology would never be enough. I felt like I couldn't talk to you at all if I couldn't figure out a way to make it all up to you. It's not an excuse, it's just... it's just what happened." His gaze drops as if he simply cannot look at Craig any longer. "I can't go back and make it all not ever have happened, and that's what you deserve more than anything else."

Craig's face falls into confusion and sadness and it breaks Alex's heart. "Can you tell me *why*, at least? Why did you do any of it in the first place?"

"If I knew that, I'd be a child psychologist, not a vet, Craig." Duncan answers the confusion with a helpless regret and sadness of his own. "The best answer I can give you was that I was a more than unusually stupid kid. I can't undo that. I hate that I can't."

It's clear as anything that Duncan sincerely means it. And Craig is an open book, so easily read as *wanting* to believe it, to accept it, but he can't seem to get over the last hurdle and go all in. Alex can only watch and hope that his support is felt.

A step in the kitchen doorway alerts them to the fact that someone is coming, but they all jump when David's calm voice fills the room. "You could tell him what you did in sixth form. That might help." He smiles in the face of their astonished stares. "Sorry. We're back. They sent me ahead to scout the mood and bring you into the front room. Or we can come in here, if you're finished eating."

At once the room is electrified; the air itself is completely charged and changed in an instant. Craig seizes on the first part of David's statement even as Duncan appears to shrink into his chair. His eyes ping-pong between David and Duncan, and his knee judders to a stop against Alex's. "Back up. What's this about sixth form?"

Given that he's built like an American football player, it is impressive to watch Duncan try to compact himself into the smallest of bundles. He shakes his head, only to wince and bring a careful hand to his sore cheek. "It's not important, Craig. I mean, it was never a big deal."

Alex looks at David and raises his eyebrows in inquiry. Whatever David means by the oblique information he's just dropped, it's having the net effect of a bomb strike on the Oliver brothers. David smiles at the seismic tremor and winks at Alex. "You might as well confess, Duncan," he says as he leans on the door frame. "It can only help. Chloe and I talked it over at dinner and we're in full agreement."

"Yeah, but it's not your information to agree on, is it?" Duncan growls, head down and eyes narrow. "It's mine and I'm not interested in—"

"It kind of is mine, as it happens," David says with a distinct edge to his voice. Under the table, Craig's knee jumps about again. "God knows it's certainly Craig's information to receive. It looks to me that you're all as done as you're going to be with those plates, so I suggest we adjourn to discuss it. Chloe and I will explain, if Duncan won't."

"It's nothing," Duncan snaps. "Seriously."

Craig holds up a hand to shut them up. Only Alex is close enough to see how unsteady a hand it is, how Craig's fingers tremble with the effort to suppress his nerves. "If it's not important, and it concerns me, and—this is the important part—if it could do anything to help us mend this damn rift, Duncan, then why can't you tell me?"

But Duncan sits in stony, sullen silence. He picks up his fork and twirls a clump of noodles onto the tines. His face is a study in stubborn withholding as he stuffs the bite of pasta into his mouth.

"As far as I'm concerned, it really will go a long way toward repairing at least some of what you want to fix." David heads to the living room. "We'll all be in here if your curiosity gets the better of you, Craig. Oh, and Chloe came back with us, Duncan. Apparently she's not calling the wedding off after all."

Craig is on his feet and out the kitchen door with the dogs scrambling at his heels before David finishes the sentence. That leaves Alex in the kitchen as Duncan does his level best to sink through the floor. It is not a sight Alex will easily forget. "What the hell was that all about?"

Duncan squirms and puffs his cheeks out in an exasperated sigh. "It's stupid. It's nothing; I never wanted Craig to know about it. It won't change anything."

"David thinks it might." The pasta is cold now, but Alex forks up another mouthful. The way the energy is crackling through the room, he'll need the fortitude of a full stomach.

"Yeah, well, David meddles…" Duncan's fork clatters to his plate. "Fuck it. Can I give you a hand out into the family room? This story is getting completely blown one way or another, and, damn it all, I should be the one to do it."

"Wasn't that David's point?" Alex asks, a split second before he's hauled to his feet and out of the kitchen at a speedy limp. "Hey!"

"Sorry. I'm in a hurry." They cross the hallway and stop in the door of the family room. Duncan bangs on the door frame with a fist and launches right in. "Fine. Start of sixth form, I beat the shit out of anyone having a go at Craig and David. They'd just gotten together. I wanted to establish that no one was to fuck with them. It was me and a couple of the guys from the rugby side and their little brothers."

The family room, full of Olivers, David, and Chloe, lapses into a silence so profound that the crickets in the front garden are loud and clear. David, the only one standing, was apparently cut off mid-sentence; one hand droops in the air as he looks back over his shoulder.

Everyone else blinks or just stares open-mouthed. Moira and Stephen look as if they can't breathe. The twins are stunned. A slow grin is making its way across David's face. Chloe has dropped *her* face into her palms, and in the window seat, Craig—Craig is shocked in a way that Alex has never, ever seen. His eyes are as round as marbles. His mouth works, opening and closing without sound. His hands are held as if he is about to catch a basketball, with fingers splayed and flexing mindlessly.

Alex is genuinely concerned that his fiancé has experienced one too many shocks in a very eventful day and is either going to snap, or have an aneurysm, or hell, go for broke and do both. Alex vows then and there to never again do anything that's even *remotely* surprising. In fact, *no one* is allowed to surprise Craig ever again. He'll have contracts drawn up.

"You... formed a brute squad?" When Craig finally gets any words out, they're steps from a frog's croak. "I... had the rugby mafia? As bodyguards?"

Duncan wiggles a hand. "Eh. Yeah, okay, more or less. I mean, if you want to put it that way. I like to think of it as more like... what's that thing you've all got in the States, Alex? The security for the President?"

"Secret Service," Alex whispers, his head throbbing as much as his ankle. "Duncan, please, my foot."

"Oh, yeah. Sorry." Duncan gently deposits Alex onto the piano bench and paces to the middle of the room. He shoves his hands into his jeans pockets and stands with hunched shoulders. "So. There you go, Craig. That's it, that's all it was."

"But... that... I..." Words still appear to elude Craig. "You could have told me about that! I would have... oh, my God. Did you, like... did you..." He clears his throat, and his face contorts hilariously, as if he's swallowed a live animal. "...watch?"

"No! No, oh God no, Jesus, we were strictly into enforcement, discipline, cracking skulls, and the like." If Duncan were to shake his head any more vigorously, it would fly off. "I told you. I have never, not *ever*, wanted to know about your sex life."

Despite the seeming impossibility of it, Craig's eyes go even wider. "Not that I had one at that age."

Moira raises an eyebrow. "We all knew about the drainpipe, darling."

That quiets the whole room. No one is able to look at anyone else.

Stephen breaks the silence by hauling himself to his feet so he can amble to the liquor cabinet. "Right, I absolutely need a drink now. Anyone else?"

"No, thanks." It has been the effort of the century to not blurt out anything stupid for the last several minutes. Alex is not about to blow that track record now.

"Yes, please," Jasmine chimes in with a sweet smile.

"Anyone over the age of eighteen?" Stephen amends. No one answers.

Craig focuses again on his brother. "Duncan, you could have told me about this. Seriously. Seriously." His hands flail. "Seriously," he repeats, a veritable broken record.

"Where'd that Lagavulin get off to, Mo?" Bottles rattle as Stephen rummages in the cabinet. "The nice one we had the other day; wouldn't you like a nip of that?"

"Dad!" The outburst comes from not one, not even two, but all *four* of the Oliver offspring. Impressive. They weren't so much as a fraction of a beat off. And it works, too—Stephen quietly produces a bottle of cognac and two small glasses and returns to Moira's side without another word.

Craig looks at Duncan. "Dunc. Come on."

"You already thought I was a thug." Duncan's shoulders move in a shrug that is a transparent effort in faux-nonchalance. "You sure wouldn't have appreciated it if you thought I was following you and hovering over you, and I'm pretty sure you wouldn't have approved of our methods. I just wanted to look out for you." He swallows. "You didn't trust me. Of course you didn't. Fucking good reasons you had for it, too. So I just did what was needed to keep you safe before I got the fuck out of your life."

"I don't understand..." Craig rubs at his forehead.

"You were so *little* back then when you came out. Just this skinny kid." The very atmosphere of the room holds its breath as Duncan pushes each word out. "I'm in gym every day with a bunch of fucking wankers snapping towels at each other and talking shit about *my* brother? No way. Fuck, Craig, you got enough shit from me all your life. I didn't know how to apologize for it, but goddamn if I was going to let anyone else make your life hell."

Fuck it. The confusion on Craig's face is too much for Alex. His ankle is on fire, but he hops across the room so he can sit next to Craig in the window seat. He gets an arm around Craig just as his fiancé whispers, "Fuck, Duncan. Fuck." He runs out of words again and leans back against Alex and grabs his hand, open-mouthed and at a loss.

"Is that why you moved home?"

Everyone's heads swivel to look at Jade, the source of the question. She fidgets with her fingers and looks as surprised to have asked the question as they all were to have heard it. Still, she takes a breath and carries on. "Did you move home from Glasgow because I came out? Because of me and Frankie?"

Alex tries his best to work out how he would describe Duncan's face in this moment. It is somewhere between *chewed on salted lemon slices* and *so that's why you don't stick forks in the socket*. It would be hilarious at any other time, a time when secrets weren't spilling out like waterfalls.

And because Duncan can't seem to recover his equilibrium, Chloe steps up to fill the void. "Yep. I was just a bonus."

Duncan swallows hard. "Someone needed to be around to keep an eye on things," he says as he turns to face his parents. "David was hearing stuff from some of the kids who came into the shop to get flowers, and he let me know. I was worried. Then the practice came up for sale. I bought it and I moved home so I could be here if Jade needed someone to be looking out."

Stephen clears his throat. "You should have told me, Duncan. The board of governors and I could have done something. You shouldn't have thought you needed to upend your life."

"We take care of each other," Duncan replies, his jaw set. "It's fine, Dad. I wanted to do it."

Moira and the twins ambush Duncan in a hug. Moira reaches up to hold her eldest child's face in her hands. "Oh, Duncan."

He squirms. "No, come on, it's nothing. It brought me home, and I got Chloe out of it. It was just important to keep Jade safe the way I tried to look out for Craig."

Don't cry, don't cry, don't fucking cry... oh, fuck it. Alex extracts his hand from the death grip Craig's got on it, the better to wipe his eyes before anyone spots how shiny they are. This family, this fucking family, damn it all, they're wacky and eccentric and slightly terrifying so much of the time, but *God*, they're so loyal and they care so *much*. It's like nothing Alex has experienced before, and he is drowning in it, amazed by it, head over heels for all of it.

Fuck, but he is so glad to be marrying into this, into all of this.

Craig goes rigid in Alex's arms, and Duncan's head lifts with curiosity writ large upon his face. "Are you?" Duncan asks, squinting and craning his neck to look over his mother's head at Alex's left hand. "Oh, hey, look at that. I guess you are. How'd I miss that?"

Alex is calling Dr. Laborteau *tomorrow*. Surely the chemist in town has some other anxiety medication. He'd spoken his thoughts without intending to, again.

"*Oh, my God.*" Chloe's words explode in an earsplitting shriek of truly epic decibel value. She bolts out of her perch in the big chair as though she's been shot out of a cannon and grabs Alex's hand. "Oh, my God! Craig! You did it!"

There's what sounds like a curse in what Alex can only assume is Gaelic as Moira pushes away from Duncan and trips over poor Newton in her haste to get to the window seat and snatch Alex's hand out of Chloe's. "Craig?" she breathes. Her eyes are huge starry pools of teary blue. "Is it... did you..."

"Can we not? This is awkward." Craig gently pulls Alex's hand away from his mother. "One, my fiancé is not a party favor; please stop trying to pass bits of him around. Two, yes, it is. I am. I have. What was the question? If it was, have I asked Alex to marry me, the answer is, sort of."

Chloe scoffs. "What, he's just trying the ring on for size?"

"No," Craig replies. "It's just that he asked me first, so I gave him the ring."

At such close range, Chloe's next shriek threatens to obliterate Alex's eardrums. "Tell. Me. Everything. Immediately." Her demand rings in his ears like a cathedral bell. "Tell me all of it. How did it happen? Was it while we were gone? Oh, it had to be; I'd have noticed that ring while we were getting Alex out of the woods." She shakes Craig's arm. "Tell me!"

Craig's mouth twitches, and he trembles with suppressed laughter. "Okay. So," he begins, "we were in the bathtub, naked—"

"I'm going to ask you to stop right there," Duncan interjects and drops his head into his hand. David's and Stephen's faces make similar pleas.

"Party pooper." Pouting, Chloe tosses the insult over her shoulder. She leans toward Craig. "You will call me and tell me later."

He answers with a smile and a quick kiss to her cheek before extracting himself from Alex's embrace to stand. Each person in the room takes in a huge breath and holds it as Craig steps over to Duncan. He's standing much too upright, much too taut. "Duncan."

Duncan is strung just as tight. "Yeah?"

The room falls silent. Craig's fists curl, and Alex worries that there's will be a second coming of Punchmageddon.

"I am still angry," Craig says at last. His gaze is so intense, Alex is surprised it's not drilling holes right through Duncan's head. "I am angry, and so much still hurts. One apology is never going to fix it all."

"I know," Duncan begins, but he flinches as Craig lifts a hand, and whatever else he was going to say sputters off into the air.

Craig keeps his hand up a second longer before he drops it. The smile that comes to his face isn't a large one, and it's still sad around the edges, but it is unmistakably a smile, and everyone's breath releases in a rush. Craig swallows. "I accept it."

Duncan looks as if he's been hit again. "Come again? Sorry?"

"Right. You're sorry, and I accept it. Your apology." Craig nods. "A very wise fellow that I hope to marry as soon as possible reminded me that... well, life is too short. Anger is... too much of it is poisonous." He casts a soft, affectionate glance at Alex, and his smile grows just a bit bigger as he turns back to Duncan. "I am looking at something amazing and new in my life, this thing that is just..." His hands rise and fall. "It's big, Dunc. Getting engaged to Alex is a whole new beginning of a different part of my life. I get now why you wanted to apologize this week. I understand it. You wanted all the big, shiny new beginnings you could get."

Duncan's face works; his mouth opens to let out a soft chuckle as he dips his head. His eyes come up to meet Craig's. "Yeah. Essentially. I mean, I meant it, but yeah, you just nailed it."

"So." Craig shifts on his feet, and his shoulders twitch. "I sort of want to rack up a few shiny new beginnings myself. I am that selfish." Quick as a flash, he shoves his hand out.

"You and me, can we start over, Dunc? You really think it's not too late?"

The laugh Duncan lets out is the shortest burst of the purest joy and is clogged with the tears that are already making his eyes gleam. "Nah. I think maybe it's just in the nick of time."

And Duncan grabs Craig's outstretched hand, pulling him close into what might be their first hug. They're laughing, just short of crying, and they're pounding each other on the back.

As far as new beginnings go, Alex never saw a better, brighter one. It is amazing.

He's really looking forward to the day that he and Craig eclipse it entirely.

"B<small>ABE," </small>A<small>LEX CALLS GENTLY THROUGH THE BATHROOM</small> door. "We have a wedding to get to."

"I'll be out in a minute," Craig calls back, and Alex takes that minute to check himself in the closet-door mirror. Hair—good. Tuxedo—very good, very sharp, well-tailored, tie straight. Shoes—nice and shiny. Yep. He's good.

Not as good as the sight of Craig when he swings the bathroom door open, though. "Whoa."

"You like?" Craig brushes his hands down the front of his Cunningham-tartan kilt. His fingers dance over the sporran, the short dress jacket with its silver buttons, the red tie at his throat. "I mean, it's not ridiculous?"

Alex's mouth goes dry. "Never. I could just drag you back to bed right now."

"Well. As per tradition..." Craig winks and lifts the hem of his kilt just high and long enough for Alex to see he's not wearing anything underneath. "I really would let you in a heartbeat. But we're already running late."

"We are." Alex reaches out to adjust Craig's collar points and brush a twist of hair out of his eyes. "Okay. So."

"So." Cocking his head, Craig lets a lopsided smile curve his mouth. "Are you ready to get married?"

"Not really." Alex grins as Craig looks startled. "I'm more used to working at weddings than being the subject of them. But I'm ready to spend the rest of my life with you, how's that?"

Craig grins back and loops his arm through Alex's. "Works for me. Now, let's go put everyone else out of their misery."

THE ONLY ONE EVER TRULY IN MISERY WAS ALEX'S COUSIN *Samantha, who inexplicably appointed herself their chief wedding planner.*

"I need you to pick a venue, dammit," are her first words to them when they disembark at Sea-Tac. "Pick a date, pick a venue."

Alex stares. "We've been engaged for less than a week. Craig's ring won't even arrive from London for another two at least."

"I can't wait for that. I love my new ring." Craig ignores the questionable-quality breath caused by drinking far too much celebratory champagne on the airplane and kisses Alex on the lips, a kiss that deepens considerably and quickly, since they are still fairly tipsy. He giggles against Alex's mouth. "My God, have we stopped drinking since Thursday?"

"Drinking with your mother for breakfast on Friday, with Chloe that afternoon finishing the cake, at Duncan's little stag thing, before the wedding, at the reception, at the jeweler's, at dinner after we saw Duncan and Chloe off, on the plane... no, I don't think—"

"A little focus, please, you high-flying drunks." Sammi shakes them apart. "Do you know how far ahead Seattle's best wedding and reception venues are booked up? If you want to get married any time in the next ten years, we have work to do. I just went through this, so I know."

She breaks off when Craig and Alex exchange significant glances and grins. "We want to get married on the rooftop at Sucre Coeur," Craig announces with a nod. "Theodora loves the idea and says she can have it ready and fit for a wedding by next July; that suits us fine."

"That Goth bartender, Katie, she talked to the owner of The Order of the Garter and said we can have the reception there," Alex adds, his grin beaming out some serious high voltage delight. "That's where we met, so there's nowhere better."

Samantha is stunned completely stupid for the first time since either of them have known her; she stands with her mouth open and hands flailing. Her husband Nate is grinning back at them, though. "That sounds perfect to me, completely amazing and absolutely exactly what both of you would do." His hug nearly squeezes them breathless. "Perfect."

"Is Sammi going to be all right, though?" Craig asks, hitching his carry-on up on his shoulder and taking Samantha's hand to lead her to the baggage carousel. Sammi's eyes and mouth are still as hilariously wide and round as saucers. "She didn't expect us to have thought ahead; she thought she was going to shock us."

"More fool her. We're both in the wedding business one way or the other; how could you even think we wouldn't be planning logistics already? Peach, we know an actual professional wedding planner." Alex nudges his cousin hard in the shoulder, jolting her out of her shock. "Don't worry, Sammi. We'll let you and Poppy handle everything else."

EXCEPT FOR THE VOWS—THOSE THEY WROTE ON THEIR OWN.

"I promise pancakes every Sunday morning, to hold your hand in mine whenever you need it, to stand by your side and support you through the easy times and the rough ones," Craig says now while he grips Alex's hand like a lifeline. "Alexander Michael Scheff, I will love you with every beat of my heart until it stops."

They, of course, kept their vows secret from each other, not even reading them in rehearsal. It chokes Craig up to speak them aloud for the first time. It completely freezes Alex's thoughts and any words he was about to speak. He swallows, and swallows, eyes bright with tears. His hand lifts to his face as he sniffles.

Craig leans forward with a swallow of his own, and whispers so that only Alex hears him say, "And I absolutely vow to never hang any posters of handsome staring men over our bed at any time, ever."

Alex's laughter peals out into the Seattle summer sky.

"WHAT DO YOU MEAN, NO?" ALEX ASKS WITH INCREDULITY, *staring at Connor as if he's just spontaneously turned into a Care Bear. "You can't say no! You're my best friend! You're practically my brother! You have to be my best man!"*

Connor picks up Kira and passes her across their table at The Finch to shove her into Alex's arms. "I can too say no, ass... butthead."

"Ass Butt Head," Kira chants in delight as her father's face collapses in a frown of chagrin and consternation. "Ass Butt Head."

Alex hides his face in her soft brown curls until he can stop smiling and resume the serious expression the conversation calls for. "Connor, come on. Why not?"

"Because I can't be your head photographer and your best man at the same time," Connor informs him while handing Kira a bagel, "and I don't trust anyone else to shoot the most important day of your life but you, and you're going to be kind of busy for that. So ask Sammi to be your best man; I got shit to do."

"Shit!" Kira shrieks with glee, bouncing and throwing bagel crumbs like confetti until she nearly falls from Alex's lap.

And so it is settled, unless Connor's wife Rayna kills her husband for continuing to inadvertently teach their toddler profanity.

ALEX GLANCES AT CONNOR, WHO IS STANDING STILL AND QUIET with his camera behind Nate and Jade—Craig's wedding party—and grins. The grin is not returned. Connor waves his free hand in a motion that clearly is intended to get Alex moving on the recitation of his own vows so Connor can catch the moment.

He's still reeling from the sweetness and hilarity of Craig's words, but Alex takes a deep breath and gives it his best shot.

"Craig Andrew Oliver," he begins, squeezing Craig's hands in his. His chest is tight, so tight; all of his emotions are expanding against his ribs as if they could burst out, and his heart is going to lead the charge. "There's not a day that goes by that I don't thank whoever's up there listening for sending you into my life. You changed everything I thought I knew about love." There's so much love in his chest, he can't get a good breath, and his voice shakes with it. "I promise to spend every day showing you how much I love you, how grateful I am that you exist. I promise to always drink tea with you in the morning. I promise to stand by you through everything that comes at us. I promise to never, ever spring too many surprises on you in a day."

Their hands are trembling in each other's grips.

"I promise," Alex says, his knees shaking as if they could give out any time, "that all the love I have in my heart is yours, and only yours, forever."

"THAT'S GOT TO GO," SAMANTHA SAYS IN ALARM AS JASMINE *takes her mass of twisted hair out of its sloppy bun to reveal that she streaked the twists with a full rainbow spectrum of color. "Oh,* my God. No. No, no, no, you are supposed to be identical. I was promised identical maids of honor."

"You were promised identical twins as maids of honor." Jasmine tosses her scrunchie to Jade, who uses it to put up her own blameless and enhancement-free braids into a much tidier bun. "We don't do full-time identical."

Samantha displays all the signs of a woman who is on the verge of a stroke. Color drains from her cheeks, and her gray eyes darken in her despair. Her hands shake, her knees give out, and she lands with a thud on one of the kitchen chairs with a measuring tape dangling from her fingers. "This is terrible."

Jasmine pulls one of the twists over her shoulder and strokes it. "I thought it was pretty. I like it."

"It's got to go." Sammi is galvanized into action; she thrusts her hand into her skirt pocket to fish out her cell phone, fingers flying. "We've got to find someone to take it out."

Craig raises his hand. "Hang on, now, it's my wedding, and I like her hair. It is pretty. Don't you like it, Alex?"

"It looks great to me, and she's my maid of honor," Alex agrees. "I say leave it."

Samantha is two steps from apoplectic. "You said I was in charge of all the rest of the details. This is a detail."

"My mother will kill you if you touch so much as a hair on my sister's head," Jade chimes in, all sweetness and light except for her narrowed eyes. "Good money was paid for that."

Samantha is cursing a blue streak before Jasmine collapses into giggles. "They're just colored extensions. I'd really like to wear them, though. Seriously, we don't do the totally identical thing. And Alex said it was fine."

"I actually sort of expected it of her," Alex says, leaning companionably against Craig. "I like it, Peach. Seriously. The dresses are lilac, it's not like it'll really clash with them, and who cares if it does anyway."

"I care," Samantha sputters, but no one else does, and when both Moira and Marina sweep into the apartment to back Jasmine up, the issue is closed.

APART FROM THE RAINBOW STREAKS ECHOED BY GOLDEN strands in Jade's updo, the twins are identical, and gorgeous in their matching dusty-lilac chiffon dresses. Samantha tore apart every vintage boutique in town and cashed in every favor she owed to her army of clerk friends to find them.

Craig is grateful to Samantha for having pulled all of this off. He and Alex drove her, Poppy Lawrence, and both their mothers up the wall with their inability to get into the wedding planning, but they couldn't help it. He and Alex just wanted to be married; everything else was trappings for their family and friends.

So everyone was getting what they wanted. Right? He sure was.

"Please present the rings." The officiant is none other than their friend Devesh, happy to volunteer his hastily-acquired services as an Internet-ordained minister.

Nate kneels to retrieve the two rings from the ribbon tied around Fitz's furry little neck. The Yorkie was an amazingly patient ring-bearer, riding imperiously in a little basket that flower girl Kira had to be helped with carrying.

Craig is glad that Connor set up a video camera array along with everything else, because the sighs and squeals that went up at the sight of Kira and Fitz were *epic*.

Devesh clears his throat as Nate places the gold band in Craig's hand and passes the burnished titanium one to Alex.

"Craig, please put the ring on Alex's finger, and recite your ring vows."

Their hands haven't stopped shaking. "Alex, I give you this ring as a symbol of my love and how much I will cherish you and every minute of time we'll have together in the rest of our lives." He slides the ring over Alex's finger where it belongs, where it will belong forever.

"Craig," Alex responds, holding tight with one hand as he pushes the titanium circle over Craig's knuckle, "I give you this ring as a symbol of my love and how much I will cherish you and every minute of time we'll have together in the rest of our lives."

Sniffles and weeping can be heard all over the rooftop. Even Jasmine is wiping tears from her cheeks. Devesh smiles and closes his little ceremony book. "Then by the power vested in me by the state of Washington and the Universal Life Church, I now pronounce you husbands and life partners. You may seal your union with a kiss."

Amid clapping, cheering, and tears, they chuckle into each other's mouths and make it all so, so official.

They are so, so married.

"I'D LIKE TO INVITE JEFF AND HIS HUSBAND," ALEX SAYS, FLIPPING an ivory card over and over in his hands. His fingers trace Samantha's tidy black calligraphy before he tucks the card into a matching envelope and pastes a stamp on the corner.

Craig pauses, a stamp of his own hanging in the air. "Seriously?"

Plucking one of the address labels from the free sheet sent to them by some charitable organization they donated to, Alex shrugs and tries to be casual as he sticks it into place on the envelope's other corner. "He won't accept it; don't worry."

"Then why?"

The envelope sails across the table to join the pile of other neatly stamped and labeled envelopes waiting to be addressed. Alex remembers a day almost two years ago now, remembers a dare. "It's just a message. He'll understand."

"THANKS FOR NOT PUNCHING ME IN THE NOSE. I KNEW I WAS right." Stephen frowns at the inscription in the otherwise congratulatory card, one of dozens opened and displayed on a table in The Order of the Garter. "What sort of congratulations is that?"

"It almost sounds like something I would have sent." Duncan peers over his father's shoulder and plucks the card away. "I didn't, though. Who are Jeff and Kevin?"

Chloe snatches the card from her husband and reads it with interest. "No clue, but I don't think they're here. I met Katie, and then Will from the bakery and his partners Ginny and James—they're all three so cute together—then Sarita and Maritza, Connor and Rayna and Kira, Nate and Samantha, Devesh and his husband Sunil and baby Nikhil, Natasha and her daughter Katerina, and Theodora, and of course Alex's parents and grandparents..." She ticks them all off on her fingers and closes one eye. "There's no Jeff or Kevin anywhere."

Moira is squinting around the bar. "Yes, that's... everyone. I don't remember a Jeff or a Kevin, either."

"Jeff the Jerk is Alex's ex. He and his husband declined on their RSVP." Samantha sails by, champagne flute held high and an inordinately pleased smile on her face. "And that's a good thing. They sent a hell of a gift, though."

Jasmine looks over from where she and Jade are poking through the haul of opened gifts that's loaded onto the adjacent table. "Really?"

"Mm. Apart from their lack of presence, which is a gift in itself," Samantha points to a long envelope with her glass, "they're sending Craig and Alex to Italy for ten days starting next week. Cake, anyone?"

NATASHA CROSSES HER ARMS OVER HER CHEST. "CRAIG. GET OUT. *Theodora's orders."*

"This is half my bakery, too," Craig protests, trying to push past his bakery manager to get into the kitchen. He fails utterly, largely because Sucre Coeur's former head decorator Sarita, who has returned to Seattle from L.A. especially for this occasion, is a formidable second line. Between the two women, he's pushed back to the bakery door. "Hey!"

"You know the drill, Craig." Sarita's liquid dark eyes are wide and sweet even as she leans around him to open the door and help shove him out onto the sidewalk. "You got to pick the flavors, but everything else is up to us. Out. You can't see it; it's a wedding present! I flew here just to make it a special surprise."

"It's going to be gorgeous. Don't you trust us?" Natasha has been shoved out onto the sidewalk with him, the better to lean against the door and defend it against his efforts to get inside. "We know the colors. We know what you like. We know what Alex likes. Don't worry."

Craig wants badly to push past her, but she's been taking Krav Maga lessons for the last two years, and it would probably be a bad idea to test his luck three days before his wedding. "Yeah, but... Tash, I just want to work. I need something to do."

Her hands come up to nudge him gently back in the direction of his apartment. "Why don't you go make out with your husband-to-be?" she suggests. "Get some practice in for the wedding night?"

On the other side of the glass door of the bakery, behind the gold and white letters spelling out his name and Theodora's as proprietors, Sarita makes a kissy face. Craig sighs. He's beaten. "Okay."

"I CAN'T WAIT FOR TONIGHT," ALEX SAYS, TWIRLING HIS FORK so that it clinks and clatters against his cake plate. He's taken a couple of bites of the raspberry-filled chocolate dream of a cake—one of the most amazing things he's ever tasted—but it sits otherwise untouched on top of a paper doily; a lavender buttercream rose rises from the frosting. "When do we get to be alone?"

Craig cocks his head to regard his husband and chews and swallows his own bite of cake before replying. "We're just going back to our flat, babe. To do the same thing we do every night." His mouth tips up in a positively wicked smile. "Not that I don't absolutely love what we do every night, mind."

"Yes, but I have never been alone with my *husband* before." Alex's tone is arch, but his eyes are full of promises and no small amount of absolute, undiluted delight. "I can't wait to be alone with my *husband.*"

"Mm. I love it. Say it again." Lifting his fork, Craig offers a bite of cake from his own plate to his husband, who accepts with a smile. "Come on, babe. Please?"

"What, husband?" Alex leans in. "*Husband, husband, husband,*" he whispers, and the two of them collapse against each other in helpless laughter. "We are the biggest idiots in the world."

"That's as it may be." Craig nuzzles in against Alex's neck. "But we're each other's biggest idiots in the world. It's legal now and everything."

Alex nips at Craig's ear. "What I'm gonna do to you tonight, *husband,* isn't legal, at least, not in the U.S." He takes in a deep breath; the warm inhalation tickles Craig's ear. But he doesn't get to say what, exactly, that might be.

"Time for our grooms to have their first dance!" shouts out the DJ, some friend of Nate's with the most inopportune timing in the world. "Come on, you two, get your hands off each other and get out on the dance floor." He scans the room and his face lights up when his gaze falls on the two of them. "I've got your song right here, ready to go."

"YOU SAID I WAS IN CHARGE!" SAMANTHA THROWS HER HANDS into the air, forgetting herself and nearly sending her iPhone flying. After she has it securely back in her hands, she glares glass daggers at Alex and Craig. "But you took charge of the date, and the venue, and Jasmine's hair, and now this too!"

Craig looks up from where he was staring, besotted, at his and Alex's intertwined fingers. Soon they'd have their rings back in their proper places. He can't wait. "Come on, Samantha, the song for our first dance is a fairly important matter."

"Which is why I should be in charge of it; I'll get it exactly right." It's not a sound argument, and her cheeks flush brilliant scarlet as the grooms-to-be level nearly identical stares of skepticism at her. "I would! I will!"

If Alex could, he'd shift his raised eyebrow even higher. "Peach, you and I have never liked the same music," he begins, covering his and Craig's entwined hands with his free one. "But even if we did? I'm pretty sure nothing by Panic! At The Disco is ever going to be appropriate."

Samantha sulks. "I only played them so you'd compare it to the one I really want and like that one better."

"And that one would be?" Craig asks, leaning against Alex's shoulder and waiting. He does not lose the skeptical expression.

Samantha's fingers twist and fidget, and her knuckles turn white even as her cheeks flush. Her eyes drop away from theirs. "'A Thousand Years.' It's by Christina Perri."

"No," the grooms-to-be state in firm, immovable agreement.

"It's totally appropriate!"

Alex shakes his head. "It's sap, Peach. Pure, unadulterated sap. No."

"We like the one we picked out," Craig says, freeing his hand to grab his phone and toss it to Samantha. "It's the first one on the Holy Fuck We're Getting Married *playlist."*

When the first notes of the guitar plunk out of the speakers, Samantha raises her own eyebrow. "You've got to be kidding me."

"I REALLY DO LIKE THIS SONG A LOT," ALEX SAYS AS HE GRINS at Craig and delights in the way the grin is returned tenfold. Over the bar's sound system, a bass guitar begins to thump out a cheery rhythm. "So glad your mother suggested it. It is actually perfect."

"We can never tell her how much we like it," Craig warns, grabbing Alex and swinging him into a shuffling little spin on the dance floor when the Reid brothers begin to sing. "Not ever. We'd never hear the end of it."

"C'MON." MOIRA'S GRIP ON HER SON'S WRIST IS AS FIRM AND secure as her footsteps are not as they wobble down the first-floor hallway. Alex follows the slosh of the alcohol in the bottle she carries as he limps drunkenly behind them in the dark. "Shhh."

It's a nearly pointless warning, because if their constant tipsy banging into walls didn't wake anyone, Moira slamming open the door of her home office surely would at least bring Stephen running.

Or not. Stephen, in his joy, hit the cognac pretty hard after all the talking and hugging. Only the twins were sober at the end of the night, and they were so exhausted by the events and stress of the day, they were punch-drunk by the time they wandered to bed. So they probably wouldn't come down either. Eh.

Alex wavers into the office after Craig and falls into the closest chair with a thump and a sigh of dust from the abused seat cushion. "Siddown," Moira commands, a second too late. Eyes glazed with much too much cognac and whatever devil water his mother served them in the wee hours, Craig has already slumped into a nearby chair.

But this, Moira insisted, they'd want to remember. They needed to hear it.

Moira fiddles her laptop to life and pulls something up on iTunes. "This song, this song is perfect for you boys," she drawls, falls a little sideways into—or really onto—her desk chair, and swigs directly out of the bottle still in her hand as a bass guitar pulses into rhythmic, cheerful life. "So perfect."

It's The Proclaimers, of course. Not the usual song. Not one Alex's heard before, actually. Craig's head lifts in bleary interest when the vocals start. "I think I remember this one. 'Life with You?'"

"It's perfect," Moira mumbles, and the longer they listen, the clearer it becomes that she's right.

Within moments, the three of them link hands and dance like maniacs in the study, not caring if they wake the household singing along.

THE TWINS ARE THE FIRST OUT ON THE DANCE FLOOR TO JOIN them, grabbing David and swinging him into a giddy laughing whirlwind. Moira, of course, is quick to follow with Stephen, Duncan with Chloe, Devesh with his husband Sunil and Sarita with her girlfriend Maritza. The floor fills with Craig and Alex's entire family, immediate, extended and adopted, everyone whirling and laughing and singing along to the chorus at the top of their lungs.

Craig laughs as he pulls Alex closer. "Babe, oh, my God, look. Even your parents are out here; it's adorable."

Alex turns to see Marina dragging Dieter out onto the floor despite his laughing protests, and, when his staid father spins his mother into a dramatic dip, he can't help but laugh and hold Craig close. "Can we be like that? My parents, your parents... Duncan and Chloe. Can we be like them?"

Craig rests his head on Alex's shoulder. "And then some, babe. And then some."

As the song draws to a close, the tempo slows, and Alex reaches for his husband. He draws Craig in for a long kiss just as the Reid brothers sing them out. The entire room falls away. There's no sound or sight in the world but each other as they let their love eddy back and forth between the two of them.

Craig pulls back first, eyes alight and fists clenched tight in Alex's lapels. "That was our first kiss as a married couple. I mean, the first one where we weren't being told to do it."

"Was it?"

"Mm hmm."

Alex smiles and wraps his arms around Craig's neck, drawing him close again so that their foreheads touch and they're just swaying in place. "I'm glad."

"About anything in particular or just in general?"

"I'm glad," Alex says, and every word is in his every heartbeat, "that my last first kiss is you."

THE END

Absolutely Perfect Cupcakes

NO ALMOST ANYTHING ABOUT THESE CUPCAKES! Chocolate stout cupcakes topped with a layer of chunky raspberry preserves and a swirl of Chambord buttercream will elevate any occasion you make them for. Say, like, a wedding, maybe?

Cupcakes:
1 ¼ c. all-purpose flour
1 c. unsweetened dark cocoa powder
¼ tsp. baking soda
¼ tsp. baking powder
¼ tsp. salt
1 c. butter (unsalted, softened)
1 ¼ c. sugar
2 eggs, room temperature
1 tsp. bourbon vanilla
1 c. chocolate stout beer

Frosting:
½ c. butter (unsalted, softened)
3 ½ c. powdered sugar
1 tbsp. Chambord (add more if preferred)
2 tbsp. heavy cream

Additional garnishes:
Chunky raspberry preserves
Fresh raspberries

Preheat oven to 350 degrees Fahrenheit. Line two 12-count muffin tins with paper liners.

Sift together flour, cocoa powder, baking soda, baking powder, and salt in a medium bowl. Make sure the dry ingredient mixture is well-blended, with no pockets or noticeable spots of white.

In a larger bowl, cream butter and sugar together until it is fluffy. Add eggs, one at a time, beating between each egg, then add the bourbon vanilla.

Add a third of the dry ingredient mixture to the larger bowl and mix until just combined. Blend in ½ cup of the chocolate stout. Add another third of the dry ingredients, then the remainder of the stout, then the last third of the dry ingredients.

Distribute the batter evenly between the muffin tins—fill each cup between half and three-quarters full. Bake for no longer than 23 minutes, until a toothpick inserted into the center comes out with just a few crumbs on it. The cupcakes will look black, because of the stout and the dark cocoa powder.

Allow the cupcakes to cool completely before frosting.

To make the frosting, beat the softened butter and powdered sugar together in a roomy bowl. Add the Chambord and heavy cream gradually, in single tablespoon increments. More cream or Chambord can be added as desired until the frosting achieves the flavor and consistency wanted. Fill a pastry bag with the frosting.

Spoon a bit of the raspberry preserves onto each cooled cupcake and spread it out. Pipe frosting on top. Add a raspberry or two to each frosted cupcake as garnish and enjoy!

Acknowledgments

Without the support and encouragement of the Interlude Press Unholy Trinity ;) the Sucre Coeur Series would not exist. Love and thanks to Annie, Candy, and Choi for all of their hard work and help!

Lex, I still can't pass a patch of clover without thinking of you and looking for a four leafer. We miss you.

Mimsy, Ali, and Julian—my advance reading team, for your Britpicking and careful checking of me and generous feedback and all of your help, I thank you to the ends of the earth and back!

Alana, my best cheerleader, especially for this book, the one you shouted the loudest for me to write! Love, love, love. This one is yours from top to toe.

Love to Angela, for all the test baking and for being the best of best friends, and to Aaron for putting up with the weekly coating of the kitchen in cocoa powder and flour! Sorry not sorry to all of Aaron's colleagues at work for all the delicious leftovers.

Love to Jessica for always being excited for me when I'm stressed out, and for all the dinners that you push on me when I'm screaming about deadlines. You're my oldest friend and the best Buffy ever, and I love you!

Love and thanks to my family, to my mom and Aunt Kathy, to David and Elena, to Drew and Nadine, to Dad and all my grandparents—I write because you all believed I could and should. Thank you.

To my Hufflepuff sisters, C.B. Lee and Rachel Davidson Leigh, the best sounding-boards and convention roommates in the world—so much love, and all the snacks, always!

To Naomi Tajedler, you are the sweetest and most wonderful person. Thank you for listening and encouraging. I love you to pieces and I am so proud of you! Even after the Brie enabling incident. Yep. You know what you did.

Lots of love to all my Interlude Press family, you're all stellar, funny, wonderful folks, and I am proud to be associated with all of you. Thank you for accepting this weirdo cookie-pusher into your ranks.

And my readers, you hilarious, supportive, excited crew— you are all so kind and delightful and make me pleased and proud to write for all of you. Thank you, with all the love I have in me.

About the Author

A NEARLY LIFELONG WRITER, LISSA REED HAS DABBLED in sports writing, blogging, poetry, and the creation of really dirty covers of popular Renaissance tunes (best we don't speak of what she did to Greensleeves). Being a Navy Brat left her with pervasive wanderlust, but it also introduced her to a wide variety of people and places, fueling her imagination and helping to populate fictional worlds that kept her occupied during cross-country drives.

The only reason she has stopped moving around is because she now owns too many books and stock pots for that to be a reasonable option.

Lissa lives in the DFW Metroplex with her two cats and her ailing balcony garden, where her pastimes include baking many, many cookies and knitting very, very slowly. *Absolutely, Almost, Perfect* is the third book in her Sucre Coeur Series.

also by
lissa **reed**

Definitely, Maybe, Yours

Sucre Coeur Series, Book One

Seattle-based baker Craig Oliver leads a life that is happily routine: baking cupcakes for an enormous family reunion, managing Sucre Coeur for its frequently absent owner and closing out his day with a pint at the local pub. He has a kind heart, a knack for pastry and a weakness for damaged people.

Habitual playboy Alex Scheff is looking to drown his sorrows, but instead discovers that he may have a weakness for Englishmen who carry cookies in their pockets. Can a seemingly incompatible pair find the recipe for love in a relationship they claim is casual?

ISBN (print) 978-1-941530-40-5
ISBN (eBook) 978-1-941530-41-2

Certainly, Possibly, You

Sucre Coeur Series, Book Two

Sarita Sengupta is in her last semester of grad school and has finally realized she doesn't have a career plan, a girlfriend, or a clear outlook on life. She works as a pastry shop's head decorator, but is otherwise drifting without direction until a friend's birthday party ends with her waking up in the unexpected company of Maritza Quiñones, a pretty ballroom dancer whose cheerful charm and laser focus sets Sarita on a path to making all of the choices she's been avoiding.

ISBN (print) 978-1-945053-05-4
ISBN (eBook) 978-1-945053-06-1

CPSIA information can be obtained
at www.ICGtesting.com
Printed in the USA
FSOW01n0525141217
41866FS